"This isn't right, Nick," said Lily softly.

Nick's head whipped up, his fingers stilled in mid-caress. Lily was sitting cross-legged like a Turk on the pillows at the top of the bed, her wings behind her echoing the curved headboard, her hands draped across her bent knees.

Why now? he thought wildly. *Why in blazes did Lily have to come* now?

"Damnation," he rasped as he glared at her. "I thought you wished to make me happy."

As she lay beneath him, Rose's eyes flew open, wounded and uncomprehending. "I thought I was making you happy, Nick, truly," she whispered uncertainly. "But if somehow I've done something wrong—"

"Nay, sweetheart, not a blessed thing," murmured Nick quickly, sweeping his mouth down on hers to reassure her. He shut his eyes and tried to concentrate on Rose, not Lily. If he tried hard enough to ignore her, perhaps she'd give up and go away.

"Of course I wish you to be happy, my dear captain," said Lily. "But you won't shed me until I've said my piece. Randy and virile you doubtless are, but lust alone isn't making you do this. And until you can sort out your reason, you truly must not be in this bed with my sister!"

Dear Reader,

Since the very first of her seven stories featuring the adventurous Sparhawk family, Miranda Jarrett's characters have gone up against all manner of villains and disasters, but Captain Nick Sparhawk, the hero of *Sparhawk's Angel*, is in real trouble. His tormentor is a meddlesome angel bent on matchmaking. Don't miss this tale that *Romantic Times* calls "delightful, unforgettably funny and supremely touching."

The third book in award-winning author Theresa Michaels's Kincaid Trilogy, *Once a Lawman*, features the oldest Kincaid brother, a small-town sheriff who must choose between family and duty as he works to finally bring to justice the criminals who've been plaguing his family's ranch.

A sensible novelist brings love and laughter to the wounded soul of a neighboring earl in Deborah Simmons's new title, *The Devil Earl*. And an indentured servant is torn between her affection for her good-hearted master and her growing love for the rugged frontiersman who is guiding them to a new life in the territories in Ana Seymour's new Western, *Frontier Bride*.

We hope you will enjoy all four titles, and come back for more. Please keep a lookout for Harlequin Historicals, available wherever books are sold.

Sincerely,

Tracy Farrell
Senior Editor

Please address questions and book requests to:
Harlequin Reader Service
U.S.: 3010 Walden Ave., P.O. Box 1325, Buffalo, NY 14269
Canadian: P.O. Box 609, Fort Erie, Ont. L2A 5X3

Miranda Jarrett

Sparhawk's Angel

Harlequin Books

TORONTO • NEW YORK • LONDON
AMSTERDAM • PARIS • SYDNEY • HAMBURG
STOCKHOLM • ATHENS • TOKYO • MILAN
MADRID • WARSAW • BUDAPEST • AUCKLAND

ISBN 0-373-28915-4

SPARHAWK'S ANGEL

Printed in U.S.A.

MIRANDA JARRETT

was an award-winning designer and art director before turning to writing full-time, and considers herself sublimely fortunate to have a career that combines history and happy endings, even if it's one that's also made her family regular patrons of the local pizzeria. A descendant of early settlers in New England, she feels a special kinship with her popular fictional family, the Sparhawks of Rhode Island.

Miranda and her husband—a musician and songwriter—live near Philadelphia with their two young children and two old cats. During what passes for spare time she paints watercolor landscapes, bakes French chocolate cakes and whips up the occasional last-minute Halloween costume.

Miranda admits herself that it's hard to keep track of all the Sparhawk family members, and she has prepared a family tree to help, including which characters appear in each book. She loves to hear from readers, and if you write to her and enclose a self-addressed stamped envelope, she'll send you a copy of the family tree along with her reply. Her address: P.O. Box 1102, Paoli, PA 19301-1145.

For Martha, with affection,
and for suffering through this one with me

Because you agree that Madame Max is a better
heroine than Lady Glencora;
because you'll understand the debt to Mr. Sargent;
and because, somehow, at six o'clock every
evening (almost) you can still find whining
children charming!

Prologue

Off the coast of South Carolina
July 1779

For the first time the odds didn't favor him, not on this pitch-dark morning in the last hour before dawn.

Furiously Nick swiped the sweat and blood from his forehead with his sleeve as he struggled to make out more of the English ship than the ten gunports bringing fire and death. Pale clouds from the flames in his *Liberty*'s hold billowed up through the hatch and mixed with the acrid powder smoke from the guns and the screams of dying men. Splinters of oak and bits of tarred cord and canvas rained down onto the deck with every uneasy sway of the sloop in the sea. Already he could feel how the *Liberty* was settling lower into the waves as the sea rushed in through the jagged holes left by the English broadsides. Another five minutes, ten at the most, and then the ocean would claim them.

If five minutes were all he had, then so be it, but he wouldn't go down without a fight, and he sure as hell wasn't going to surrender. With grim satisfaction he glanced up at the two tattered flags overhead—the red, white and blue stripes of the American cause and below it the scarlet pennant of Sparhawk and Sons. He'd sooner cut his own throat than strike either one of them to the British.

Though maybe that was what they expected. Maybe that was why the English captain, the devil take him, hadn't fired at all on the *Liberty* this past quarter hour, believing instead that the Americans were too battered by now to do anything but surrender. Softhearted coward, thought Nick scornfully. If he'd been the one blessed with twice the men and guns, *he* wouldn't have been so overnice.

Nor would he be now. With a roar of pure fury Nick hurled himself down to the lower deck to one of the last functioning cannons.

Intent on firing at least one more time at the enemy, the five men in the gun crew only barely acknowledged their captain as he helped them muscle the heavy cannon into position. He'd done it before; it was one of the reasons they'd follow him anywhere. With his long black hair held back by the makeshift bandage around his forehead, his coat gone and his ruffled shirt torn and filthy, the captain was no different from the rest of them, all joined together in their hatred for the English.

Shielding the faint spark of the linstock's slow match in his cupped fingers, Nick concentrated on his target, the English ship that was only a faint outline in the early dawn.

"Steady, lads, steady!" he shouted hoarsely, holding the match over the little ring of gunpowder on the back of the gun. "We've got her now, don't we? Now—*now—fire!*"

The cannon roared to life, spitting fire and smoke as it jerked back with the force of firing. But in the same instant came another explosion, bright white and blinding and louder than thunder. Nick felt himself being thrown into the air, high into the sky and then higher still, far above the top of the *Liberty*'s mainmast until the sloop and the English brig looked like carved toys on the water so far beneath him, and yet still he rose, all six feet and more of him floating weightless as a feather, with the pale light of dawn turning the clouds around him pink and orange, and suddenly he knew, he *knew,* that he wasn't going to fall back to the *Liberty*'s deck or the waves around her or to earth at all.

So this, then, was how his luck would end. His luck and his life and his run as the most fortunate American captain in a notoriously unfortunate war, every last bit of it done and over in one bright blast of gunpowder. Already he could predict the notice in the Charles Town papers: "Captain Nickerson James Sparhawk, master of the twelve-gun privateering sloop *Liberty,* lost at sea with all hands after a most gallant engagement with the enemy."

Lost, hell. He'd never lost a blessed thing since the day he'd been born, and he didn't want to begin now. He wasn't ready to die. He was only thirty-two, in his prime. Damnation, he would *not* die!

"Oh, bother and hush, you're not going to!" declared a woman's voice. "Do you truly believe I would have squandered so much time and effort on your well-being heretofore only to watch you tumble off now?"

Nick twisted about, searching for the source of the voice. He found her perched on the edge of one of the clouds as if it were as solid as stone, her legs crossed gracefully at the knee, and without a doubt she was one of the prettiest young women he'd ever seen.

One of the most elegant, too. He'd never had much of an eye for female frippery, but he did have three younger sisters, and thanks to them he knew that this lady's gown—white silk taffeta over a painted China silk petticoat, edged with silver embroidery—was very fashionable, and doubtless very dear. Around her pale throat lay a double strand of pearls hung with a Roman cameo, and more pearls swung from her ears. A pink sateen ribbon threaded through her extravagantly curled hair, golden auburn, he guessed, beneath the ladylike dusting of powder. Her eyes were large and blue beneath arching, elfin brows, and her rosy lips were winsomely curved for the kind of tempting little smile she was giving him now, her head tipped just so and one brow cocked as she twitched her wings—

Her *wings?* The devil take him, here he was ogling her like any other chit when the creature had wings like a swan's sprouting from her shoulder blades, right beneath the crossing of her sheer white-work fichu. *Wings.* He shook his head and swore.

"La, what a pretty greeting for a lady!" she scoffed. From beneath the curve of one wing she drew a fan of ivory *brisé* and spread it with a practiced flick of her wrist. "I'd thought better of you, sir."

But Nick was in no mood for bantering. "Just who—or what—in blazes are you?"

She laughed merrily over the fan. "I've blessed little to do with 'blazes,' Captain, for which you should be quite thankful."

"You're a bloody angel, aren't you?" he demanded hoarsely. "You're rigged out like some sort of Vauxhall doxy, but still—"

"But still you're quite right, my darling captain." Her eyes were as blue as the Caribbean, dancing deliciously with the pleasure of teasing him. "I'm entirely what you wish me to be. Though that Vauxhall remark rather stings. I'd hoped for an effect more passing genteel than that."

"Blast your effect!" Desperately Nick looked down to where his ship had been, but the *Liberty* and her enemy and the sea, too, had vanished entirely, swallowed up by the same ethereal wisps of clouds that somehow were supporting him. "I'm dead, and all you can damned well think about is the cut of your petticoats!"

"I know it will be difficult for you, Captain Sparhawk, but you really must learn to heed what I tell you." She sighed, the tops of her breasts quivering above her stays. "If you'd only listen, you'd discover how you have it in yourself to be the happiest man alive."

"I was plenty happy before this," he growled, shoving his hand back through his hair. His fingers brushed the blood-stiffened bandage tied around his head, and the wound beneath it throbbed so that he winced. But that was good, wasn't it? If he were dead, he'd be beyond pain, wouldn't he?

Wouldn't he?

"I told you before that you're not dead," she said placidly, answering his doubts as if he'd spoken, "and you're not."

"I'm sure as hell not alive!" Furiously Nick grabbed for her, and as he did she seemed to fade into the intangible distance, melting away like mist in the morning. "Come back here, madam, and show yourself!"

"You must learn to heed what I say," she said again, softly, her voice but a whisper in his ear. "For your own good, you truly must."

He was slipping away himself, not falling exactly but drifting into something close to sleep. This was all her fault, he thought as he struggled to keep his wits, all the fault of some fancy jade trumped up with angel's wings. Why the devil should he heed her about anything? And as for happiness—war and happiness weren't made for each other, but he was still the most contented man he knew.

But the clouds were turning darker now, the sun behind them fading, and with a final, mumbled oath of frustration, he let the darkness claim him.

Chapter One

"It's a hopeless case, Mr. Cole," the surgeon was saying sadly. "Quite, quite hopeless. Three nights and three days, sir, and look at him. Scarcely a mark on the man beyond this poppycock scratch to the cranium, yet already he's slipped beyond our reach."

Cautiously Nick dared to open one eye, and then the other. Dr. Barker's broad back in the worn blue coat was unmistakable as he turned away to fold his spectacles, and beyond the surgeon stood the *Liberty*'s lieutenant, Gideon Cole, with his hands folded and his face as solemn as if he were already staring into an open grave. If Nick's head hadn't ached so badly, he would have laughed out loud, for solemnity from Gideon was as rare as piety from a brothelkeeper. Did Gideon really believe he'd cock up his toes so easily?

Nick shifted slightly in the bunk, intending to reassure his friend, then stopped and frowned. The bunk wasn't his. The mattress was newer and softer than the old wool-stuffed one he'd bought years ago when he'd first outfitted the *Liberty,* and there were two—no, *three*—plump pillows beneath his head, each in pressed linen cases that certainly had no place aboard any sloop of his.

Uneasily he forced himself to focus on the cabin around him. There was his own battered, familiar sea chest, and the spindle-back armchair with the black paint worn off the front rail from his boots. That was his spyglass on its high-front shelf, his logbook and his sextant in the leather case, his favorite gray coat hanging from the peg on the back of the cabin door, and there was certainly no mistaking either Gideon or Barker. But as for the rest of it—the sweeping windows across the stern, the massive wooden desk with the stars carved into the front, the polished brass lanterns swinging in their gimbals, this bunk—none of it belonged to the *Liberty,* and none of it was his.

He closed his eyes again, trying to remember how he'd come here. They'd been surprised in the night fog by an English frigate or privateer twice their size. There'd been no place to run, and they'd been forced to fight or surrender outright. And Nick, of course, had fought.

But then things grew muddled. They'd been losing, badly, and the sloop was sinking, and he and Jemmy Roberts's crew had tried to fire one last shot when the gun had misfired, and finally that infernal woman with the wings, the angel, had hauled him up into the clouds and promised him all manner of claptrap before dumping him back to earth to wake in some stranger's bunk.

He'd been dead, or mighty close to it. And now, somehow, he wasn't.

He could just make out his reflection in the glass of a small framed map of the Mediterranean bolted to the bulkhead beside the bunk. He looked like hell, true enough, but that wasn't particularly out of the ordinary. His thick black hair stuck out at crazy angles from the bandage, and the heavy brows that came together over the bridge of his nose seemed even more inclined to scowl than usual. Someone had washed the gunpowder and grime away from his face since the battle, but his green eyes were ringed with red and his jaw was unshaven and bristling with those three lost days' worth of dark whiskers. More the face of a pirate than one to set the maidens swooning, but then the only difference between him and, say, Blackbeard was the scrap of paper from the Continental Congress that promised he'd fight and plunder for the good of his country and not just his own pocket.

Gingerly he reached up to touch the bandage around his forehead. At least that much was real. He hadn't imagined that. But hadn't he thought the same thing when he'd been up there in the clouds?

"Captain Sparhawk!" Dr. Barker rushed to his side, his jowls quivering with alarm and surprise. "Please, sir, you must not disturb yourself when your situation is so delicate!"

"There's not a blasted thing about me that's delicate, Barker," growled Nick, his voice gravelly from disuse. "You know that as well as I."

Gideon came to stand beside the surgeon, his face returned to its customarily sly expression. His hair was as thick and red as a fox's brush, and the quizzical sharpness of his features, too, gave him a vulpine air. He'd grown up with Nick in Newport, even as a boy willing to play the small, quick fox to the larger, more menacing wolf that was Nick.

"What Barker means, Nick," he said cheerfully, "is that he'd just about given you up for dead. Ready to toss you over the side to the fish, he was."

"Certainly not!" declared Barker indignantly. "I was properly concerned by the gravity of your condition!"

Nick grunted, unconvinced. He'd given himself up for dead. Why shouldn't the surgeon feel that way, too? "Then you'll get me a drink, Barker, and be quick about it."

"Water, sir, that is all," ordered Barker as he went to pour from the pewter pitcher on the table. "No spirits, though perhaps I'll permit a thin broth later if there's no fever."

Glaring at the surgeon, Nick bit back a groan as he pushed himself higher on the pillows and took the tankard. Even that tiny effort made his head throb like the devil, but he refused to give Barker any more reason to fuss over him. What he needed now were answers.

"So where the hell are we, Gid?" he demanded. "Where's the *Liberty?*"

"In Charles Town by now, God willing." Without waiting for permission, Gideon pulled one of the chairs close beside the bunk and sat, leaning forward eagerly with his hands on his knees. Though he'd signed on as Nick's lieutenant, the two men had been friends too long to stand on ceremony. "And us—ahh, we're aboard as fine a little privateering brig as you'd ever fancy."

Nick scowled. "The truth now, Gid. I'm in no humor for fancies, mine or yours. Last I recall we were on our way down."

"Aye, and that's the beauty of it, Nick! We were going fast, like you say, and you and Jemmy's boys fired that last ball, and those hen-wit Britishers up and struck!"

"Struck?" Nick stared in disbelief. "You mean we *captured* her?"

Gideon grinned with delight. "Her captain was killed early on, and the feather brains left in the crew hadn't a clue what to do next, so they struck. Gave it up, just like that. 'Twas a rare sight to watch their faces when the sun come up, and they could see how sorry the poor *Liberty* was."

"Struck," repeated Nick again, stunned by this twist of fortune. "What was the cost to us?"

Gideon's grin vanished. "Twelve of our people killed outright," he said soberly, "four more dead since, another ten in their hammocks, may God keep them all."

"Amen," said Nick softly. Though every man who signed on to a privateer knew the odds, as captain he still hated grim accountings like these, and mourned the men he'd lost. Yet this time Gideon's tally seemed somehow worse. Why, he wondered, had these men died while he'd been spared? Why hadn't they, too, been sent back by that silly Vauxhall angel?

"If it's a comfort," said Gideon, "the Britishers fared worse. Lost their captain and their two lieutenants and the gunner's mate and a dozen others besides. I sent the rest as prisoners in the *Liberty* to Charles Town, and then shifted us over here. I figured you'd want it that way."

Nick nodded. How could he want it otherwise? Switching vessels like this in the middle of a cruise wasn't covered by either his commission or his Articles of Agreement and he'd have the devil of a time sorting it out through the prize court, but he'd be a fool to let a chance to improve his lot like this slip through his fingers.

Swiftly he glanced around the cabin with new appreciation. So it all really did belong to him now. Three years of wartime scarcity and blockades had put luxury on this scale beyond the reach of any American privateer, and his excitement grew when he remembered how heavily the brig was armed, long guns that now would fire at his command, beneath an American flag instead of English. Lord, what he'd be able to accomplish for the cause with a ship like this!

"She's only six months out of a shipyard in Portsmouth, Nick," continued Gideon, gloating. "Twenty guns, all of 'em new. Don't think she took even one prize under that fool of a captain. But I expect that'll change now that you're master of the fair *Angel Lily.*''

"*Angel Lily?*'' repeated Nick uneasily, his pleasure in his good fortune thumping to a halt. "That's her name?''

Gideon shrugged. "Queer sort of name for a privateer, I know, but that's what the brig was christened, and that's what she'll stay, unless you wish to risk ill luck and change it.''

"I'd warrant *Angel Lily* is most appropriate,'' intoned Barker with pious conviction, spreading his fingers wide across his waistcoat. "Considering it's a veritable miracle that the captain's alive to enjoy his victory, the celestial name seems altogether proper.''

Proper or not, Nick didn't like it. An angel named Lily, a dream more real than reality, a miracle bringing him back from the dead—no, it was far too much coincidence for comfort. Though he wasn't as superstitious as many sailors, Nick still didn't like things he couldn't explain, and this all made so little sense that he was ashamed to confide it even to Gideon.

Instead he threw back the coverlet and swung his legs over the side of the bunk. His head still throbbed as if a thunderstorm had settled into his skull, but what was that beside his sanity?

"Enough of your nattering,'' he said as he reached for his breeches and Barker blustered with disapproval. "If I'm captain of this angel of a ship, then it's high time I met her properly.''

He spent the rest of the afternoon with Gideon at his side, inspecting every inch of the brig from the depths of her hold to the tallest tip of her foretop. He critically sighted one of the new guns with the gunner, and he grinned like a boy on Christmas morning when he saw the cache of other weaponry the English had stowed below. He congratulated the crew members who'd come over from the *Liberty* on their victory and tossed back a dram of rum with them between decks, and he welcomed the handful of Englishmen who'd decided to cast their lots with the Americans rather than sit out the war in a South Carolina prison. He drove himself mercilessly, intent on learning everything about his new command and determined to banish the ill-gotten memories of angels and miracles.

He nearly succeeded. Almost, but not quite. As the sun was dropping low to the horizon, Nick ordered one of the boats lowered so he could be rowed around the brig to see how she sat in the water. At Gideon's suggestion he'd brought along one of the English turncoats to answer any questions. The man's name was Hobb, and he took the first oar so he faced Nick sitting in the sternsheets. A fisherman from Guernsey Island, Hobb had hoped a turn at privateering would improve his station enough to marry, and because he was new at it, he'd none of the careful reticence of the more experienced hands around officers. He needed no prompting from Nick to begin a monologue of all that was right—and wrong—about the brig and her former master.

"Th' ol' cap'n didn't know what-for th' jewel he had," said Hobb sorrowfully as he pulled at the oar. "Master Everard, he be th' owner, he spared nothing on 'count of *her.*"

"'Her' being the brig?" asked Nick absently, suspecting that he'd drifted off while the man had droned on about the wickedness of the dead captain.

"Nay, sir, *her* bein' Miss Lily, o' course!" Hobb smiled, pleased that his new captain was listening after all. "Miss Lily Everard, Sir Edmund Everard's first daughter, th' one what he named this brig for, sir, an' th' one that died so tragical. She be there now, sir, if you only but look."

Hobb cocked his head toward the *Angel Lily*'s bowsprit, and even before Nick turned to look, he knew what he'd see. Part of him had known ever since he'd learned the brig's name. With a sigh he pushed back the brim of his hat and forced himself to look at the *Angel Lily*'s figurehead.

The carving was life-size, a beautiful young woman gazing out to sea with the hint of a smile on her painted lips. Her auburn hair was piled high on her head, one wooden curl artfully tossed across her shoulder, and her white gown swirled against her body as if blown by the same wind that filled the brig's sails. Behind her her wings were raised and spread against the bow, each white feather neatly carved, and over her head hung a halo bright with the same gold leaf that trimmed the hem of her gown. Apparently Miss Lily Everard had inspired the wood-carver to the limits of his craft, for

Nick had never seen another figurehead more real, and as he stared at it he could almost hear the merry laughter rippling from her lips.

It wasn't until the boat had finished circling the brig and Nick had climbed back on board that he realized he was damp with sweat and that his heart was pounding with something perilously close to fear. Alone at last in his cabin, he sank into his chair with his head cradled in his trembling hands.

Of course there must be an explanation. There had to be. Even if he'd been unconscious, he still could have wakened enough to glimpse the figurehead when they'd brought him aboard. He could have overheard Gideon or Barker talking about the brig, maybe one of the Englishmen, maybe even Hobb himself, discussing Edmund Everard's tribute to his daughter Lily.

"Well, then, do you approve of my namesake, Captain Sparhawk?" asked the woman's voice behind him. "You've certainly been more thorough in your perusal than Captain Fotherill ever was. Whatever your conclusions are, you may be sure that *I* approve of *you.*"

This time Nick didn't turn toward the voice, nor did he answer. He closed his eyes, willing himself to be calm. It was his imagination, that was all. He was giddy now from exhaustion and the head wound, but in the morning, once he'd rested and—

"You don't believe in me, do you?" The edge of irritation in her words was clear. "You've only to look my way, you know, and trust your eyes to tell you the truth."

But Nick kept his eyes resolutely shut. "I don't believe in you because you're not real. You're no more than the rum I drank this forenoon, come back to addle my wits."

He heard a little *shush* and a snap as she opened her fan. "Oh, bother and stuff, Captain! You've spent the past fifteen years of your life with a tankard of rum near to hand, and precisely how often have you toppled so far into your cups that you began to see apparitions? You're stubborn and you're horribly accustomed to having your own way, but my goodness, you're also far too sensible to be a drunkard. Captain Fotherill, now, there was a man who could disappear into a bottle for days at a time!"

Nick frowned in spite of himself. No one had ever called him sensible before, particularly not a female, and it didn't sit well with him. Privateers were supposed to be reckless and daring and wallowing in rum, not bloody *sensible*.

"You're rum and the hot sun and this blasted ruddy gash on my forehead," he said doggedly. "You're not real, and you never have been."

She sighed. "Very well then, my dear captain, you've left me little recourse but to prove you wrong."

At that Nick's eyes crept open. What the devil was she about, anyway? Did she really mean to—

The water rushing over his head was so cold it made him gasp, and he lunged to his feet, swearing, as the empty pewter pitcher crashed to the deck before him.

"There now, Captain Sparhawk, was that real enough for you?" asked Lily as Nick sputtered and shook the water from his hands. "I vow it seems a bit like a parlor trick, but if it serves to convince you—"

"You've convinced me of nothing, ma'am, except that you're a damnable nuisance, and I want you gone immediately!" Nick was too angry to pretend to ignore her any longer, and he glared at her, sitting on his bunk with her legs crossed and hands linked casually around her knee as if she'd every right to be there. "Go on, shove off!"

"Oh, pish." Idly she circled the toe of her shoe, the lantern's light glinting off the square paste brilliants on the buckle. "I told you before that I've no intention of leaving. I can't, you see, not until I've accomplished what I've been sent here to do. It would, of course, make things vastly more agreeable for us both if you'd try to be a bit less like an old bear and cooperate instead."

She wasn't real, he told himself fiercely. *She was not real.* She couldn't be, and plague take him if he couldn't prove it. With a growl that was very much like a bear's, Nick scooped up the now-empty water pitcher from the deck and hurled it at the bunk directly where Lily sat. But as the pewter pitcher flew through the air, she raised her fan. The pitcher stopped in midair, hovered for a moment and then settled itself once again on the table.

"Parlor tricks," said Lily with a contemptuous little sniff as she smoothed the feathers of one wing.

"I've refilled it for you, though, to save you the trouble."

Nick glanced at the pitcher, but refused to give her the satisfaction of looking inside. Besides, he had the uncomfortable conviction it would be filled, just as she'd said. "You've caused me trouble enough already, ma'am, and if you don't—"

"Nick?" The door to the cabin opened and Gideon cautiously stuck his head through it. Behind him, cowering in the shadows of the companionway, was the boy with Nick's supper. "Nick, you old rogue, are you all right?"

"Of course I'm all right!" he shouted with exasperation. "At least as well as I can be when I'm being hounded by this *creature!*"

"What creature, Nick?" Slowly Gideon pushed the door open, his gaze sweeping around the cabin before pointedly coming to rest on Nick's soaked shirt. "The boy here heard you railing on fit to burst, and when you didn't answer his knock for supper, he fetched me. Was there someone in here vexing you?"

"It was that infernal strumpet with the wings again!" declared Nick, standing to one side to point to the bunk where Lily sat behind him. "I swear, Gid, she's becoming a bloody nuisance!"

Gideon looked, and frowned, and looked to Nick again. "A strumpet with wings, you say?" he asked doubtfully. "You've seen her before, Nick?"

"Damnation, stop looking at me like I've lost my wits! If I can see her, than you bloody well can, too!"

But neither Gideon nor the boy did; that was clear enough from the doleful looks on their faces. Swearing, Nick swung around to face the now-empty bunk.

"Almighty heaven, Lily, show yourself! Now, ma'am! *Now!*"

"Lily?" asked Gideon warily, his fox-colored brows raised with skepticism. "Like the name of the brig? You're seeing the poor lass herself?"

"Aye, damn her, and she's playing me false now, hiding herself away to make me look the fool!" Nick tugged his wet shirt away from his chest. "How do you think I came to be this way? Lily did it, that's how, dousing me with that entire pitcher of water to prove she could!"

Gideon lifted the pitcher from the table with both hands and held it, testing its weight. "It's full, Nick. To the brim."

Nick roared with angry frustration. "That's because *she* refilled it!"

Gideon set the pitcher back on the table and sighed. "If you've seen her, Nick, well then, that's fine," he said carefully. "Barker said you were pushing it too hard this afternoon, and maybe he was right. Best to rest now, eat your supper here and turn in early."

"Hell, Gideon, I'm still your captain, not some puppy needing a nursemaid!" Furiously he slashed his hand across the table and once again sent the pitcher sailing through the air. This time, though, it struck the deck with a resounding clank that turned into a gurgle as the water spread into a puddle.

Avoiding Nick's stony gaze, Gideon gave the cabin boy's shoulders a shove. "Swab that mess, lad, and be quick about it."

"Nay, leave it!" countered Nick angrily. Blast Gideon! Friend or not, he was only the lieutenant, and he had no right to be giving orders in the captain's presence, even orders about wiping up spilled water. "And leave *me,* both of you. Out!"

Immediately Gideon stiffened to attention, his eyes wary yet wounded. "Aye aye, Captain Sparhawk," he said curtly. "Come along, boy, you heard the captain. Out!"

Without turning to watch them leave, Nick heard the cabin's door latch shut. He'd done it now, hadn't he, ripping Gideon's head off like that. He'd done it right royally, and over what? Furiously he kicked the empty pitcher across the deck and into the bulkhead, swearing at his own temper even as he couldn't contain it.

"I'm sorry, Captain Sparhawk," said Lily softly behind him. "I didn't mean for that to happen. I'd every intention of explaining how only you can see me, but somehow we've never quite had the time."

With a groan halfway to a sigh, Nick dropped heavily into his chair. "It doesn't matter now anyway," he said with disgust. "Doubtless the word's already racing tween decks about how the captain's gone daft, hearing voices and talking to the figurehead and quarreling with his own shadow. Fine sort of courage that will give the men. Aye, who wouldn't want to follow a raving lunatic into battle?"

"The ungrateful wretches! They wouldn't truly believe that of you, will they?" she asked indignantly. "You're supposed to be one of the very best American privateers, and certainly the luckiest. Why, you've made the fortune of every man in your crew! Not a morning passes but that every last governor in the Windward Islands has merchants clamoring for your neck, you've brought them that much grief by capturing so many of their ships!"

He looked to where she was sitting now, on the center of the carved desk, her skirts spread over the top and her wings resting on the back. Strange how he was beginning to feel resigned, if not exactly pleased, to having her there.

"So my reputation's spread from the Caribbean heavenward?" He smiled bleakly. "Perhaps next you can whisper a word to the keeper at Bedlam on my behalf."

"I can do better than that, Captain," she said eagerly. "I'll give you a way to regain your crew's confidence."

"Keep it." He shook his head. "I don't want your help."

"But I don't see why—"

"Because I'm American, and you're English," he said roughly. "Or at least you were once. Our countries are at war, mind? Maybe it don't bother you, helping the enemy like this, but I sure as hell don't forget how many friends, good friends, I've lost to English guns and swords since this infernal war began.

What of the first master of this brig, eh? Don't it concern you at all that he's dead?''

"Captain Fotherill? Mourn *him?* La, no!'' She narrowed her eyes and and wrinkled her nose as if she'd smelled something foul. "He, sir, was an odious, mean-spirited, cowardly cheat of a drunkard, who took advantage of my father's trust and inexperience in privateering ventures. Whether a gentleman's British or rebel makes no difference to me, and it never has. Consider you who took care to shift Mr. Fotherill into the path of one of your cannonballs.''

"*You* killed him?'' asked Nick, incredulous.

"More correctly, you did,'' answered Lily sweetly. "I merely made certain he was standing in the proper spot.''

Nick frowned, remembering how neatly she'd stopped the flying water pitcher. It would, perhaps, be in his best interest not to quarrel with Miss Lily. "I thought angels were supposed to do good.''

"For good people, yes, we do. And you, Captain Sparhawk, have it in yourself to be a most excellent gentleman, with a proper bit of guidance. The dear Lord knows you're already handsome enough.''

She smiled, a smile that could outshine the sun, and Nick caught himself wondering what she'd been like when she lived. Nothing but trouble, likely. Women like her always were.

"How did you die, anyway?'' he asked sourly, intent on putting distance between them. It was bad enough to be having a conversation with her; beyond bearing for him to start taking her compliments to heart. "Did you drive your poor old father to horse-whip you to save the family honor?"

Her laughter rippled through the cabin. "Nothing so fearsome, nor 'tragical,' as the sailors say. At Sir George Carruthers's Christmas ball I insisted on dancing outside in his garden in the new snow. It was a lovely night, the snowflakes like crystals as they fell, but I caught a chill and a fever and died, just like that." She smacked her palm on the top of the desk with emphatic finality. "Just like that! The only true tragedy was that I missed the next ball on Twelfth Night."

She swept her fan shut and tapped the last blade twice against her lips. "I might not be precisely what you expect, but I've always been vastly fond of gentlemen, and that is why you've been…*given,* shall we say, to me."

He glowered at her, his green eyes dark beneath his drawn brows. "I don't consider myself 'givable,' especially not to you for haunting or whatever it is you're doing to me. What's to separate you from a common ghost, anyway?"

"What's to separate *you,*" she said archly, "from a common, thieving pirate?"

That took him by surprise, and almost made him smile. "I've a commission from the Continental Congress that makes me honest, but I doubt that that's what you're steering toward."

"Indeed I'm not! In your way, you mean to do good, both for what you believe and for your fine, new rapscallion country. And I'm here to do the same." A glow of triumph crept into her smile. "You're my first real challenge, Nickerson. I may call you Nickerson, may I not? 'Captain Sparhawk' seems so dreadfully cold and cumbersome."

He sighed deeply, realizing that the luckiest Yankee captain in the Caribbean had just lost again. "Will it make any real difference to you what I wish?"

She shrugged her wings with charming nonchalance, all the answer that Nick knew he'd get to that particular question.

"But I do wish you well, Nickerson. You'll see." She leaned forward off the desk to study their course on the charts spread across the table. "I've plans—oh, such plans!"

Abruptly Nick rose, moving to stand between her and the charts. "I won't have you interfering with my orders or with how this vessel is sailed."

"And I vow I won't. I only wish to offer you the chance to redeem yourself in the eyes of your crew, just as I promised. If you'll but consider this course I've suggested here—"

"Damnation, ma'am, I won't have it!" Across his chart now ran a bold red line to the northwest, a course no sane privateering captain would ever choose, and once again her audacity infuriated him. "I'm still captain! You keep your lubberly suggestions to yourself, and let me be!"

"As you wish, Captain Nick." She settled back on the desk with a sigh, uncharacteristically contrite. "But if you truly wish to decide whether I'm real or not, sir, you'll follow my course for, oh, eight hours. If by then you've found no other ships to tempt your piratical inclinations, then you'll know for certain that I'm nothing but the rum-induced will-o'-the-wisp you claim. But I don't believe you shall."

Nick scowled down at the ugly red line that disfigured his immaculate charts. As if he'd ever waste his time on such a misguided course! The crew would mutiny for certain.

"The devil take you, Lily Everard," he grumbled to himself. "The devil take you straight to blazes where you belong."

But still she heard him, and laughed. "I fear I've already been taken by the other side," she said merrily, "and before I'm done you'll be mightily glad I was."

Chapter Two

"It's a rebel pirate, miss, no mistake," said the captain of the English ship *Commerce* as he squinted through his spyglass at the horizon. "And they're gaining on us so fast we might as well be standing still."

Beside him Rose Everard clutched the rail more tightly, her fingers trembling inside the black gloves. The Americans were gaining on them, and there was no use pretending otherwise. Even without a spyglass, she could now make out the shape of the enemy ship that had been chasing them since dawn. To think that they'd come within four days of St. Lucia after a hard twelve-week passage from Portsmouth only to fall prey to *pirates!*

"Are you certain we cannot escape them, Captain Richards?" she asked, thankful that shouting over the wind hid the fear she was certain must mark her voice. "We must be close enough to some island that would give us sanctuary."

Unhappily Richards shook his head, his gaze still fixed on the American ship. "Nay, Miss Everard, we're not, not since the French jumped on the rebel side against King George. We're still days away from St. Lucia, or even Anguilla, and they'll catch us long afore then. My poor *Commerce* doesn't have a chance, miss, not after beating clear across the Atlantic and not against a ship like that one. That Yankee's built for hunting, fast and mean as a gray-bellied shark."

"I should like to see for myself, Captain Richards." Rose held her hand out for the spyglass. "If you please?"

Richards looked from her outstretched hand to her face and back again, and doggedly shook his head. Even facing into the chill wind off the water, he was sweating, his weathered cheeks shiny and flushed.

"Nay, Miss Everard, you belong below," he said glumly. "I only let you come topside because you begged so, but now you've seen your sight, and I'll ask you to go below again to your cabin. I'll have enough to answer for from your father without having you on deck with rebel guns trained our way."

"Please, Captain. I wish to see them before they capture us." She forced her mouth into a smile, looking up at him from beneath the curving brim of her black straw hat. She'd never have her sister's effortless charm with gentlemen, but because Captain Richards was a friend of her father's and equally old, he didn't expect much in the matter of flirtation. "Please, Captain Richards. Then I promise I'll go below."

Yet still Richards shook his head. "You're a lady, Miss Everard, and a pirate ship like that's a fearsome sight."

"Less fearsome now at a distance than when they capture us, as you claim they must." Rose's smile faltered. All of her twenty years she'd prided herself on being calm and capable. Why should this be any different? She swallowed hard, raising her chin with determination.

She tried not to remember the dreadful tales from Aunt Lucretia, horrifying stories of the rebel sailors who called themselves privateers, but were in truth no better than pirates. How could they be otherwise, her aunt had asked in a horrified whisper over her needlework, when they thumbed their noses at His Majesty and took their commissions from the anarchists and rogues pretending to be a government? One had only to read the papers to know it all. Torture and rape and murder, pillage and robbery: nothing was too low for such knaves.

And now, thought Rose as her smile disappeared entirely, she'd learn the truth for herself. No wonder her hands were shaking as she took the spyglass from the captain and lifted it to her eye.

Unfamiliar with the glass, Rose struggled to steady the heavy brass cylinder long enough to focus it. First she saw only blue sky, then the white-tipped waves of the sea, and then, finally, she found the stern of the American ship, the blue, red and white striped flag of the fledgling country flying briskly from her jackstaff.

The brig was exactly as Captain Richards had said, low and mean as a shark as she bore down upon them. Her deck was thick with men, and though her gunports were still closed for the chase, Rose knew well enough what lay behind each neat square on the brig's side. How could she not? The war had so inflamed her father that this year he'd begun outfitting privateers himself, and Rose had had to listen to endless discussions of this gun's merits versus that type of boarding ax.

And, of course, the profits he hoped to make. She could never forget that. Patriotism was all well and good, but for Papa, the profits would always come first, where for him they belonged. Profits and prestige, position and power. Would she be making this journey now at all if he believed otherwise?

Carefully Rose shifted the glass along the brig's black-painted sides, forcing herself to think of something else. Pirates or not, even Papa would have to admit the Americans knew how to sail. The brig sliced like a knife through the water as she edged closer and closer with a speed and deadly grace that the poor *Commerce* could never dream of matching. Soon, too soon, the Americans would be within range to open those gunports, and then—merciful heaven, let these men not be the savages Aunt Lucretia swore they were!

"I know I must strike to them, though it pains me worse than death to do it," said Richards angrily beside her. "And, well, forgive me, miss, if it weren't for you being on board, I'd sooner damn their heathen souls to the devil where they belong than surrender my *Commerce* into their filthy hands!''

Rose didn't answer. She couldn't. She'd just discovered the brig's figurehead through the glass, and it was taking every last bit of her concentration simply to remember to breathe.

"How they found us in these waters I'll never know," continued Richards, too caught up in his own outrage to notice Rose's silence. "I've never seen a Yankee ship this far to the east, blast their impertinence! It's almost as if they'd been led to us, and—"

"They're not Americans," blurted Rose.

Richards frowned and shook his head. "Of course they are, missy," he said, testy at being interrupted. "You've the glass, and you can see their flag plain as the sun. And why else would they be chasing us, eh?"

"I don't know," she said slowly, her voice half-strangled in her throat. "But that privateer is British, not American."

Richards sniffed. "Forgive me, Miss Everard, but what would you know of the matter?"

"I know because that brig belongs to my father." Rose handed Richards the glass so he could see for himself, her own eyes too blurry with tears to look any longer. "She's the *Angel Lily,* and if you don't believe me, you'll find my sister's face on her figurehead."

"That's not possible," snapped Richards as he swung the glass to his eye. "Not possible in the least."

But Rose knew it was. Father had paid extra for the carving and gilt on that figurehead, wanting a fitting tribute to his elder daughter's beauty, and the likeness to Lily was extraordinary, the effect breathtaking.

Exactly the way Lily had been while she lived.

"By thunder, it *is* the *Lily!*" exclaimed Richards. "They must have captured her and made her their own, the thieving jackals!"

The brig was near enough now that Rose could make out the figurehead's white gown as it dipped in and out of the waves. The sight of her sister's image in the hands of the enemy was a hideous, unimaginable joke.

"But they can't do that!" she cried, her anguish real, as she seized Captain Richards's sleeve. "They've no right, none at all!"

Yet as she spoke the other ship's gunports flipped up in unison. She saw the burst of flame and the smoke from the first gun an instant before she heard the dry, percussive sound of the firing across the water. All at once the *Commerce*'s mainsail flew apart, the severed lines whipping like snakes as the taut canvas shredded into streamers in the wind and the massive spar splintered and dropped to the deck with a thunderous crack.

With the careful balance of sail and wind broken, the *Commerce*'s bow pitched crazily downward, and Rose's feet skidded out beneath her. She shrieked and grabbed the rail with both hands, her black skirts swirling around her in the wind as she struggled not to be swept along the canting deck and over the side. Wildly she looked for someone to help her, but Richards had joined the others running and sliding away from her and toward the wreckage of the mainmast. Waves crashed and broke over the side and across Rose, white foam washing like soapsuds across the pine planks, and as slippery as soapsuds, too, beneath her leather-soled shoes. Her sodden skirts and petticoats were dragging her down, heavy as lead to tug against her weakening hold on the rail.

God help her, she was going to die as surely as had Lily, drowned if she wasn't killed first by cannon fire, and not one of those bloodthirsty American savages in her father's ship would lift a finger to save her!

"Miss Everard!" Richards's arm circled her waist to steady her, his shout filled with fear and concern. "Are you harmed, miss?"

He was trying to lead her toward the companion-way, but she refused to abandon the security of the rail just yet. Slowly the ship was beginning to level herself as the crew cleared away the wreckage and trimmed the remaining sails, and she'd much rather wait until she could walk on her own with dignity than lurch along with his assistance.

"Thank you, no, Captain Richards," she huffed breathlessly. "though it's certainly through no wish of those—those *jackals!*"

"I told you you should have gone below, miss, indeed I did, but you would not listen." Bunched beneath his other arm was the *Commerce*'s flag, faded and frayed after their long voyage, and much like the woebegone resignation on Richards's own face at the thought of surrender. "If that warning shot had gone awry—"

"*Warning* shot!" exclaimed Rose indignantly. With the immediate danger of being killed gone, at least for now, her anger swelled to fill the gap left by fear. "That was a low, murderous shot meant to kill us all! Those Americans were mean-spirited cowards to steal my father's ship and then turn his very own guns on *me*, and so I shall tell them, the first opportunity I have!"

Richards looked beyond her, his eyes bleak. "Then ready your words, missy," he said grimly, "for here come the bastards now to hear you out."

Swiftly Rose turned in time to see the first Americans climbing up over the side, and without stopping to consider the consequences she pulled herself free of Richards's support and marched across the deck to the red-haired man who appeared to be their leader. Dressed in breeches instead of sailor's trousers, a long green coat with pewter buttons and a reasonably clean shirt, he looked more like a prosperous shopkeeper than a bloodthirsty pirate.

"Who are you, sir?" she demanded.

"Gideon Cole, ma'am, your servant." He smiled and lifted his three-cornered hat to her with a courtly little bow, as if a pistol in his belt and a battered cutlass in his hand were nothing more than gentlemanly props. "Dare I ask, ma'am, if I have the pleasure of addressing the fair wife of the captain of this fine vessel?"

"You may not dare, sir, nor will you find any pleasure at my expense," she said tartly. "You presume entirely too much."

She lifted her chin a fraction higher, challenging him to contradict her. Everything he said was meaningless honey, she thought fiercely, treacly nonsense that he'd pour before any woman he chanced to encounter. She knew well enough how she looked, bedraggled and sallow in salt-stained mourning, just as she knew that men who made pretty speeches to her never meant a word of it. She wasn't Lily and she never would be, and she deeply mistrusted anyone who pretended otherwise.

But instead of his accepting her reproof, the man's smile widened to a grin, his dark eyes teasing beneath his rust-colored brows. "Then you must be the master's daughter, eh? Gone to sea with the old gentleman?"

"She's Miss Rose Everard, the only daughter of Sir Edmund Everard," said Richards warmly as he came to stand beside her, "and you'll treat her like the lady she is or answer to me, damn your eyes!"

"I've no intention of doing otherwise, sir," said the American, ignoring the other captain's hostility just as he'd ignored Rose's. He narrowed his eyes, studying her so closely that she felt herself blush. "Not a wife, nor a daughter, nor a widow despite those weeds. You're English, no doubt there, and a lady. Somehow you seem deucedly familiar to me, Miss Everard, but I can't conceive of a way we might have met."

"Nor, sir, can I, because I'm quite certain we haven't." Impatiently she brushed a loose lock of hair back from her face. Heaven only knew where on earth—or in the sea—her hat was by now. "You listen to me, Captain Cole, and if you—"

"I'm not the captain, miss," interrupted Cole. "I'm only the lieutenant, here to take this gentleman's surrender and make you all our prisoners."

"You'll do nothing of the kind until I speak with your captain!"

Richards took her arm and stepped in front of her. "Best to hold your tongue with this rascal, miss," he cautioned. "Better you let me handle him."

But Rose wriggled around him. "Don't you go surrendering to him, Captain Richards," she said warmly, "at least not until I've spoken to his so-called captain!"

Cole laughed. "Oh, aye, how he'd like to hear that! Nickerson Sparhawk a so-called captain!"

"Well then," snapped Rose, "I'll oblige us both and tell the man so to his face!"

"Ah , Miss Everard, don't!" pleaded Richards, his spirit suddenly gone. "Don't sully yourself quarreling with the likes of him!"

Rose sighed impatiently. "I am not quarreling. I'm merely attempting to retrieve what by rights belongs to my family, and I can do that only by speaking with this Mr. Sparhawk."

"Let it go, miss!" Richards begged, his flag forgotten beneath his arm. "The man's Black Nick Sparhawk, and he's captured a score of ships if he's taken a one! There's not a more wicked, desperate Yankee sailing these waters, miss, and we'll all be lucky if we get clear with our lives!''

Rose looked at Richards's flushed, frightened face and frowned. She supposed she should be as terrified by this *pirate* as Captain Richards seemed to be, but somehow she found it difficult to be frightened of a grown man who let himself be called such a ridiculously schoolboy *nom de guerre*. For all love, she thought with disgust, if *he* fashioned himself Black Nick, then why didn't *she* start calling herself White Rose?

Slowly she shook her head, sorry to distress Captain Richards but determined to do what she must. ''Forgive me, Captain, but I feel I have little choice but to speak to the man.''

Cole laughed again. ''You'll have the devil of a time doing that, miss, with you here and Captain Sparhawk—'' he waved ''—there.''

''Then he must come across here to me, to the *Commerce*,'' she answered promptly. ''Unless, of course, he's too much of a coward.''

''Oh, you'd find him brave enough,'' Cole said softly, the expression in his eyes changing subtly as he watched for her response. ''But what of yourself, miss? If you wish so much to speak to Captain Sparhawk, would you be willing to go across to him?''

''Damn your impudence!'' cried Richards. ''I won't allow it!'' Roughly he shoved Rose to one side and lunged at Cole, his fist tensed and ready to strike. But he never reached the lieutenant; he didn't even come close. In the first instant he'd begun to move two of the American sailors had jumped to stop him, each seizing one of Richards's arms to drag him unceremoniously backward. As he struggled against their hold, his boots scrambling against the deck, one of the Americans flipped the pistol in his hand and raised the butt to hit the older man's head.

"No!" shrieked Rose. "Don't hurt him, please! He was only trying to protect me, that was all!"

The sailor stopped, looking to Cole, whose infinitesimal nod was command enough to spare the English captain.

But not Rose. "So tell me, Miss Everard," he said again, his eyes cold and all traces of his earlier good humor gone. "Do you wish to speak to Captain Sparhawk so much that you'll go to him, or shall you stay here and keep silent?"

Her heart pounding at the sudden violence, Rose stared down at the deck, struggling to sort her thoughts. Because of her impulsiveness, Captain Richards had suffered, and would suffer more if she unwittingly erred again. Yet beyond Cole's shoulder she could see Lily's familiar face on the figurehead to remind her of why she'd spoken in the first place.

Lord help her, she only wanted to do what was right!

Slowly she bent to gather the English flag from the deck where Richards had dropped it in the scuffle, folded the faded fabric into a neat packet and held it out to Richards, his eyes still pleading with her in silence. As she'd hoped, the sailors released his arms so he could take it, and with a last, troubled smile for the English captain, she turned again to the American lieutenant. Her father, she knew, would expect no less.

"What I have to say to Captain Sparhawk will not wait, sir," she said, her voice sounding far too loud and brittle to her own ears, "and I'll be much obliged if you will take me to him directly."

She'd only wanted to do what was right, yet as she was rowed across to the *Angel Lily,* she couldn't help but wonder what under heaven that might be. Cole had stayed behind on the *Commerce,* as had all the other Americans who'd come with him except for the two huge, stone-faced men sitting opposite her at the boat's oars. One was a Yankee with a queue that reached his waist and bare arms covered by inked designs, the other an African, his face cruelly scarred by some long-ago knife. Neither man looked at her as the boat flew across the water, and neither spoke except to hail the brig as the boat drew close. The *Angel Lily* was larger than the *Commerce,* her glistening sides rising up from the water like a black, curving wall of oak.

"You knows th' cap'n's rules on th' chits, Ned," called a man over the side high above them. "Can't keep her on board, even if she do be a prize."

Raucous laughter greeted his words, and Ned and the African both grinned as Rose's cheeks grew hot with shame and indignation. Automatically she shot to her feet, wobbling with the motion of the boat.

"I am not a chit, sir," she shouted back at the man's face overhead, "but an English lady and a loyal subject of His Majesty King George."

Someone on the deck made a loud, disrespectful noise, followed by more laughter and a handful of oaths, and Rose gasped with outrage. Her aunt had been right. Americans were little better than savages.

"If you are quite done," she shouted when the laughter faded, "I should wish to speak with your captain directly."

But before anyone answered the boat bobbed against the brig's side, and ignominiously Rose toppled backward into the seawater that had gathered in the bottom of the boat. Close to tears with humiliation and dread, she climbed back to her bench, her skirts soaked, and waited for more of the laughter that she knew must come again at her expense.

But to her surprise, it didn't. Instead Ned tugged on the front of his knitted cap and held his hand out to her. "Bos'n's chair's ready for you, miss," he said gruffly. "Mind yerself, now."

"Thank you," said Rose with a little sniff, and gingerly she climbed into the makeshift sling that would preserve what was left of her modesty as it lifted her swaying to the deck. Balanced in the bos'n's chair, she felt like some market-day acrobat, as she swung precariously up into the air. It seemed odd to be able to see the *Commerce* from a distance rather than to still be walking her decks, and with a pang of homesickness for the other ship, Rose noticed that a new American

flag now flew at the masthead. So Captain Richards
had finally surrendered, she thought bitterly; nothing
she could say now would be able to change that.

She was level with the main deck now, and with a final pull on the line she was lifted over the side. She
smiled her thanks to the man who held the chair steady
while she climbed down, but he was as careful to avoid
her eye as the men in the boat had been at first. Her
smile faded as she noticed the same reaction all around
her; although she sensed that every seaman on the deck
was watching her, not one was actually looking *at* her,
and beneath their furtive scrutiny she'd never been
more self-conscious, or more uncomfortable, in her
life. Nervously she touched her hair, wishing again that
she hadn't lost her hat.

"So you've come a-calling, have you, Miss Loyal
Subject of King George?"

The man's voice boomed out over the deck, deep and
effortlessly commanding. It was a voice that instinctively made Rose want to hop to attention, the same
way it undoubtedly did everyone who heard it, but instead she forced herself to count to five, then five more,
before, slowly, she turned to face Captain Nickerson
Sparhawk.

To face him, and to stare. There were no gentlemen
in Portsmouth like this. There probably weren't any in
the entire rest of the world. He was immensely tall with
shoulders and a chest to match, and even clothed
though he was, Rose was acutely aware of the strength
and energy that his oversized body contained. His hair

and brows were black as tar—the black, guessed Rose, by which he'd earned that foolish prefix—and so was the beard that darkened his jaw. In the middle of all that black his eyes were an astonishing green, pale yet brilliant as they studied her with an intensity that made her blush from her toes clear to her cheeks. No wonder he'd succeeded so as a privateer, she thought stupidly. One look from those eyes and his enemy would simply turn to jelly where she stood.

Yet that wasn't quite right. The enemy would most likely be male, a *he,* not a *she.* And the only jellified *she* right now was herself, Miss Rose Everard, spinster. She could have counted to a hundred in the time she'd let slip past here gawking on his deck. She blinked, forced herself to think once again and finally remembered to speak.

"Good day, Captain Sparhawk," she said as briskly as she could. "I am Miss Rose Everard of Portsmouth in Hampshire, and I have come to speak to you concerning this vessel, which, you should know, belongs to my father, Sir Edmund Everard."

"Oh, hell," he said with disgust he didn't bother to hide. "Miss *Rose* Everard. Why the devil didn't I guess?"

Chapter Three

A ghost, thought Nick furiously as he stared at the woman before him. She had to be a ghost.

But how could she be a ghost, too, when the ghost, the real ghost, was the one she so resembled? She must be the living version of the ghost or angel or whatever Lily was, which would make this girl—what?

Lily's sister: he'd settle for that. If he considered it any further he'd lose his mind or his temper or most likely both. The wonderful prize Lily had promised, the improbable course on the chart that he'd reluctantly followed, the chase and the shamefully easy capture of the English merchantman: every bit had been somehow contrived by Lily to bring her sister here.

It wasn't even as if she was Lily's twin. Far from it. This girl was smaller, not even to his shoulder, with dark hair drawn severely back from her pale, serious face, and though the shape of her eyes was similar to Lily's, their color was only a faded gray version of her sister's brilliant blue. Mourning wasn't supposed to be attractive, but the hideous black gown she wore drained her cheeks of any color and hid whatever feminine roundness she might possess beneath its stiff, salt-stained folds. She had none of Lily's laughing merriment, none of her teasing charm, but somehow the similarity was still intangibly, annoyingly there, in the shape of her face and the way she lifted her chin to talk to him.

And in how *much* she talked.

"There's not much guessing involved in it at all, Captain Sparhawk," she was saying. "It is merely the simple truth. I expect by now you've rifled through the *Angel Lily*'s papers enough to recognize my father's name, and it wouldn't take a great scholar to determine the rest."

Rose sighed. She hadn't expected the man to be gracious, or even civil, but she had hoped he'd at least listen. But he wasn't. He wasn't even pretending to hear what he said, instead staring at her with an ill-humored scowl.

"It's the simple truth, sir," she said again, hoping repetition would make it sink in. "And this vessel—"

"You're Lily's sister," said Nick abruptly, closing the distance between them. Before she could react he took her chin with one hand and turned her face up toward his. "You can't be anyone else."

Instantly Rose jerked away, the heat from his touch burning into her skin. "How dare you?" she gasped. "How *dare* you?"

And without a thought for the consequences, she reached up and slapped him as hard as she could.

Nick didn't flinch, even though his face stung like hell. All he'd wanted to know was if she were real, or if somehow he was imagining her, too. He hadn't meant to set her off like this. Now he knew every man on deck was watching and waiting for him to toss her over the side at the very least for striking the captain. Damnation, why did she have to hit him before the entire crew?

"Insolent creature," he said sharply, loud enough for them all to hear. "I should have you strung up for that."

But she was still too furious to care. "I'll do it again if you dare touch me!"

"Damnation, I had to know if you were flesh and blood!"

Her silver eyes flashed her scorn. "Whatever else would I be? Tea cakes and India tea?"

"Nothing half so sweet, I'll wager." If he wasn't careful he'd be babbling next about seeing angels in his cabin. "Good day to you, ma'am, and back you go to your ship."

"Not yet, I'm not." She gave a little shake to her fingers, still smarting from the impact of slapping him. She might as well have struck a rock covered with nettles as this man's face. "And you've absolutely no right to be issuing orders to me."

"You forget yourself, ma'am, just as you forget that I'm the captain of this vessel."

"You're not *my* captain." She glared up at him, wishing he'd back away. He was still too near for her comfort, his sheer size and undeniable maleness a more potent threat to her equilibrium than the pistols thrust into his belt or the sword at his waist. No wonder she was finding it so difficult to behave in a reasonable fashion. "And I'm not yet a married woman, so I'll thank you to stop calling me 'ma'am'."

"*Miss* Everard, then. Why am I not surprised, *Miss* Everard?"

Rose flushed. "Where is Captain Fotherill? I wish to speak with him so we might settle this business directly."

Nick made a rumbling noise deep in his chest. As far as he was concerned, there wasn't any business left to settle, except to send her back to the other ship. "You'll have a blessed hard time of it. Fotherill's dead."

"*Dead?*" repeated Rose incredulously. "Captain Fotherill's dead?"

Nick looked down his nose at her, satisfied that at least in this he'd have the final word. "Aye, miss, dead and gone with the fishes."

"Oh, the poor man!" She had met Captain Fotherill only once, on the day the *Angel Lily* sailed, but though she hadn't known him well, she did regret his death, for it was going to make her task that much the harder. "Poor Captain Fotherill!"

"Poor man, hah," said Nick contemptuously. "Fotherill took a dozen of my lads when he died and a share of his own with them. More than a score of good men lost because your blessed Fotherill preferred to waste his powder on long shot rather than haul in and close for a decent hand-to-hand."

"I see," said Rose, though she didn't. "What have you done with the rest of the Englishmen? You didn't kill them all, did you?"

"I'm a privateer, ma'am, not an executioner, no matter what you English might think. When I sent my own sloop into Charles Town for repairs, they took Fotherill's men to the prison there."

"Charles Town?" she echoed faintly.

"Charles Town," he repeated firmly. He was explaining too much, more than she deserved. Blast the woman, he was beginning to chatter as much as she did. "In South Carolina. Where, I can assure you, your countrymen will be a sight better cared for than the Americans your King George has taken."

"They're traitors," she said defensively. "They're treated as they deserve. Or have you forgotten that my king was also yours not so long ago?"

"I remember it every morning upon waking, ma'am, and thank the Lord for change." He smiled, pleased he'd discovered exactly the way to irritate her the most. She looked a hundred times more appealing with that flush in her cheeks, and it would be a perverse challenge to keep it there. "That could be why so many of Fotherill's old crew decided to toss in their lots with us. A taste of our kind of freedom can do that to a man. Or does that make them traitors, too?"

She took a deep breath, wishing he hadn't smiled and confused her wits. "I'm not going to quarrel over politics with you, Captain Sparhawk. You'll believe what you please because, after all, you're a rebel, too."

"Thank you," he said dryly, reaching for her elbow to guide her toward the side. "Now back to the boat."

But Rose shook him off. "I suppose, Captain Sparhawk, being a rebel is why you've behaved so dishonorably by capturing the *Angel Lily*. Privateers aren't supposed to attack other privateers, and that's exactly what you did to poor Captain Fotherill."

Nick's smile lost some of its gleam. Pride kept him from confessing that Fotherill had attacked him, not the other way around, and that the Englishmen had come horribly close to winning.

"Any vessel that sails under a British flag is fair game," he said, dodging the truth, "just as we Americans are always in season for your gunners. Doesn't make one whit of difference whether it's a doryman or another privateer."

"But that can't possibly be true!" said Rose indignantly. "It's not fair!"

"This is a war, Miss Everard. It's not supposed to be fair."

"I still don't believe it. My father is a cautious man in matters of business and trade, and I can't conceive of him taking on such a risk, especially with such a costly vessel that is named for my sister!"

Nick frowned, staring at her for a long, unbelieving moment. He wasn't the mad one. She was. "Your father's caution doesn't figure in it at all," he said. "He may have his eye on his ledger book, but the rest of us are here to fight a war. The rules haven't changed much since the Greeks, unless your Admiralty Board's taken on a few other petticoat despots to alter them to suit you.''

Rose stiffened. ''Foolish nonsense like that won't change the facts. You've unfairly captured the *Angel Lily,* and I'm not leaving until you admit it.''

''I'm not admitting anything, and you're leaving regardless.'' This time he took her arm before she could wriggle away. Lord, she was thin, he thought, nothing but little bird bones inside her sleeve. ''Come along.''

''No, I'm not!'' Stubbornly Rose tried to pull away, but her efforts were as ineffectual as a child's against a parent's will, and, humiliated, she felt herself being almost carried across the deck. She struggled harder, raising her voice. ''I'm not leaving, I say!''

''And I say you are. *Now.*'' She was light as a thistle and nearly as prickly, thought Nick with grim satisfaction as he pulled her across the deck, and he'd rejoice to see the last of her. So much for Lily's grand plans. He'd show *her* he was still the master.

But as soon as Nick reached the side to send Rose back to the boat, Gideon slung his leg over the rail and clambered onto the deck.

''Everything's squared away as you ordered, Nick,'' he said with a hurried, haphazard salute as three more Yankee sailors followed him up the rope ladder and over the side. ''We stowed the English in the hold with nary a squawk, jury-rigged the mast and sent them on their way. I left Hibert in command, as you said, and he'll have her in Charles Town in two days if this wind holds."

Nick looked across to where the *Commerce* had been, and then to the east, where she was already making good progress with the wind at her stern.

"Damnation, Gideon," he demanded, "why did you have to be so bloody quick about it?"

Gideon looked at him strangely. "Because that's the way you always want it. The faster Hibert can get her into Charles Town, the faster the prize courts can declare in our favor and sell her off, and the faster we'll all be paid off. Your orders, Nick," he said defensively. "And damned good ones they are, too."

"Well, they're not much good to me now, are they? Now they've stuck me with this wretched woman!"

Gideon folded his hands across his chest, tucking his hands beneath his arms, and frowned. "I thought that was what you wanted. You kept her long enough."

"What *he* wanted!" sputtered Rose indignantly. "What of my wishes in the matter?"

Nick ignored her. "I wasn't keeping her, Gideon. I was trying to send her back."

"Why the devil would you?" asked Gideon. "Do you know who she is, Nick?"

"She's a damnable pest, that's who!"

Gideon stepped closer and lowered his voice so that Rose and the others couldn't hear. "She's the last surviving daughter of Sir Edmund Everard, the man who built and owned this brig, and she's gold to us, Nick. Nay, better than gold." Gideon glanced at Rose before he edged closer to Nick and lowered his voice. "Can't you see the value of keeping her with us? Her old man's a grand, rich lordling back in England, and now with her in your hands you can make him dance to whatever tune you play."

"A lord's daughter, you say." Nick frowned, rubbing the back of his neck as he considered. "If she's very dear to him, she could be worth five hundred guineas to us. Maybe six."

"Oh, aye, six, no mistake." Gideon's grin returned with renewed eagerness. "And she won't be the most disagreeable prisoner we've ever had aboard."

Nick shook his head, still not completely convinced. The girl did look harmless enough now, standing by the rail to stare after the last of the *Commerce*. Could the ransom her father would pay bring the happiness that Lily was always promising?

He rubbed his neck again and sighed uneasily, trying not to think of the other Everard sister. "Still and all, Gideon, you know I can't abide women on board. And this one will be a trial, a regular trial, what with her sis—her shrewish ways."

Nick glanced at Gideon, praying the other man hadn't noticed how close he'd come to saying Lily's name again.

"That little mite a trial?" Gideon's eyebrows rose skeptically. "You'll scarce know she's aboard. And if you spare her a thought at all, just remind yourself of that six hundred guineas I asked from her father's business people in the letter that went with the ship for Charles Town."

Nick glared at him. "Didn't leave a blessed thing to chance, did you?"

Gideon flushed beneath his tan. "I figured Miss Everard was the same as any other cargo we'd taken, Nick. Your orders are always for me to dispose of the goods as I see fit." He shifted uncomfortably. "I only meant to make things easy for you, Nick, that was all. I didn't want you bothering yourself over nothing right now."

But Nick knew what Gideon really meant. It didn't matter that Nick had just led them to the richest prize they'd taken in months; Gideon and all the others still believed their captain was mad as a hatter. And so, in some ways, he did himself.

"I don't think Miss Everard would take to being called cargo," he said wearily. "And for your trouble, Lieutenant Cole, you will give our lady prisoner your own quarters."

But at that moment an excited cry rose from the lady prisoner, and together Nick and Gideon wheeled around toward her.

"My trunk!" cried Rose, leaning over the side. "Oh, please, pray, take care with that!"

With a final, protesting squeak from the hoist-pulley, the trunk was lifted clear of the rail and, with a sailor's guiding hand, thumped to the deck. Rose ran to kneel beside it, brushing away the drops of seawater from its hide-covered sides.

"I can't begin to fathom what manner of foolish presumption this is, bringing my trunk clear over here after me," she said crossly, as much to the trunk as to the men behind her. "Why ever would anyone go to the trouble of doing such a thing?"

Grumbling to herself, she used the edge of her skirt to begin blotting the worst of the water spots. With the trunk's elaborate pattern of brass nailheads, it was better suited for traveling by carriage or coach than by sea, and the constant damp of the voyage had rotted bald patches into the hide despite Rose's best efforts. Carefully she worked her way around one side and the front, but when she reached the second side she stopped with a gasp.

Trailing from beneath the locked lid was a long, torn length of white linen trimmed with lace, and unhappily Rose ran her fingers along the tattered scrap. She sat back on her heels and looked up at Nick and Gideon, her gray eyes flashing.

"Well, captain," she said to Nick. "You see the work your men have done."

Once again Gideon shifted uneasily from one leg to another. "I sent Mackenzie to stow her dunnage, Nick. I told him not to tarry, but he seems to have been a mite hasty."

"Hasty!" Rose held out the torn lace as testimony. "This is careless, not hasty, and now it's quite ruined, and I hadn't yet worn this—this—"

"Shift?" supplied Nick automatically. Besides his growing up among three sisters, his firsthand experience with a wide assortment of friendly barmaids and lonely widows had made him familiar enough with all the layers women wore beneath their gowns. "Underskirt? Petticoat? Or was it a nightrail?"

But Rose had had the disadvantage of neither brothers nor lovers, and her cheeks flamed with embarrassment. Never before had she heard a man say such words to her, and certainly not a dark, devilish man like this one, who could make the mildest nothingness seem indecent. Quickly she wadded the torn strip into her fist where Nick could no longer see it or comment on its nature.

The modest little gesture unsettled Nick. Before this he had thought of the girl only as a shrewish, inconvenient female, but to see her this way, crouched before that ridiculous monstrosity of a trunk with her cheeks on fire and her eyes wide with misery, changed everything. She seemed small and pitifully young, and shamefully innocent, too, if the mere mention of her shift could cause her such mortification. It wasn't as if he'd seen her wearing the wretched thing. Damnation, how *were* genteel females raised in England, anyway?

"You tell me the cost of the damage, miss," he said gruffly, "and I'll make it up to you."

"Oh, no!" Rose gasped again and shook her head violently. "I couldn't let you do that!"

"Of course you can. My man caused the damage, didn't he?"

"The damage isn't the question," she said, struggling to explain. "That is to say, I mean, that because you are a man, for me to let you pay for—for such personal effects would be most improper. I could not possibly accept such an offer from you without acknowledging a familiarity between us that certainly does not exist."

Nor ever would, thought Nick as he clasped and unclasped his hands behind his back. How could such an undersize chit of a girl have so blessed much to say for herself? She spoke in such overbred circles around him that he had to concentrate, really concentrate and not just listen, to understand what the hell she was trying to say.

Blast Lily for doing this to him!

"If you won't clear my reckoning, then will you accept my apology?" he said with more care than gallantry. "Lieutenant Cole should have let your maid look after your things, instead of having a ham-fisted oaf like Mackenzie—"

"He couldn't," she said abruptly. "He couldn't ask my maid for assistance because I don't have one."

"You're traveling alone?" Nick's surprise was genuine. No woman with any pretensions to being a lady would dream of doing such a thing. "Why'd that father of yours pack you off without a maidservant?"

"He didn't." Her dark head bent over her lap and her voice grew so muted that Nick had to strain to hear it. "My maid perished a fortnight after we'd left Portsmouth."

There was little else to say of the maid that Aunt Lucretia had chosen. She'd been mean-tempered even before she'd fallen ill, and though Rose knew it was un-Christian of her, she'd been almost relieved when the woman died.

"But you're well enough yourself, Miss Everard?" he was asking. "Your own illness is past?"

Rose's head jerked up at the new gentleness in his voice. The galley stores on board the *Commerce* had dwindled during the overlong crossing and there hadn't been enough to eat, but he assumed instead that she'd been ill, too, because she was sallow and too thin. She didn't want his pity, wanted it even less than she wanted his contempt. She was what she was. Swiftly she rose to her feet, the length of torn lace from her shift fluttering from her fingers.

"I am perfectly well, Captain Sparhawk, thank you," she said, meeting his gaze as levelly as she could. She would be strong before him. She *must*. "Perfectly well."

He looked at her closely. "Perfectly?"

"Perfectly perfect." She raised her chin a fraction higher and prayed it wouldn't tremble. "As you see, I have lost my hat, and the brightness of the sun in these latitudes struck me for a moment. But I am quite well now. Quite."

"That's because you're English," he said with the hint of a smile that made his dark face briefly, alarmingly boyish. "You're not accustomed to much except fog and foul weather."

She could tell from his eyes that he didn't believe her, but that he wasn't going to bother quarreling about it.

At least she could be grateful for that much, and to prove it she wouldn't jump to defend the English weather the way he expected.

Instead she glanced briefly over her shoulder to where she'd last seen the *Commerce*. "You will think me quite presumptuous, I know, but shouldn't we be sailing after them before we're left entirely behind?"

"We haven't been left behind, Miss Everard, because we're not trying to catch them." Restlessly he tapped his fingers on the hilt of his sword, looking past her toward the other ship. "They're bound for Charles Town, and we're not."

Rose gulped. Sweet heaven deliver her, she'd been kidnapped, and it was all her own fault. While she'd been fussing over that infernal trunk, this man with the black hair and the green eyes had carried her off just as he'd captured the *Angel Lily*.

And just like the brig, she was now his prize. No wonder he'd smiled at her like that.

She folded her hands in front of her to keep them from shaking. She told herself she wouldn't panic and she wouldn't weep, no matter how much she wanted to. She would be calm and reasonable and firm. That had always worked for her before. And what other choice, really, did she have?

"Then I must implore you, Captain," she said, her tangled hair blowing back from her face as she lifted her chin so she could meet his eye, "to please change your course to Charles Town, too, so I might join them."

Avoiding her gaze, Nick squinted up at the sails and the men working aloft. Why couldn't those big silver-gray eyes of hers look somewhere other than at him? It wasn't his fault that she'd been sick and unhappy, just as he could hardly blame him because she was the daughter of a wealthy Englishman with influence. She was the one who'd decided to go sailing into the middle of a war. All he'd done was capture the ship in which she'd been a passenger.

"You're my prisoner, Miss Everard," he said evenly, "and you're not going to Charles Town because you're staying here on board the *Angel Lily* with me. That's what you wanted in the first place, wasn't it?"

"But not like this!" Stunned, Rose dug her nails into her palms as she struggled against her panic. "I came to speak to you on my father's behalf, not to be—to be carried off!"

"And because of your father, you're too valuable a prisoner to lose," said Nick, still staring aloft. "You should be grateful that Gideon at least brought over your trunk, so you'll have your comforts."

Aghast, Rose shook her head. "But this is only one trunk! I had more with me in the *Commerce*—much more. What will become of all my other things, my belongings?"

"Enough, Miss Everard." Finally he lowered his gaze to meet hers, his expression as stern as he could make it. He had to end this now; he'd wasted entirely too much time on her as it was. "We are in the middle of a war, not some English country house party, and though I'll treat you as decently as I can, you are still my prisoner. A prisoner of war, mind? The *Commerce* will be condemned by the prize court in Charles Town, and she and all her contents will be sold at auction."

He thought she'd been pale before, but somehow the last bit of color managed to drain from her cheeks.

"Including my things?" she asked in a woefully small voice.

He nodded, though he'd give half his shares not to be having this conversation with her. "This is a war, miss," he repeated in his best stern captain's voice. "If you'd wanted to keep your gowns and bonnets safe, you should have left them snug in England."

"But I had no choice," she said miserably. "I am to be wed on St. Lucia, you see, where my—my intended resides. Everything I'd brought with me was for my new home, things that can't be replaced, like my mother's looking glass and her tea chest and the Chinese vases that have always, always stood on the mantelpiece in the dining room at home, and then the—"

She broke off abruptly, her hands twisting. "But you would not understand, would you, Captain Sparhawk," she said miserably, "just as I cannot understand your cursed rules of war. You'll never understand at all."

Yet Nick did understand, more than she'd guess and far more than he'd ever dream of telling her. Fleetingly he thought of his own mother's looking glasses in the big house in Newport where he'd been born, now looted and gutted by the British, how he'd come too late to save his parents or his youngest sister—one more time he'd failed them when they'd needed him most.

Oh, aye, he understood.

But that was why he was here now, wasn't it? To harm and harass the enemy, to rob them just as they'd robbed his own family? Every chance he could, he willingly—no, eagerly—risked his life and the lives of his men to bring as much destruction as he could to British property and British ambitions, and no one had ever been able to question his bravery or his loyalty.

At least not until now.

He knew the girl was waiting for an answer, those enormous silver eyes brimming with reproach, and his jaw tightened. What was the matter with him, anyway? If he'd let himself turn all sentimental and soft over one little Britisher grieving over her lost Chinese pots, then he might as well turn in his commission now. He could always go back to Narragansett Bay and become, oh, a shepherd on Patience Island until the war was over.

Damn Lily's wings, this was all her fault, every bit of it!

He shoved his hat down lower on his head, wincing at the little stab of pain as it slid across the half-healed cut on his forehead. The bridge of the girl's nose was sunburned, the skin pink and shiny, and he focused on that instead of her eyes.

"I don't mean to keep you forever, you know," he said gruffly. "Only until your old papa comes up with the proper ransom."

She lowered her gaze to her hands. "Or until my friends from St. Lucia come after *you.*"

"Not ruddy likely," scoffed Nick. "Those fat-bellied merchants from Cul de Sac Roseaux have been after me since summer last, and you can see how lucky they've been."

"The gentleman I am to wed, Captain Sparhawk, is no potbellied merchant." She was speaking quickly, her voice no more than a soft, breathy rush that Nick had to strain to hear. "He is Captain Lord Eliot Graham of His Majesty's frigate *Goliath,* and I do believe, Captain Sparhawk, that his guns will more than compensate for your luck."

Nick stared down at the top of her head with disgust and dismay. His luck, hell. His blessed *luck* would now have some titled jackass in a frigate out for his blood, all on account of the two Miss Everards. And there wasn't a single thing he could do about it.

Close to smothering from his own frustration and fury, Nick unleashed such a torrent of oaths on the British navy in general and the dubious ancestry of Captain Lord Eliot in particular that even Gideon turned to smile with admiration. The girl's expression didn't change, but her pallor vanished as her cheeks turned as red as the skin on her nose.

"Forgive me if I've offended you, Miss Everard," said Nick at last, feeling somewhat relieved and not the least bit contrite. "But until your honorable jacka-napes can rescue you, you'll have to pardon our rough ways here on board."

For a long time she looked at him, simply looked, while to Nick it seemed those silver eyes turned to pure Sheffield steel.

"As you wish, Captain," she said with an evenness that made the back of his neck prickle. "I'll forgive you whatever sins you please. As long, of course, as you're willing to forgive mine in return."

Gathering her skirts in one hand she headed toward the companionway after the two sailors carrying her trunk, her back straight and her head held as high as if the *Angel Lily* still belonged to her father. With one last muttered oath for all infernal British women with flower names, Nick turned on his heel and stalked across the deck in the opposite direction.

He'd been fighting the British already for three long, hard years. So why, then, did it feel as if the war had just begun?

Chapter Four

"Aye, miss, this be your cabin." Hobb thumped the massive trunk down on the deck and slid it through the doorway. "Mr. Cole cleared out so's you could have a space all to yourself."

"That was very kind of Mr. Cole," said Rose faintly as she peered past Hobb's broad shoulder at her new quarters. "I must be sure to thank him."

Hobb shook his head vigorously. "Oh, nay, miss, 'tweren't Mr. Cole's notion. 'Twas the cap'n's orders that you have a cabin of your own, on account of you being a lady an' Sir Edmund's daughter an' all. It's the cap'n you should be thanking."

"Indeed." To Rose's mind, *cabin* seemed far too grand a word to describe this tiny, murky closet of a space, tucked in tight against the curved side of the ship. Built along one bulkhead was a bunk with a wool-stuffed mattress and a mottled looking glass beneath a single shelf, and that, it seemed, was the extent of the accommodations. The space was so small that with her trunk on the deck she had perhaps eight inches clear between it and the edge of the bunk. Longingly she remembered her cabin on board the *Commerce,* with a chair and a writing table and more than enough space for both Phoebe and her to turn around.

"Aye, miss, 'twas the cap'n's doing, no mistake." Hobb reached up to light the single oil lamp, a small brass lantern that swung from gimbals fastened to the bulkhead. He rested his hands on the wide belt at his waist, in no hurry to leave. "He's a good man, is the cap'n, an' a sight better mariner than that sorry rascal Fotherill, though I 'spect your father don't want to hear it."

"You're English, then?" asked Rose in disbelief.

Hobb nodded. "As English as any man, I 'spect."

"You signed on to sail on behalf of my father, and then when these rebel pirates killed Captain Fotherill, you joined them instead? You're a traitor, that's what you are, a traitor and a turncoat!"

"Aye, miss, and what of it?" Hobb shrugged carelessly. "What the king an' his fine, fancy ministers decide don't mean much to me, miss. The way I sees it, this war's no different from that of Cromwell's time, with Englishmen fighting with Englishmen, an' me, well now, I'll throw my lot with him that treats me best. An' that be Cap'n Sparhawk."

"Captain Sparhawk, Captain Sparhawk!" cried Rose irritably. "I am sick unto *death* of Captain Sparhawk!"

Hobb looked at her with surprise, clearly amazed that she didn't share his admiration. "He's a good master, miss,'' he said staunchly. ''He has his share of temper, and he goes daft sometimes, but he's a good master, no mistake.''

''Then I vow I must be the most mistaken woman in creation, for I can see none of the man's merits at all.'' Rose pressed her fingers to her temples. ''Now if you will please leave me, I rather wish to be alone.''

''Very well, miss.'' Hobb tugged at the front of his shapeless knitted cap and slammed shut the door with a rattling force, latching it from without.

With a sigh, Rose perched on the edge of the bunk and lifted the lid of her trunk. She'd been careless not to lock it, but on board the *Commerce* such precautions hadn't seemed necessary. One look at the trunk's contents now, though, showed her the price she'd paid for her trust. Everything from her other cabin had been thrown and squeezed into this single trunk, shoes on top of gowns on top of stockings and her hairbrush. The thought of these strangers pawing through her personal belongings sickened her, as if they'd touched and defiled her the same way, and again she felt tears sting her eyes when she remembered how cavalierly Captain Sparhawk had disposed of everything else.

She untangled the shift with the hem that had been shut into the lid and torn, the ragged strip hanging forlornly, dirty and damp, from the otherwise spotless linen. She closed her eyes and pressed the fabric to her cheek, smelling the faint fragrance of lavender that still clung to it, the scent that Lily had so favored. The shift had belonged to her sister, as had so many of the other garments and even the trunk itself, all of it ordered for the bride that Lily had planned so confidently to be.

And now, instead, the wedding clothes and the lace-trimmed linens belonged to Rose. It had been easy enough to alter the garments to fit her, but with a little shiver Rose wondered again if Lily's bridegroom would prove as accommodating.

With the shift still clutched in her hand, Rose curled on her side on the bunk, fighting the fear and misery that at last threatened to claim her now that her anger had cooled. Think of Lily, she ordered herself as she breathed the lavender scent on the torn linen. Think of what Lily would do. Lily would not be afraid; Lily hadn't been afraid of anything, especially anything male.

But then Lily wouldn't have insisted on being brought to this ship to speak to the captain, for Lily wouldn't have cared a fig if Papa had been robbed of every last ha'penny he owned.

And Lily most certainly wouldn't have quarreled with Captain Sparhawk. She would have tipped her chin, peeked up at him from beneath the brim of her hat—for she wouldn't have lost her hat, either—and charmed him so thoroughly that he might have given back the *Angel Lily* without a fight, just for the privilege of having her smile at him. Men had always given presents to Lily. Rose had never quite figured out why, but she was sure that it wasn't because she hit them in the jaw like an indignant fishwife.

Rose groaned at the memory of how she'd slapped the American captain. She was supposed to be the clever Everard sister, not that anyone would guess it from how she'd behaved with Captain Sparhawk. Ladies who were prisoners didn't hit their captors. True, she'd been shocked when he had seized her face and she'd reacted from pure instinct alone, but she was lucky that was all he'd done.

He certainly wasn't the first man who couldn't believe that she and Lily were sisters. That familiar startled look had been in his eyes the instant she'd turned and faced him, and there'd been moments when he hadn't even been able to meet her eye, he'd been so eager to look away.

Because Lily had loved her, she'd tried to convince Rose otherwise, but Rose knew the truth. There wasn't any help for it. She *was* plain and small and insignificant, and she always would be in the eyes of gentlemen. But it still hurt to be reminded.

Especially by a man like Nickerson Sparhawk, the handsomest man she'd ever seen. A traitor who'd stolen the ship with her sister's name and face, a lawless rogue who'd robbed her father and kidnapped her, a powerful, ruthless man from whom she'd somehow have to escape if she wanted to reach St. Lucia in time for her wedding and spare her poor father even more disgrace.

With a smothered sob Rose pressed her face into her sleeve, and wished to heaven she were the one who was dead instead of Lily.

* * *

"Lily!" roared Nick as he slammed the door to his cabin shut. "Damnation, woman, show yourself!"

"I should be the one to swear at you, sir, and not the other way around!" Lily's image sharpened into focus instantly, framed by the stern windows as she stood with her arms folded defiantly across her chest and her wings twitching with anger. "How dare you behave so barbarously toward my sister?"

"Oh, it's to be my fault now, is it?" Furiously Nick ripped off the belt with his sword and flung it onto the desk. "What kind of fool are you playing me for? All this claptrap about following your special course on the chart to an easy prize so I could salvage *my* pride and *my* crew's respect, when all you had in mind the entire time was finding *your* blessed sister!"

"And what's the harm of it?" demanded Lily. "Why couldn't both things be accomplished at once?"

"Because your sister is as great a nuisance as you are." He jerked his arms free of his coat and let it fall to the deck, and began unfastening the long row of buttons on his waistcoat with a quick, angry tug at each buttonhole. "Nay, make that a greater nuisance, since she's betrothed to some ruddy royal frigate captain who'll doubtless now dedicate all his days to chasing me!"

"Oh, pish!" Lily swept her hand through the air dismissively. "As if you'd be afraid of the likes of Eliot Graham!"

"What kind of idiot wouldn't be?" He glared at her as he let the waistcoat fall onto his coat and began yanking his shirt free of his breeches. "Thanks to you, I've stolen the man's bride out from under his nose. That should be insult enough to rouse even some addlepated aristocrat to action, and to help get her back he has thirty-two guns and a crew of a hundred at his disposal."

"What of it?" she said impatiently as he pulled his shirt over his head. "You have the *Angel Lily,* don't you? That should be more than enough to even the match."

Nick grunted sourly as he poured water into the washbasin. He had hoped that by stripping to his breeches he'd offend her enough so she'd leave—he'd noticed before that she never appeared in the morning until he was fully dressed—but still she stayed, unperturbed and unimpressed by his bare chest.

He lowered his face over the bowl, sluicing the water over his head. Nay, it was worse than that, for *he* was the one who felt uncomfortable. Angel or not, she was still female, and he wasn't accustomed to females ignoring the splendid breadth of his chest or the width of his arms. It didn't seem natural.

"Besides," she continued behind him, "Eliot doesn't even know you have Rose."

"He'll know as soon as the *Commerce* reaches Charles Town with the prize crew," grumbled Nick. "The British spies—*your* spies—are remarkably efficient that way. Why the devil I listened to Gideon and didn't ship her off to Carolina when I had the chance is beyond me."

He recognized the familiar little crack of her fan being snapped open, and absently wondered why she needed one at all. Wouldn't a good flap of her wings accomplish the same thing?

"I still don't believe Eliot will bother you, Nick," she said. "He may be intent on marrying poor Rose, but he doesn't love her in the least."

"Understandable enough," said Nick as he splashed the water over his arms and shoulders. "Your sister's a small, shrewish, ill-favored article that would test any man's soul to—damnation!"

The desk chair caught him in the back of his leg, the turned maple slamming against him hard enough that he had to grab the bulkhead to keep his footing.

"You should be more careful, Captain," said Lily mildly. "With all your experience at sea, I would have thought you'd know to be wary of how furnishings can shift about in a high sea."

"The devil take your high sea! There's barely a ripple on the water today, and you know it. That was all your doing, you wicked little creature!" Nick rubbed his leg, feeling the knot of a bruise growing already. "And it *hurt.*"

"It was supposed to." Lily smiled sweetly, and with a sinking feeling Nick remembered the exact same expression on Rose's face after she'd told him about her frigate captain.

"I won't have you speaking unkindly of my sister."

"I'll say whatever I damned well please!"

"Oh, I know, because you're the almighty captain and the master and goodness knows whatever else." She sighed dramatically and shook her head. "But I thought you were a gentleman, too, and a gentleman would never be so quick to judge a lady. Or didn't your mother teach you that?"

Nick grumbled to himself as he shook the water from his black hair like an oversize spaniel. His mother had in fact taught him exactly that about ladies, as well as a good many other things he'd tried equally hard to forget over the seventeen years since he'd left home. Twice now today he'd been reminded of his family and his past, jarring loose the memory of how he'd been born into a genteel family, with expectations of him that he'd never been able to fulfill. But why should he care? He liked the life he'd made for himself just fine.

At least he had before the Everard sisters had come careening into the middle of it.

"She didn't care for me any more than I did for her," he said defensively. "Nigh sliced my head off."

"What did you expect, bullying her the way you did? She's lost and frightened and grieving and lonely, and though she's betrothed to a man she's only met once, still she's determined to wed him to please Papa." She stepped closer, beseeching, her silk skirts rustling softly. "Rose needs a friend, Nick, not another enemy."

"Then she doesn't need me." He raised his jaw, wary of her intentions. "You're her sister, or leastways you were. If her life's such an all-fired disaster, then why don't you go and start arranging things for her and leave me alone?''

"Because I can't," said Lily sadly. "Since I always scoffed at her advice while I lived, she in turn will never be able to hear me now, or even see me. It's my—well, it's my punishment, I suppose, for being so headstrong. As much as Rose needs me, I can only change things for her through you."

Nick sighed. "So that's why you had me capture her? To brighten her cheerless life with a little gunfire and brimstone from Black Nick Sparhawk?''

"You needn't be flippant. It doesn't become you." She sighed, too, a breathy rush behind her fan. "All I ask is that you be civil to Rose while she's in your custody. You could invite her here to your cabin, say, for a light collation.''

"'*Collation*'?" Nick cocked one scornful black brow. "Oh, aye, why not? Next you'll be expecting tea and currant scones with clotted cream. Your wretched little sister should consider herself fortunate if I ever invite her here for grilled onions and toasted cheese.''

"Ah, my dear captain," said Lily, her smile beatific. "What a perfectly wondrous idea.''

The folded white paper shot beneath the cabin's door and across the deck, the messenger who'd brought it gone before Rose had lifted her head from the pillow. For a long moment she stared at the white square on the smooth-sanded planks. She knew no one on board

who would write to her, and she could not imagine that
these wild, rough Americans corresponded with their
prisoners on white vellum.

She leaned off the bunk to reach the paper, lifting it
carefully as if she feared it might somehow explode in
her hand. She turned it over and traced her fingertips
over the seal stamped into the frozen puddle of car-
mine wax that held the letter shut. An eagle with outstretched wings perched on a branch—a symbol,
perhaps, of the American cause?

Frowning, she tipped the seal toward the lantern's
light and gently slid one finger beneath it to crack it
free. The handwriting was bold and confident, broad,
black slashes across the white paper, and immediately
she knew who had written it. Not an eagle graced the
sealing wax, then, but a hawk, not a branch from a tree
but a bit of ship's timber, a spar.

Miss Everard, will you do me the honor of joining me in my cabin as my guest for a light collation.

Yr. S'v't N. Sparhawk

Her frown deepened. She wouldn't have expected
such civility from Captain Sparhawk. A light collation in his cabin? Was this some form of apology for
all the ill he'd brought her, or only a mockery, another
way for him to goad and torment her? She touched the
seal, remembering how he'd tried so purposefully—and
so successfully—to shock her with his profanity and the

appalling catalog of her undergarments. No, if he wished to torment her further he wouldn't bother with anything as subtle as this prettily worded note. But why, then, would he bother with an apology, either?

She read the invitation again. There was no time or date to the invitation, and she decided with a sniff that privateering captains must consider themselves above such niceties. Rose had seen how every man on board the *Angel Lily* jumped to carry out Captain Sparhawk's every order, and doubtless she was supposed to do the same. She wasn't one of his sailors, and he'd no right to expect her to obey his commands. Instead she should tear the invitation in two and send it back to him, and she smiled to herself as she pictured the look on his face when he received it.

But both her smile and her defiance were short-lived. Except for a few moments' satisfaction, what would she gain by crossing him again? When she'd slapped him, he'd threatened to hang her, and she didn't doubt he'd do it if she provoked him too far. He'd already shown how little regard he had for laws and decency. She'd be nothing but a fool if she antagonized him again, and she'd never reach St. Lucia for her wedding.

With a sigh she laid the invitation on the mattress and began to sort through the tumbled contents of her trunk. All of her new gowns, made for her life as Lady Graham, had been left behind in the hold of the *Commerce*. The three that had been unceremoniously stuffed into the trunk were black and severe, all in the same grim mourning she wore to honor Lily, and none any more attractive than the one she was wearing already.

She propped her traveling mirror upright in the trunk's open lid, unpinned her dark hair and brushed it smooth before she twisted it once again onto the top of her head. She'd had to learn to dress her hair herself after Phoebe's death, and the most she aspired to was tidy rather than elegant. At last she pinned a tiny lace cap onto the crown and let the narrow ribbons curl down around her cheeks, her single, modest touch of frivolity.

Not that it helped, not really. With dismay she noted how crying had made her eyes a perfect red-rimmed match for her sunburned cheeks and nose, and she wrinkled that same nose at her reflection. All the lace caps in the world weren't going to make much difference. Captain Sparhawk would simply have to accept her as she was.

Finally she reached deep into the trunk, shifting aside her clothing as she felt for the carved indentation in one corner. She pressed it hard with her thumb until she heard the muffled *sprong* as the latch gave way and the trunk's false bottom lifted back. With relief she saw the privateers hadn't discovered it, for the leather pouch with the new banknotes and the hundred polished guineas that Papa had given her as wedding gifts were still untouched. Beside it were the two flat boxes that held her mother's jewelry, and another smaller, square box covered with black plush. This she

Rose's eyes narrowed. Impertinent, indeed. She'd never met a man this rude before, and she was sorely tempted to turn on her heel and forget all about his foolish invitation. Except, of course, that he would think she'd fled from fear alone, and she refused to let him believe her a coward. With her hand firmly on the latch she swung open the door.

And every last word she'd planned flew from her consciousness in an instant.

He was standing turned away from her, leaning across a pewter washbowl to peer into the mirror on the bulkhead while he shaved, and he wore absolutely nothing except the breeches slung low on his narrow hips. Rose stared; she couldn't help it. Her only experience with undressed males was the plaster casts taken from antique statues that the gentlemen in Portsmouth brought home as souvenirs from Rome, and those white, lifeless forms were nothing like the man before her.

He kept his legs angled, effortlessly adjusting to the ship's motion with an ease that riveted Rose's attention to the broad, muscled planes of his back and shoulders. Little droplets of water trickled down from his wet, sleek hair along the shallow valley of his spine, and helplessly Rose followed their course to the neat bow at the back of the waistband of his breeches.

"Speak, man," he ordered, deftly sweeping the razor's blade along his jaw to the edge of his throat, "or did the Britishers take your tongue, eh?"

"Oh—oh no, indeed not," she stammered in confusion. "That is, it's not possible, is it?"

He swiveled around to face her, clearly surprised but not shocked to find her there. "Not possible, nay," he said as he reached for a cloth to wipe away the last of the soap on his jaw. "Even you British can't take what you already have."

She nodded as if this made perfect sense. His eyes seemed greener here away from the sunlight, and she felt her cheeks grow hot beneath their scrutiny.

Think, Rose, think! Don't stand here like an open-mouthed imbecile!

"You said to enter," she said, and winced inwardly at the defensive banality of it. If only the man had the decency to cover himself with his shirt so that she might think clearly! "I did not mean to intrude."

"You're not, if you've a reason for being here." Nick smiled, intrigued and pleasantly surprised by her new ingenuousness. Because of how she'd spoken to him on the deck before the others, his impression of Rose Everard was of an ill-favored shrew, and so he'd told her sister. But though she'd never be a great beauty, he now noticed the fine bones of her face, the feathery dark lashes that set off her gray eyes, and how her little pink mouth twisted unconsciously as she watched him, the way a child's would when tempted by a sweet. Far more satisfying that than her sister's ethereal indifference.

Lazily, he widened his smile and watched with amusement as the blush on her cheeks grew to match the rosiness of her sunburned nose. "You did have a reason for coming here, didn't you, Miss Everard?"

"You invited me," she said, bewildered. "You had a note delivered to my cabin asking me here for a—a light collation. I presumed you meant supper?"

His smile vanished, done in by that word *collation.* "*I* invited you?"

"Oh, yes." Rose fumbled in her pocket for the note, relieved to have an excuse to look away from his chest. "Here you are."

He took the note from her, barely glancing at the writing and the seal before he looked over her head toward the cabin's stern windows. "This is your doing, isn't it? Doubtless you opened her door as well," he said crossly. "And nay, I am not swaggering!"

Belatedly Rose recalled that she'd heard him in conversation earlier through the closed door, and swiftly she turned to see who the other person might me. But the bench below the long sweep of windows was empty, as were the chair at the desk and the two at the table. They were, it seemed, quite alone together in the cabin. Perhaps he was speaking to her instead, though his comments made little sense.

"I don't see how it can be my doing," she said slowly as she turned back around. "You can't deny that that's your ink and paper and seal, or your invitation, either."

But still he scowled past her, his brows drawn together in a single black angry line. "Damnation, I know she can't see you! All the easier for you to make a fool of me, eh?''

"I beg your pardon, Captain Sparhawk?" Uneasily Rose glanced again over her shoulder. The sailor Hobb had told her that the captain turned "daft." Was this, then, what he meant? "Perhaps I should come back at another time."

"Nay, Miss Everard—Miss *Rose* Everard—you'll stay directly where you are." Irritably he raked his fingers back through his wet hair as he looked away from the empty window seat and back to Rose.

"You believe I'm mad, don't you?" he demanded, his green eyes brilliant. "Acting like some blessed dog whose hair's all on end from seeing ghosts? Talking at shadows like an inmate in Bedlam?"

But before Rose could answer there came another knock at the open door.

"Yer supper, sir," said the towheaded boy as he balanced the heavy tray with both hands before him. "All as ye ordered, sir. Grilled onions an' toasted cheese an' some o' th' ham Cook's kept special from Sunday last, sent up on account o' th' lady."

"Set it there on the table," ordered Nick as he reached for a clean shirt. He wouldn't give Lily the satisfaction of looking her way. He knew she'd expect him to thank her for her interference, but blast her, he wasn't going to do it. "Then leave us."

Rose ducked her chin, trying to hide the little smile of foolish pleasure as the boy arranged the meal. It had been so long since anyone had done anything with her happiness in mind that this simple meal and the knowledge that it had been ordered for her were almost beyond bearing.

Yet he is still your enemy, Rose. You must not forget that, and you must be careful. He is still your enemy, and still a dangerous man.

A very dangerous man...

She nodded to the boy as he left the cabin, and then went to stand beside the table, resting her hands on the back of one of the chairs. The smoky fragrance of the toasted bread and cheese and the onions cooked so perfectly that their rings had just begun to separate on the plate made her realize how long ago she'd eaten breakfast on board the *Commerce*.

"This is very kind of you to do this for me, Captain Sparhawk," she said carefully, concentrating on the carved, polished wood beneath her fingers instead of the man opposite. "Very kind indeed, especially since we are enemies."

"Save your thanks," he said curtly as he dropped into the second chair, not waiting for her to be seated. He stabbed his knife into one of the onions and lifted it dripping to his mouth. Irritation was making him intentionally boorish, and he didn't care. Lily had been the one who said he was a gentleman; he'd never made that claim himself. "This is none of my doing."

Rose frowned, impatiently running her fingers back and forth along the chair's back. "But this is your cabin, your crew. Who else could have ordered it?"

"Who else?" He leaned back in the chair and laughed humorlessly. "The only one who'd care enough to do it. Your sister Lily."

Chapter Five

"My sister Lily." Rose's voice was flat and emotionless, too stunned by the audacity of his claim to be otherwise. "Dare I ask, Captain Sparhawk, how you believe that is possible?"

"The devil knows, for I surely don't." Nick tugged a corner from the toasted cheese and tossed it into his mouth. "Not that Lily's about to confide in me."

"Indeed not." There was a chance, a faint chance, that he'd somehow been one of Lily's less reputable followers who might not have heard of her death. "You knew my sister, sir?"

Nick shrugged carelessly, his unfastened shirt sliding across his shoulders. "Depends what you mean by knowing. But there's no denying that she's caused me trouble enough these past five days with her mischief."

"Then you didn't know her at all," said Rose sharply, "and you are most cruel, sir, to pretend otherwise. There is no possible way Lily could bring you any 'mischief.' You've no right to accuse my sister of anything, for she died eighteen months ago, may God rest her soul."

"Amen to that," agreed Nick. "But in the meantime, I tell you she's here, on this ship."

"And you, Captain Sparhawk, are every bit as mad as you fear." She couldn't help striking the back of the chair with her fist for emphasis as she turned to leave. "Perhaps then this imaginary Lily will share your company, for I shall not. Good day, Captain."

"Nay, you're not going yet." In an instant he was around the table and at her side, seizing her arm so there was no chance she'd escape.

She fought the desire to struggle, forcing herself to seem calm even as her heart pounded in her breast. Struggling would earn her nothing but grief, she told herself firmly, and fighting back would only make him angry. But, oh, dear Lord, he was so much larger than she, so much stronger!

"You have no reason to keep me here, Captain," she said as evenly as she could. "As a prisoner you've every right to confine me to the little cabin you've granted me, but not here, not in your quarters, while you mock the memory of my only sister."

"Nay," he said softly, "she is the one who mocks me. For I tell you, Miss Everard, your sister is here."

His fingers dug into the soft flesh of her arm beneath her sleeve, drawing her closer. A drop of water from his wet hair fell onto her bare wrist and she shivered.

"You *are* mad!" she cried desperately. "No one knows better than I that Lily is dead!"

"I never said she wasn't, did I?" he said roughly, his breathing harsh. He was looking beyond her again, his green eyes unnaturally brilliant as his gaze swept across the cabin. "It's her spirit, her soul, that's haunted me ever since I took this ship!"

"I don't believe you," whispered Rose. She could feel the tension building in him, transmitting itself like a current through his fingers into her arm. "How can I?"

He laughed again, a hollow, bitter sound. "Oh, aye, and why should you? Would you listen if I tell you how she's dressed, all in white with pink ribbons twisted round her head? Her wings are white, too, like a swan's."

"Her *wings?*"

"Wings, aye," he said defensively. "How could she be angel Lily otherwise?"

She ducked her chin, realizing too late there was no graceful way to explain. "I didn't mean to question you," she said. "It is only that—well, as much as I loved Lily, her actions often weren't quite fit for an angel."

"No matter. She plays the part well enough now." Nick's black brows came together as he concentrated on remembering Lily clearly. "Her hair's right for an angel, too, though more copper than gold, and all fussed up on top in curls. Not a bit like yours, for all that you're sisters."

He squinted critically at Rose. "Though there's something about her eyes that's akin to yours, too, even if hers, of course, are blue instead of gray."

Inwardly Rose winced, though she offered nothing in her own defense. How could she, when her hair was dark and unfashionable and her eyes a dull, drab gray, just as he'd said?

"Anyone could know that of Lily," she said stiffly. "You could describe her hair and dress simply from seeing the figurehead of this ship. Papa was most particular with the carver about such details."

"Then how would I know that Lily cracks her fan like a whip when she's crossed, and tips her head to one side when she's pondering mischief? Would a bit of gilded, gaudy wood be able to tell me that?" His large fingers tightened on Rose's arm, his voice low and rough with the urgent need to convince her. "How would I know the sound of her laughter, rippling up and down as if played on a flute?"

Rose shrank back, not so much from him as from what he was saying, and in her confusion looked down at his fingers as they held her arm. His wrist was twice the breadth of hers, with dark curling hairs over sun-browned skin, and his hand was scarred and callused from a life of hard work and battles long past. Not the smooth, elegant hand of a gentleman like Lord Eliot, nor the ink-stained one of her father. But how could Captain Sparhawk possibly be as honest and direct as his strong, blunt hands implied?

He believed what he told her of Lily, as emphatically as Rose believed that he was wrong. She had seen Lily's body sewn in her shroud, and had stood by her sister's grave when the shoveled dirt had dropped with such awful, empty finality onto her coffin. She knew without doubt that her sister was dead, just as she knew, as a member in good standing of their grim stone church at home, that she must not believe in such things as ghosts or spirits.

But how, then, could an American sea captain like Nickerson Sparhawk have come to know so much of her sister?

"You must have found some Englishman here on board, one of Fotherill's men, who knew my sister and told you these things," she said breathlessly, grasping for a rational explanation. "Lily was often seen in Portsmouth. She was a great beauty there, a belle. Most anyone from Hampshire could have described her."

"And what would be the point of that?" he demanded. "Why should I care that much about some lord's giddy daughter? It's Lily's doing, not mine. She shows herself only to me, and in ways I can't explain. Even now she's toying with me, hiding herself away in the very air to make me question my own sanity."

"But you must—"

"Nay, don't say it," he said sharply, his fingers tightening around her wrist. "It's nothing I haven't told myself already. No wonder you and Gideon and likely every other man on board believe by now that I've lost my wits, when I wonder the same thing a hundred times a day."

She lifted her gaze to stare at him, and found her own fear and uncertainty strangely mirrored in his face. He had seemed so strong, so invincibly powerful to her that the desperation she now discovered in his eyes confused her all the more.

And even worse was knowing he was, somehow, inexplicably right.

"My sister often did such things to me when she lived," she said haltingly. Though a year and a half had passed since Lily's death, still it hurt to speak of her. "It was, as you say, a game with her. When we were little girls, sometimes she'd hide from me until I wept from frustration, and then she'd show herself and laugh and hug me and call me a goose for fretting."

"Aye, that would be like her." Nick nodded with a grim eagerness. "She'll jibe and play me false, then laugh and call it parlor tricks." His gaze swept past her, around the cabin another time. "Just as she's doing now. More of her wretched parlor tricks."

"And yet you say you never met her," whispered Rose as she searched his face for the truth. "Dear Lord, how can I dare believe you?"

"You will," he said roughly. "You must."

She was, Nick knew, so close to believing him, to believing *in* him, that he would do anything to convince her. Without another thought he pulled her after him through the cabin's open door and up the narrow companionway. On the steps her feet tangled in her skirts and she stumbled, pitching backward with a startled little cry. Instantly he was there, his broad arm curling around her waist as he lifted her upwards to the windswept deck.

Against his body she was so stiff and tense with fear that he wasn't surprised she'd made a misstep. She reminded him of some tiny wild bird ready to fly the second he lifted his hands free, and beneath his forearm he could feel how her pulse raced and her breath quickened. He knew he'd no right to be holding her like this, at least not so long as he wanted to be thought an honorable privateer and not some renegade pirate. The laws were very clear about the treatment of prisoners, particularly lady prisoners with titled fathers.

But he couldn't let her go, not yet. First he had to make her understand about Lily, and prove to her—and himself—that he wasn't mad. And damnation, he *wasn't.*

He was breathing hard himself as he drew her as far forward as he could, to where the ship narrowed above the bowsprit and the figurehead below and where none of the men on the first watch could overhear them. He pulled her close against his chest, his arm tight around her waist as he steadied her against the ship's motion.

It was nearly night, the last breath of evening when the western horizon still glowed dimly pale with the final traces of sunset and the sky overhead had already turned to blue-black ink. The sliver of a new moon hung low above the sea, while the same wind that whisked the sky clear of clouds rushed the *Angel Lily* through the white-capped waves so swiftly that the ship seemed to fly over the water.

To fly on wings, white wings like a swan's....

"You can feel her here, can't you?" he said hoarsely, his mouth close to her ear so she'd hear him over the wind. "She's nearby somewhere, on the ship or in the wind. Lily's *here.*"

Rose closed her eyes, struggling to find sense in a world that had gone crazily beyond reason. If she'd been tossed into the waves below she'd feel not a whit more lost and helpless than she did right now. To be taken as a prisoner by the enemy and dragged here to the bow at his whim with the black, deadly water crashing below should have been bad enough.

But it was worse than that. Far worse, for as hard as she tried she could not blot out the new sensation of her body pressed so shamefully against the hard, muscled wall of Nickerson Sparhawk's chest, or how easily he held her, his forearm as thick and strong as the branch of an oak. The thin linen of his shirt and the bombazine of her gown seemed to vanish between them, and the layers of her petticoats offered no real barrier as she stood tensed against his thighs.

It was Lily's fault that she'd given in like this. If he hadn't spoken of Lily, of how she'd inexplicably chosen to visit him or haunt him or whatever it was Lily was doing, then Rose wouldn't have let herself be dragged from his cabin in the first place, and she certainly wouldn't be here in this dreadful, humiliating position with him now.

But for Lily, of course, it wouldn't have been dreadful at all....

No man had ever embraced Rose like this—no man except her father had ever embraced her at all—and even realizing that this one meant nothing by it did little to ease the unfamiliar warmth that spread across her body at his touch. Yet as his arm curled more tightly around her, his fingers spreading to cover her protectively from waist to hip, still she gasped at the intimacy of the touch—the touch of a madman.

"She's here, lass, isn't she?" he rasped, his breath seductively warm on her ear. "Your sister's here."

Rose shuddered and tried to pull away, from him and from the truth. For if he was truly mad, her conscience told her, then so was she. Somehow, in some way, Lily *was* here on this deck, in the wild unpredictability of the wind and sea and in the beauty of the night sky dappled with diamond-bright stars. The feeling was as intangible as that, yet the aching grief that had become a part of Rose's life since Lily's death seemed wondrously to lift and ease. Lily wasn't gone; she was with her here again, to tease her, to guide her, to comfort her as only a sister could.

Blindly Rose turned her face to the wind as it tugged away at her hairpins until, at last, she felt the heavy coil of her hair slip and fall free over her shoulders, the thick waves tossing and whipping around her. That was Lily, too, for Lily had always chided her for dressing her hair so severely. "Gentlemen," Lily would declare as she tipped her head, "fancy a becoming degree of disarray.'' And then she'd click her tongue with resignation as Rose had pinned hers back anyway.

But this time Lily had won. The hairpins were gone, never to be recovered, and the prim little lace bonnet with them, and this time Rose didn't care.

"Oh, Lily," she whispered plaintively. "Lily, please don't go!"

"She won't," came the hoarse reply beside her, and Rose's eyes flew open. Instead of Lily's laughing blue eyes, she was staring into the green depths of Captain Sparhawk's, only inches away, as his black hair, untied like her own, tossed across his broad forehead with its fresh scar.

This, then, was reality, this man and the ship and the night wind at sea, and her sister no more than a bittersweet dream. Rose pressed her lips tightly together, fighting back the tears as she reached up to press her palms against her cheeks.

"It was so real," she said miserably, her voice breaking with disappointment. "I cannot explain it, but I knew Lily was here with me and now—now she's gone, and I've lost her once more."

"Nay, lass, don't think too hard on it," he said with a gentleness Rose hadn't expected from a man so given to arrogance and shouting orders. "Accept the feeling for what it is."

"But how can I?" Still fighting tears, Rose shook her head, sweeping aside her hair from her face. "What we are saying is impossible, and yet I felt her here with me again, as plain as day."

"Then let that be enough. God knows that's what I've had to do." He reached up and brushed his fingers across her cheek, his calluses rough against her skin, and smiled sadly. "And Lily won't take no for an answer."

"She never would before. Why should she now?" Troubled, Rose drew her face from his fingers, and saw how his smile turned wry as he let his hand drop back to his side. "Yet you swear you've seen her as an angel, the mirror of the figurehead below."

"Aye, I'll swear to that, and a good deal more." He sighed. "We can make it our secret, little Rose, between you and me alone, for I doubt there's another on board who would believe in Lily. Or in us."

Again she shook her head, and to Nick the silence that followed stretched endlessly between them. Damnation, he *knew* she'd felt Lily's presence! Why the devil wouldn't she accept it?

And why, too, did it matter so much to him that she would, this small, solemn girl who was the living shadow of her sister? It had been so long since he'd needed anything from anyone else that the intensity of it now frightened him. He'd spent the greater part of his life shying away from dependence of any kind, priding himself on how little he was bound to others. Was Rose Everard really such a link to his own sanity and self-respect that he'd let himself hang here while he waited on the favor of her reply, as tongue-tied and fearful as some landlocked plowboy?

Blast, he should never have been so familiar as to call her "little Rose," even if she was—

"There can be no confidences between us, Captain," she said, carefully keeping her eyes focused slightly below his chin. "You are my enemy, and you have caused a great affront to my father by capturing this ship and claiming me as your prisoner."

Strange how he'd almost forgotten that himself. "We were speaking of your sister, not your father," he said warmly. "Damnation, doesn't that mean anything to you?"

She lifted her gaze to his, and Nick wondered how he'd ever thought her plain. She'd taken the moonlight for her own, her pale skin luminous and her gray eyes bright, and if it had been for him to decide, she would never pin up her hair again, but leave it instead loose and wild about her shoulders as it was now, a dark, tangled cloud around her face.

"It means more than you can ever understand, Captain," she said softly, her words barely audible over the wind, "but I promise you I shall consider what you have said."

Eagerly Nick leaned closer to hear more, but instead she slipped both hands to his arm around her waist and gently eased herself free. She hesitated for a moment, her black skirts swirling around her as she clung to the rail for balance, then bowed her head, turned and made her way alone to the companionway.

And Nick let her go. His arms felt strangely empty without her in them, his body now chilled where she had warmed it, and absently he rubbed one hand across his chest as he stared out over the water.

By bringing her here, he'd found the answer he'd sought. What he hadn't counted on were all the new questions that came with it.

"I cannot believe you would do something so unspeakably cruel!" cried Lily as soon as Nick returned to his cabin. "Unconscionable and cruel!"

"Was it now?" Nick dropped heavily into his chair. He'd known Lily would be waiting for him, so much so that he'd half expected her to appear on the deck. But this time, after three hours of walking back and forth on the quarterdeck while he considered what next to do, he was ready.

"It was indeed, and you know perfectly well why!" The air in the cabin seemed to crackle around her with her fury as she paced back and forth, her wings twitching with little jerks of irritation.

Nick sighed and leaned back in his chair, purposefully stretching his legs out before him so she'd have to walk around him. Whatever force had sent an angel in the form of Lily to him had chosen well, for she was exactly the kind of woman he generally chose for himself—buxom, brazen lasses who knew how to please men. If any woman could influence him, living or dead, it would be one like Lily. So why, then, did his thoughts keep returning to her little sister, awash in moonlight?

"You left me no choice, Lily," he said. "If you'd but shown yourself to your sister, then I wouldn't have been reduced to that dumb show of taking her up to stand over your figurehead."

"I told you before that I can't do that!" She cracked open her fan, fluttering it rapidly before her face. "You are the only one among the living who can see me!"

"And because of that, the rest of the blessed living judge me completely mad. Except now, of course, your sister." He smiled slowly, thinking of Rose. "I'll wager whatever you please that she believes in you with all her heart, with or without your consent. The only marvel to me is what you've done for her to earn that sort of devotion."

"How else should it be?" sputtered Lily indignantly. "Mama died when we were little, and there was no one else for us to turn to but each other. I should have been equally bereft had she died first. But for you to play upon her grief as you did was shameless!"

Nick remembered the eager, wistful look on Rose's face when she'd first sensed Lily's presence, how her lips had parted breathlessly and her whole face had seemed to glow from within. He'd have had to be made from granite not to have been touched by that, or to wish it hadn't happened.

But it would make what he planned to say next come easier.

Nick slanted his gaze at her, warning enough to those who knew him well. "I'll play upon a good deal more of her, Lily," he said softly, "if you do not agree to leave me alone. As you said yourself, Rose is not as ill-favored as first I judged her. A mite small for my tastes, but fair enough for passing amusement.''

Lily gasped, her face frozen in horror. "You wouldn't dare! You wouldn't *dare!* Rose is a sheltered innocent, without the slightest guile or defense against the traps of men like you!"

"Traps of men?" Nick scoffed. "That's a pleasant take on it. Remind me to put the ratsbane beneath my pillow."

"You know well enough what I mean, just as Rose would not!"

"Oh, I'll warrant she may know more than you think. As a younger sibling myself, I recall how desperate my elder brother was to keep me in leading strings beyond my time." He linked his hands behind his head. "Besides, she's agreed to wed this man Graham, hasn't she? Surely even some empty-headed lordling wouldn't offer for a woman without sampling her wares. Likely I'd be but widening Rose's... *experience.* That is, if it's your choice."

Lily practically spit her words. "You are a common and vulgar swine, sir, and if you believe what you say, I cannot begin to fathom how marriages are arranged in your country!"

"Neither can I," said Nick dryly, "for I've kept blessedly clear of the whole marriage carnival. Who would have me, anyway, seeing as I'm so common and vulgar? Not that it will matter with your sister. She doesn't seem to be so besotted with her intended that she'd be averse to my attentions. And marriage wasn't what I had in mind for your dear little Rose."

"You are not behaving at all the way I intended, not at all!" she sputtered. She slammed her fan down on the edge of the table, hard enough to shatter any earthly *brise,* and spun around with a swish of her skirts so that her back was to Nick. She stood there for a long moment, her wings heaving as she struggled to control her anger.

Nick waited, enjoying how he'd turned the tables on her. Lord knows he'd been furious enough at her that he could afford to be patient for once in turn.

"I'm sorry I've disappointed you, sweetheart," he called amicably. "But I have a long history of being contrary."

"Oh, a pox on your history!" she said irritably. "If you could but understand Rose's situation, then you would not even jest at such a thing."

But Nick wasn't jesting, not any longer. "The only situation I give a damn about is my own. You've made a shambles of my life, Lily, and I'd rather you'd have let me die than continue on like this, with my men all whispering about me behind my back and me wondering what mischief you've planned next. I have to be my own master, and with you fluttering about, I'm not. I don't want your help or your happiness or whatever other blessed name you give it. I want you gone."

She turned to face him with her hands outstretched, beseeching. "I cannot leave you, Nick," she said unhappily. "Not now, not yet, not until you've changed yourself for the better."

"So we're back to that, are we? Making me over into a better man?" Unmoved by her appeal, Nick shook his head. He hadn't expected her to call his bluff like this, but it wasn't in his nature to back down, and he wouldn't now. "Well, you wished to make me more contented, and few things content me more than a pretty little wench twisting and sighing with joy beneath me in my bunk. Your sister won't have cause for complaint, I promise you that."

"Seducing Rose wasn't part of the plan," said Lily with a clipped edginess. "I told you she needed a friend, not a—not a debauchee."

"Then you should have thought of that before you tossed her into my path." Nick leaned forward, his expression ruthless and his eyes glittering with anticipation. "I'm not a gentleman, Miss Everard, no matter how much you wish to pretend otherwise. If you want to play games with your sister's virtue as the stakes, then you're free to do so. But don't try to paint me the villain if I accept."

Resolutely Lily folded her arms across the front of her gown. "So that if, against your wishes, I remain in your life—which of course I am bound to do—then you will ruin my sister."

"Aye." Nick nodded. "That's the whole of it."

"So that if I continue trying to help you better yourself, you shall reward me instead by committing an act that can serve only to make you an even greater rogue and rascal.'' She sighed deeply, her full breasts quivering above the low-cut gown. ''You aren't making this in the least manageable for me, are you?''

''I didn't intend to. You're a woman, and you're dead, and you might well be no more than a dream brought on by my being struck on the head. If I can't win against you, well then, I should cash it in now and be done.'' His smile was humorless. ''Go on, heave all the water pitchers you please. But if you vanish now, this night, I give you my word that your sister will be delivered untouched to her bridegroom the moment her ransom is paid.''

''As you wish then, my dear captain, though you are sadly misled if you believe a woman, alive or dead, is of no use as an adversary.'' With the air of a general preparing for battle, Lily tapped her folded fan against her shoulder once, twice, three times. ''And I should warn you, too, that I'll have considerably more than water pitchers on my side.''

The memory of what had happened to the *Angel Lily*'s first captain flickered through Nick's mind, and swiftly he shoved it aside. His situation bore not the slightest resemblance to Fotherill's. He had an unbeatable trump in little Rose Everard, and if Lily forced his hand, he'd no compunction whatsoever about playing it.

Or at least that was what he told himself, and perhaps, at that moment, he believed it.

"You can try whatever you wish, Miss Lily," he said softly. "But mind that it's your choice. And mind, too, that when I play, I play to win."

Chapter Six

Gideon held on to the brim of his hat as he craned his head back to point at the top of the mainmast.

"That man there's the lookout," he explained as Rose, too, leaned back to squint upward into the sun. "His task is to scan the horizon for enemy ships. 'Course we hope he sights a slow, overburdened merchantman, but we want to know if he spots a frigate, too. Either way he'll bawl out the instant he spies a sail, and if we chase and close and take the vessel for a prize, then the cap'n awards him one hundred dollars for his trouble."

"One hundred dollars!" marveled Rose with open wonder too sarcastic to be genuine. "And does your captain take the money himself directly from the pockets of his poor captives, or must the same lookout man do that task, too?"

Gideon frowned. "It comes from his own pockets, Miss Everard," he declared soundly. "I've seen it a score of times myself. Besides, Nick—er, Cap'n Sparhawk goes as proper by the rules as he can. He doesn't countenance looting or helping himself the way some privateering masters do. He sends everything in to Charles Town to be auctioned and sold at the prize courts, and waits until then to claim his shares.''

Rose nodded absently. She hadn't intended to be so sharp, but in the hour since she'd come on deck she'd heard nothing from Lieutenant Cole but the most overblown praise for his captain, and by now she half expected the man himself to come walking across the waves like the saintly paragon Cole was so eager to describe.

If, that is, Captain Sparhawk decided to show himself at all this morning. From the bells that rang to mark the changes of the watch, she guessed the hour must be close to noon, and he'd yet to come on deck. Though after what had passed between them last night, she still wasn't sure what she'd say to him if—or when—he did. As furtively as she could, she glanced around again toward the companionway that led to his cabin.

''If you're looking for the captain, you're likely to have a good long wait,'' said Gideon, reading her thoughts with such ease that she blushed. ''Concerns of the ship kept him from his sleep until late, and I don't expect him to appear any time soon.''

''I wouldn't think Captain Sparhawk would be so plagued,'' said Rose. *She* had managed to rise at a decent hour, she thought crossly, no matter how many sleepless hours he'd given her thanks to his foolishness about Lily. The least he could do was the same. "This ship seems to be run quite effortlessly without him."

That, at least, was true. Especially considering the *Angel Lily* had belonged to the Americans for such a short period of time, the ship and her crew appeared in perfect harmony. Every rope was coiled in exact loops, every unused sail furled with precision, and each sailor seemed almost to be able to anticipate the lieutenant's orders, so effortlessly did they move to execute his wishes. Beneath the cloudless sky the *Angel Lily* sliced through the waves with an easy assurance that Rose had never seen before.

"Thank you, miss." Gideon beamed and touched the front of his hat in acknowledgment. "'Tis one of the reasons the cap'n's been so successful. Twenty-two prizes, miss, more than any other Yankee captain."

"Twenty-two!" This time her amazement was real. From her father, she knew even the most successful English privateers in this war had captured no more than a half dozen American and French merchant ships.

"Twenty-two," said Gideon with obvious satisfaction. "Makes for a pretty piece of ciphering, figuring all those shares among two hundred men! When we finally pay out, he'll send every last jack home a rich man, and that makes for a happy crew. But that's only part of it. He had his pick of the best seamen on the coast, and he knows enough to treat them like the gems they are. Respect and tolerance, miss, that's his secret. Be firm, but treat every man in the crew like you'd want to be treated yourself. But coming from King George's England, you can't be expected to understand.''

Automatically Rose opened her mouth to protest, only to swallow her defense unspoken. If the red-haired lieutenant had just set her down as she suspected, then she deserved it. He was right. She didn't understand the reasons behind this American war, and she dutifully parroted the views of her father and his friends. Respect and tolerance were supposed to be English virtues, too, but the men on board the *Commerce* had grumbled at their minuscule wages and cowered beneath their officers' discipline. Even on her launching day the *Angel Lily* hadn't had this same spark and dash to her under Captain Fotherill that she so obviously had under Captain Sparhawk, and certainly none of the Americans' success.

''Does he—Captain Sparhawk, I mean—often have difficulty sleeping?'' she asked tentatively. Insomnia seemed a far safer topic than politics. ''I can suggest a receipt for a special powder given me by my aunt that's guaranteed efficacious.''

''Ah, now, we'd best leave that to the surgeon,'' said Gideon. ''But I thank you for your concern, Miss Everard. I do thank you for that.''

Gently he took her arm, holding her by her elbow alone as lightly as if she were made of porcelain. He would never be as handsome as his captain, but there was a certain offhanded charm to his freckled face that made Rose forgive his forwardness when he brought his face close to hers to speak to her alone.

"You are a lady of breeding and sensibility, Miss Everard," he began nervously, "and I pray I can trust your confidence."

Curious, Rose nodded. She wasn't truly a well-bred lady, her father having been knighted only five years before, but she saw no reason to mention that now.

"Good, good." Warily the lieutenant glanced over his shoulder. "It's the captain, you see. I wish to heaven that whatever disturbs his sleep could be cured by ordinary potions or powders, but I fear it's something worse. He suffered a grave blow to his head in the engagement a fortnight ago, and ever since he has taken to talking to himself in his cabin. Whole arguments and quarrels and smashed crockery, yet he's alone the entire time. As an old friend, I fear for him, Miss Everard, indeed I do."

Our secret, little Rose, between you and me alone: that was what Captain Sparhawk had asked for, and though Rose had refused to share his confidence, she now realized that simply by hearing it she'd been forced to agree. There'd been a desperation in his eyes and voice that had been as impossible to deny as his embrace, and in the long, sleepless night alone in her cabin she'd heard and felt him in her head over and over again. The too-brief moment of solace she'd had when she'd sensed Lily's presence had come with a steep price. Like it or not, Lily had become a secret she was bound to share with Captain Sparhawk.

Because, God help them both, Lily *was* here.

"As much as I admire your concern for your captain, Mr. Cole," she said slowly, hoping she kept the guilty flush from her cheeks, "I do wonder why you share it with me, a stranger and an enemy prisoner."

But to her surprise it was Gideon who colored more, deep beneath his freckles and weathered tan. "Ah, Miss Everard, forgive me, but I tell you because of who you are, not what. It's your sister, Miss Lily, this vessel's namesake, that Nick claims to converse with, and I wondered if he had mentioned to you—"

"Mentioned what, Gideon?"

Nick couldn't remember two such guilty faces as Rose's and Gideon's turned in unison toward him. Of course they'd been talking about him, and none of it good. The proof was painted across their miserable faces. These two, of any on board, he'd thought he could trust: his oldest friend in the world, and the woman who shared his secret.

But what did he expect? He should never have dragged her out on the foredeck last night, clinging to her like a dying man in clear sight of the men on watch. He should never have raved on like a lunatic before witnesses like that, witnesses who'd immediately carry the tattle back between decks where it would grow and blossom beyond his control. No wonder they'd been talking about him. He'd feel less vulnerable standing here naked with a score of British marines aiming their muskets at his chest than he did right now, and it took every last scrap of self-possession and courage not to turn tail and race back to his cabin.

Damnation, what was happening to him?

"Mentioned what, Gid?" he asked again, looking hard at his friend. "What exactly was I to be discussing with Miss Everard?"

But it was the girl, not Gideon, who stepped forward to speak. "Mr. Cole was telling me how many prizes you have taken. Twenty-two, he said, though when I asked if that included the *Angel Lily*, which I still maintain wasn't yours to take in the first place, he said only the captain would know the exact tally. Which, I suppose, you must?"

She was lying, of course. Her cheeks were as red as cherries, and she was twisting her hands so tightly into her skirts he marveled that the fabric didn't shred beneath her fingers. But her eyes told the rest of the story, begging him, pleading silently for him to accept the sorry little fib she'd offered on his behalf.

Dear Lord, could she really be lying to save him?

"Twenty-two or twenty-three, it's still a great sum," she continued, lifting her chin bravely. "I should be vastly impressed, Captain Sparhawk, if your accomplishments weren't such a grievous drain to my own country's resources."

She was lying, and because it was for him, he didn't care. She could have destroyed his entire pretense of sanity with a few short words before Gideon and the rest. But for whatever reason, she hadn't done it, and he felt a weight like lead lifting from his shoulders.

"Cole's wrong," he said. Even to his own ears his voice sounded almost normal, booming out across the quarterdeck as if nothing had changed. "It's twenty-three, including that old brig you were sailing in and the *Angel Lily* which, as I've told you, we captured fair by every law of sea and man."

He began to smile, from relief as much as anything, then frowned instead. Now that his first dread over her reaction had passed, he noticed that she wore the same sad mourning gown as yesterday, spattered with white salt stains and rusty around the hem. Considering how long and hard her voyage from England had been and that she had no maidservant to look after her, the gown was, he supposed, forgivable. But instead of a hat or bonnet she'd tied some sort of drab black kerchief around her head and under her chin, drawing the front far over her face into a hideous head-size tent. Her hair, all that richly glorious hair, was hidden beneath it, and she looked for all the world like some convent-bound French novitiate ready to take orders.

And here he'd taken special pains this morning with his own dress, choosing the best of his weekday coats, the green superfine with the darker green waistcoat embroidered in pale blue. He had fussed with his neck cloth and shot his cuffs more times than any Bath macaroni, all with the goal of impressing Miss Rose Everard. Lily had yet to appear to him this morning, but he didn't believe he'd be rid of her so easily, and when he remembered how sweetly Rose had filled his arms in the moonlight, he almost wished Lily back.

Self-consciously Rose patted at the kerchief, and only then did he realize he'd been scowling at it. "I've had to make do, you see," she explained apologetically. "I lost my last hat over the side yesterday, and even those few hours in the sun burned my nose to a quick."

"I'll wager we can do even better, Miss Everard, and save your poor nose in the bargain," he said, even as he mentally cursed himself for an insensitive brute. After all she'd just done for him, why the devil had he singled out her headgear like that? "We Yankees are known for being able to jury-rig anything. A lady's bonnet should be no challenge at all. Johnny!"

One of the ship's boys scurried over to stand before Nick.

"Johnny, fetch the straw tricorne from my cabin." As the boy ran down the companionway, Nick smiled at Rose, or at least at the top of the offending kerchief that was hiding her face. How much he longed to tear away that blasted scarf for himself and rediscover the girl he'd seen in the moonlight! "No milliner might claim it, true, but at least the brim's wide enough to keep the sun from your face. We can stuff that kerchief into the brim to make it fit you."

"That is most kind of you, Captain." She bobbed a lopsided curtsy, the best she could manage on the shifting deck. "Mr. Cole here was telling me himself how generous you are to your men, and now here's the proof that you're kind to your prisoners, too. Even an *English* prisoner."

There, thought Rose miserably, she'd done it again, spoken all wrong and muddled things worse than molasses. After last night she'd wanted to be civil to Captain Sparhawk for Lily's sake, and she'd tried, she'd really tried. She'd even covered for him before the red-haired lieutenant.

But she had no experience talking to men like this, and the more she'd babbled on, echoing her father's sentiments for lack of her own, the more stern and disapproving his handsome face had become. No wonder he'd sent below for another hat. She was a shabby, makeshift disgrace to his impeccable deck, a shameful excuse even for a prisoner. When she'd first turned to see him standing behind her, dauntingly perfect in the elegant green coat that turned his eyes to emerald, her heart had both twisted with hopeless admiration and plummeted with despair. She didn't miss the irony that it was Lily who was their single common bond, for, oh, how much more Lily would have made of the same opportunity!

She heard the boy's bare feet trotting back across the deck, and didn't bother to look. Of course she'd put on whatever hat Captain Sparhawk produced. He'd been right: most anything would be an improvement over the kerchief. She only wished he hadn't been the one to say so.

"I warranted this be what ye wanted, Cap'n Sparhawk." The boy's voice was full of doubt. "It bein' for th' lady an' all. There weren't no other."

At that Rose turned to look, too curious not to, and gasped with wonder. In Captain Sparhawk's right hand was one of the hats from her trousseau that she'd believed was gone forever, her favorite, a Leghorn straw with the broad brim pinned up on three sides in cunning mimicry of a man's, and crowned with pink silk ribands and a dyed pheasant's feather. Miraculously the hat was as uncrushed and fresh as the day it had come from the milliner's, the ribands fluttering in the wind.

"Oh, thank you!" she cried as she rushed forward. "And after I was so hateful to you about my trunks being stolen!"

She tore the kerchief from her head and stuffed it in her pocket, heedless of how her hair came tumbling down with it, before she took the straw hat from him and gingerly set it on her hair. Determined not to let the wind claim this one, too, she carefully tied the long pink ribands beneath her chin before she looked up at Captain Sparhawk.

"Thank you so much," she said softly, his image blurring because of the tears in her eyes. Once again he'd surprised her with a special gesture for her alone, and she longed to be able to tell him how much it meant. "You cannot know, but—oh, thank you!"

"You're welcome," he said gruffly. He held out his arm to her. "I'll wager you'll be wanting this to go with it."

Stunned, she saw that the coral-colored gown draped over his arm was hers as well, and could only shake her head in amazement.

"Go on, lass, take the gown, too," he urged. "Go below and change if you wish. Don't wait on ceremony on my account."

She was beyond thanks, beyond words—Nick could see that from how her eyes shone too brightly as she'd taken the gown from his arm and hugged it to herself before she ran back to her cabin to change—but it wasn't greed that had made her so. He'd seen that enough in other women to recognize the difference, when he'd rewarded one or another of his mistresses with some new bauble that made them squeal with acquisitive delight. But Rose's reaction clearly came from the giving, not the gift itself, and uneasily Nick recognized that, too.

And it was fine with him that she'd been left speechless. At least no one would notice that he was in much the same state as well. He had never in his life seen either the hat or the gown, let alone expected the boy to bring them from his own cabin. But obviously they were Rose's, and he could guess how they'd come to be in his quarters.

"You've made my little sister monstrously happy, you know," said Lily from where she sat in the mainmast shrouds, the toes of her slippered feet tucked daintily through the ratlines and her wings folded snug against the wind. "And oh, my, when she finds the second trunk of hers you've managed to squeeze into that abominable little cabin!''

She laughed merrily, showing the tip of her tongue. ''I vow, my dear, darling Nickerson, that you couldn't have chosen a better way to charm her. Though I shall venture that your coat today is most splendidly cut across the shoulders. Even Rose might notice. Your tailor does you proud.''

Nick glared at her, his suspicions regarding the hat and gown confirmed. ''Why the devil are you still here, anyway? If you don't recall the consequences of your continuing to plague me, be certain that I do, and that I damn well mean to act upon them.''

''Aye, aye, Nick, I'll leave,'' grumbled Gideon, already moving away. ''If you wish to be left alone with the little chit when she returns, then you've only to ask civilly.''

But Nick grabbed his arm. ''Wait, Gid, no, I didn't mean—oh, blast and hell!'' In frustration he looked again to the rigging where Lily had been and now, naturally, was no longer.

''Is it the woman in the figurehead again, Nick?'' asked Gideon, his voice low and serious. ''Are you seeing her again? The surgeon says—''

''Rot the surgeon! There's not a blessed thing wrong with me!'' Nick stared at the empty rigging, furious. The hat and the gown and now her popping up here on the deck: Lily was taunting him, daring him pure and simple. With all her dithering about him becoming a better man, she didn't believe he was capable of coldhearted seduction. Well, he was and he knew it, and so did the long line of women in his past. She was gambling against him, and so help him, she was going to lose. The sooner she realized that, the better.

Gideon cleared his throat. "I was about to clear for gunnery practice, Nick," he said. "You said yesterday you wanted the crews faster with the firing."

"Use your wits, Gideon!" snapped Nick. "Run out the long guns this close to the Carolina coast? Why not simply write out our intentions and deliver them to every frigate captain in range?"

"Why not indeed?" answered Gideon sharply, at last forgetting rank. "Maybe then you'll remember why we're here and stop chasing ghosts and petticoats!"

Stunned, Nick stared coldly at his friend before he broke down and swore with exasperation, rubbing his fingers into the back of his neck where that lead weight had returned.

"Nay, Gideon, you are right," he said gruffly, "and it's my temper that's wrong. My apologies, if you'll have them. I wonder that you stay with me at all."

Gideon shrugged carelessly, though as the anger faded from his dark eyes the questions and the concern remained. "Who else would have either of us?"

"Who else, indeed." Nick sighed. "Still and all, we'll stay the gunnery until tomorrow. I've no taste for it today. Keep the helm to this course for now, and call me at once if there's a sail. We should be directly in the lines of the—ah, Miss Everard!"

The difference nearly took his breath away. Freed from the heavy, dowdy mourning, she seemed years younger, a bright figure in coral sarcenet that captured the eye and interest of every man on deck. She'd tied her dark hair loosely back with another ribbon, and beneath the hat her face was glowing with pleasure. The gown's close-fitting bodice emphasized the narrowness of her waist and her small, high breasts, and the sweep of her flounced skirts, the pinked silk edges rippling in the wind, made her look as if she were dancing even as she stood still.

"Captain Sparhawk." She smiled shyly, her face dappled with the sunlight that filtered through the straw brim of her hat. "I suppose I must thank you again. Though I can't conceive of how you did it, I'm most grateful for the return of that second traveling case, even though there's scarce room for me in my cabin now. You cannot know what a relief it is to wear clothing that is clean and dry, even if I feel disloyal to Lily for putting aside the mourning."

"Ah, I doubt she'd take it to heart," said Nick, his throat strangely dry. If Lily had wanted to keep his sister safe from his attentions, she should have left her in rusty black, and not tricked her out in this charming, delightful, and sorely tempting fashion. "She didn't strike me as the kind who'd fancy wearing black for long herself."

The long pheasant feather on Rose's hat bobbed as she nodded. "That's true. When our grandmama died four years ago, Lily outright refused to wear mourning beyond a month. She said that black made her too sad for words, and turned her cheeks sallow besides. Finally Papa had to stop her bills at Madame Dusonnet's to make her comply, and even then she wore red ribands over the black.''

''Your sister must have been a trial for your poor old Papa.'' As offhandedly as he could, Nick glanced around the deck and through the rigging to see if Lily had returned to listen. Stopping her credit at a mantua maker's certainly seemed a far easier way to bring her in line; a pity it wouldn't work now. ''A regular trial.''

Rose sighed wistfully. ''I suppose she was. But she was also kind and generous and vastly amusing, and she always took my side against Aunt Lucretia.'' Her shoulders drooped as she ran her fingers across her skirt. ''You can tell this gown was made for her, not me. I'd never dare to wear anything so bold, but Lily— why, Lily would dare anything.''

''Hush now, no more of Lily,'' ordered Nick. ''The gown is yours, and with your grace you have made it your own in a way no other woman could.''

Swiftly she raised her gaze to his, startled by his tone and unsure of his meaning. He was captain, true, but what reason or right did he have for sounding so blatantly possessive?

''You speak to turn my head, Captain Sparhawk,'' she said, just breathless enough to prove how well he'd succeeded. ''Or does wearing a bold gown draw bold words?''

"Not so bold, Miss Everard, only true. A pretty lady, prettily dressed—what greater verity can there be?" He smiled, slowly and lazily and, to Rose, very boldly indeed.

"Verity has nothing to do with it," she replied, feeling rather bold herself. "Except, perhaps, to confirm my country's opinion that Americans are not to be trusted as far as they can be tossed."

"Cruel words, Miss Everard!" He sighed dramatically even as his smile winked wickedly higher. "Last evening we parted before I could share my humble bachelor's meal with you. Will you grace me again with a second chance, and join me this hour for dinner instead so I might defend the honor of my country to you?"

Rose knew she should be blushing, blushing furiously to the tips of her toes, at such an outrageously inappropriate invitation. But she wasn't, not in the slightest. Pleasantly warm, yes, though that could be from the sun on her shoulders or from the sheer heat of Captain Sparhawk's green-eyed gaze, but that was all. Instead she was meeting his scrutiny with ease, her palms dry and her hands still as she bantered with him.

Almost, thought Rose with an inward premonition of disaster, as if she were Lily.

Uneasily she remembered how strongly she'd sensed her sister's presence while standing near the figurehead that bore Lily's face. Could putting on this gown have had the same effect?

And then, of course, Rose's cheeks turned as bright as the coral silk sarcenet. "Oh, Captain Sparhawk, I— I cannot say," she stammered. "That is, I should be honored, if I could agree, but I doubt that—"

"You'll doubt nothing," said Nick easily, "and I shall take that as acceptance."

He reached out and captured her hand before she realized what was happening, his large fingers swallowing hers in their clasp. Still smiling, he bowed over their hands, his eyes never breaking away from her own.

"I fear, Miss Everard, the ship demands my attention for a moment or two," he said, his voice low and intimate, "but if you'll wait for me below in the cabin, I promise I'll join you as soon as I can."

She nodded dumbly, drew back her hand and fled.

Gideon snorted. "The ship demands, hell," he scoffed. "We could have twelve feet of water in the hold and an admiral's flagship raking our stern and you wouldn't be giving this poor scrap of oak and pine another thought, not with that sweet little piece waiting below."

"No wonder I don't as a rule allow women on board. But this one's turned out most handsomely once she changed her rig, hasn't she?" Nick looked fondly in the direction Rose had gone. What he felt for Rose Everard was more complicated than her appearance alone, but he wasn't about to confess that to Gideon. "At least by the time her blasted intended comes chasing after us, I'll have given him more reason to be wasting his time."

Gideon winked broadly. "So you mean to give his lordship a pair of horns before he's even wed?"

"Gideon, Gideon, where is thy sense of shame?" asked Nick, clucking his tongue in mock outrage even as his eyes glittered wickedly. "The lady is our prisoner and our guest. How could I ever serve her gallant sweetheart so basely?"

"The same way you've served every other husband whose wife you've craved." Gideon chuckled. "At least I know you're on the mend, Nick. You couldn't have picked a better way to prove it."

Nick's smile widened. He hoped Lily, wherever she was, had heard—and believed—every last word.

Chapter Seven

Gingerly Rose touched the hilt of the cutlass on the captain's desk. She had never seen a sword that wasn't attached to a gentleman's waist, making this the first she could actually study without seeming ill-mannered.

In comparison to the elegant creations of polished steel, gilt wire hilts and enameled or jeweled guards that she'd seen in Portsmouth parlors, Captain Sparhawk's cutlass was sturdy and serviceable, with a horn grip worn smooth from use and a curved guard of battered steel. Obviously left on the desk where the captain had tossed it himself, his belt was still threaded through the black scabbard, and Rose's heart beat faster as she thought of the belt and the cutlass swinging low on his narrow hips.

With her fingers still on the hilt, Rose hesitated, listening for footsteps or voices in the companionway. The captain had kept her waiting a quarter hour thus far, and she'd little reason to believe he wouldn't remain on deck another quarter hour more; he was, after all, the master, and for all he'd flirted so wickedly with her, he did have responsibilities. Besides, when would she have another chance like this to satisfy her curiosity? Quickly, before she lost her nerve, she lowered her chin with determination, tightened her fingers around the horn grip, and pulled the cutlass from its scabbard.

It swept free with an ease that caught her by surprise, the weight sending her staggering backward. Swiftly she clapped her left hand over the right to brace it, steadying her wrists to balance the unaccustomed weight. The guard might be dented and scratched, but the long, curving blade was sleek and cared for, gleaming dully in the sunlight. Remembering what she'd overheard from men bragging about swordplay, she circled the blade clumsily in the air before her.

Once long ago, before her governess had confiscated it, she had found and devoured a cheaply printed romance about pirate queens a hundred years before, women as ruthless and daring as any men. As she held the cutlass in both hands, she pictured herself as Anne Bonney, commanding her own destiny with a crew of desperate men behind her.

"Avast there, you rogues and dogs!" she muttered fiercely, narrowing her eyes at the imaginary crew crowding her quarterdeck. "Else I'll see you hung from the yardarm, see if I don't!"

"Not if I can help it, you won't," said Nick dryly from the doorway. "Or do you plan to serve your king by running me through with my own blade?"

Rose gasped and spun to face him, the cutlass still clasped in her hands. "Oh, no, please, that wasn't my intention at all!"

"I'll be grateful unto eternity." And that long, too, Nick knew he'd never forget the image of her standing there with the cutlass drooping from her little hands and the elegant new hat perched jauntily on her head, her cheeks as bright as the silk of her gown and her eyes the perfect guilty circles of a child caught with a hand in the sweets. "I knew I was late, but I would have come sooner if I'd realized the consequences."

"It wasn't that at all. It's only that I've never seen a sword this close, you understand, and though I know I shouldn't have touched it at all, I didn't believe you'd notice or see the harm and I'm truly, vastly sorry." She took a deep breath. "Truly."

"Vastly sorry?" Nick asked sternly, his black brows drawn together in a single menacing line. He was also having the very devil of a time not laughing out loud.

She nodded vigorously, the pheasant's feather bobbing in counterpoint above her face.

"Then surrender your weapon, Miss Everard, and I promise I won't hang you from the yardarm, either."

He held out his open hand to her, and she awkwardly transferred the hilt from her fingers to his before contritely scuttling back to the far side of the desk. Shamefaced though she already was, he still couldn't resist making a few showy, elegant passes with the blade through the empty air to make her gasp with admiration before he deftly slid the cutlass back into its scabbard. He told himself he should be ashamed, playing to her so openly like that.

He wasn't. "I suppose I should be doubly thankful you weren't curious about the pistols," he said as he hung the belt and the cutlass with it on the peg where it belonged and hooked his hat on top for good measure. "You could have done a great deal more damage with gunpowder."

"I should think you'd do sufficient damage with the sword." Her eyes were still round, but at least she seemed again able to speak coherently.

"Not as much as you think," he admitted, accepting the telling of this truth as his punishment. "The whole point of privateering is to take prizes with as little fuss and damage as possible to either party. Most merchant shipmasters—like the one you were sailing with—will strike after a single warning shot. We try not to close and board to fight hand to hand unless we can help it. It's too costly."

"Oh." She sighed and glanced wistfully one last time at the cutlass on the bulkhead peg. "So you have not been forced to kill anyone?"

"I didn't say that." Nor did he wish to say more, not to a face as innocent as hers.

Once he, too, had been that young, that innocent. Once he had believed the same foolishness as other young men, that killing was glorious if the cause was just, and that only the fallen enemy suffered. He was barely fifteen, serving on one of his father's ships in the last of the French wars, when he'd first killed another man. Another boy, really, also pretending to be a man, and Nick had watched both his dreams of glory and his own innocence die along with the French boy weeping for his mother.

"Forgive me," said Rose softly. "I had no right to ask such a question of you."

She was standing beside him, her hand resting lightly on his sleeve, and the depth of the sympathy and understanding that showed on her face shocked him, almost as much as the need that suddenly surged within his soul.

What comfort could she possibly offer him? For God's sake, she was but a little girl playing at pirates, his prisoner, the sheltered daughter of an English lord, a pretty pawn with silver-gray eyes in the middle of a wager to test his sanity....

"I know I often say the wrong thing," she went on, "and I am far too inquisitive. I should have remembered you were a—a warrior."

"Warrior? How blessed Homeric." He tried to smile, and when he couldn't, he went to the cabinet that held his rum and other spirits and busied himself with the glasses and decanters. All she'd offered had been the simplest of apologies; he'd been the one who'd read so much more into it. "Because I wished to offer you something grander than toasted cheese, I'm afraid that dinner won't be here for a bit yet. But this might help to pass the time. Not quite everything I capture, you see, reaches the auction house."

He handed her a glass of sherry wine, noting how she held it with both hands the same way as she'd held the cutlass. Was she already sensing she'd need two hands to hold herself steady?

"Oh, I know, Miss Everard, I know the wine is French," he said lightly as he filled a glass for himself, "and the French are at present my allies, but before you take me to task, I swear I took it from an English ship, and everything is as it should be. Drink up now, lass. Shall we be evenhanded, and drink confusion to the enemy, whichever side it is?"

More likely confusion to herself, thought Rose unhappily as she drank to his toast. Without his hat, the small, barely healed scar above his left brow was still pink and jagged across his sun-browned skin, one more sign of how badly she'd erred. For all she knew he might have been close to death himself from that very wound. She'd seen how his face had closed against her when she'd blundered about the cutlass and the war, his green eyes as shuttered as if he'd stepped behind a wall.

And who could blame him? Toying with the man's belongings hadn't been bad enough; she'd been prying and thoughtless and outright rude, her childish apology only making it worse. He had treated her with far more kindness than any prisoner deserved—he still was—and this was how she repaid him.

She swallowed hard, the sweet wine bitter in her mouth. If somehow Lily had been guiding her earlier on the deck, then it had been Rose herself, all on her own, who had brought this current disaster down upon her shoulders. As if a new gown alone could change what had always been wrong with her!

Swirling the wine gently in her glass, she stared down into the amber-colored liquid rather than meet the captain's gaze. Through the wine she could see her fingers as they circled the glass, distorted and magnified by the curve, and there on the third finger the heavy ring with the oval aquamarine, the stone greenish through the wine. Lord help her, did she really need another reminder?

With an unintentional thump she set the glass half-filled with wine on the table. "I thank you for your courtesy, Captain, but I believe it will be better for us both if I leave now."

"Nay, Miss Everard, stay!" he said, moving swiftly between her and the door. He wasn't about to let her go yet, not with so much hanging unsettled between them. "Please, I ask you. Simply . . . stay."

Blocked, she looked anxiously from one side of his body to the other, vainly willing him to step aside. Level with her eyes was the wide expanse of his chest, crossed by the line of buttons on his waistcoat, each one embroidered with a tiny blue flower. Forget-me-nots, she realized foolishly, as if she'd ever forget him, and at last she raised her eyes to his face.

Simply stay, he'd asked, but already she'd learned that nothing with him would ever be simple. He was watching her closely, his half-shut eyes shadowed by his lashes, and though the smile of a genial host curved his lips, there was still an uneasy tension between them that showed how much her response would mean to him.

"Please, Miss Everard," he said again, his voice dropping low. "Rose. You will stay to dine with me, will you not?"

He had used her given name once before, when he'd held her in the moonlight, and she knew it was doubly wrong for him to do it again now. Wrong, and yet she did not stop him. In eight endless weeks, no one had called her Rose, not since her father had kissed her farewell, and that sharp-felt loneliness, soothed for a moment by the sound of her name, kept her silent.

"Dinner, and no more," he said softly. "What harm is there in that?"

She raised her chin but lowered her eyes as she nodded more from resignation than agreement, and then, before he could speak again, she retreated from the door to the stern windows. If only he had blustered and shouted at her the way he had before, or at least mocked her for being a plain, empty-headed Britisher; that she would have expected and understood. But this kindness, this gentleness, bewildered and disturbed her, and made her weak with longing for things she could never have.

Retreat, she warned herself, *hold back and keep yourself safe. Do not commit the folly of seeing, accepting, believing more than is there simply because you wish it so.*

"It is a pity you did not bring my pianoforte from the *Commerce*'s hold, Captain Sparhawk," she said, her words brittle with forced cheerfulness. Oblivious to the view before her, she pressed her palm to the cool windowpane and left the mark of her fevered skin on the glass. "I could have played for you to pass the time. I'm told I play tolerably well—the Italian masters, Mr. Handel, Scottish and other country airs arranged for keyboard. Though of course I don't play nearly as well as Lily did. She was truly gifted, while I must toil and work for proficiency. But Lily—"

"Damnation, I'll hear no more from you of Lily!"

She turned swiftly, startled by his vehemence, and found that while she'd rattled on he'd closed the gap she'd put between them. With the window behind her, she could not run again. This time, whether she wished to or not, she would have to stand her ground.

"No more of Lily, mind? Not a blessed word!" He sliced his hand through the air, so near her face that she felt the air across her cheek. "She couldn't possibly have bettered you in everything. She was your sister, not a saint!"

"But if you'd known Lily, you would understand," she protested.

"Nay, I doubt I would," he said flatly. "Instead I want you to tell me one way—only one, when there must be scores!—in which you surpass her. Come now, Rose, tell me!"

She shook her head, her thoughts turning blank before the intensity of his demanding gaze. Why should it matter so much to him, anyway? Oh yes, there were plenty of things that she did better than Lily: she could

coax her roses to bloom a fortnight earlier than anyone else's in the county; she recognized by name and
face every wife and child of every man who worked in
her father's shipyard; she knew the secrets of hiring a
first-rate cook and firing a footman given to thievery;
and she was the only one who could coddle and humor her father when his gout kept him in his bed.

But none of these were valued as much as Lily's
beauty and talents and indisputable charm had been,
not by the world and certainly not by a man like Captain Sparhawk. Sadly Rose knew the truth. Ten minutes in Lily's company and he would have fallen under
her spell as completely as had every other man alive.

"One way you're better than she was, lass," he insisted. "Tell me one, that's—"

"I'm very good at draughts," she said defensively.

"Drafts?" Nick turned his head a fraction to look at
her suspiciously. She was Lily's sister; she could well be
ridiculing his request. "What sort of drafts?"

"Draughts," she repeated. Without trying she'd
managed to throw him off-balance, and the knowledge renewed her confidence. "You know, the game. I
played Papa every evening except Sunday, and it's
been, or was, years since Lily could beat me."

"Draughts." He couldn't help glancing around the
cabin for Lily, convinced this must be another trick of
hers. He wasn't sure how he'd expected Rose to ex-
cel—in fancywork with crewel threads, perhaps, or
good deeds among the poor. A game played in taverns
and much favored by apprentices and stable boys

wouldn't have been his first choice, or even his hundredth. But if draughts were her special gift, then by heaven he wasn't about to scorn her for it.

"I shall play you if you don't believe me." Suddenly she smiled with surpassing sweetness. "If, that is, you will agree to play for stakes. Papa and I generally played for a penny a game."

"Done."

It took only a minute for Nick to send the word throughout the ship for a draughts board and pieces, and less than five for a game set to appear at his cabin door, courtesy of the gunner's mate, who'd made it himself.

Nick set the board in the center of his dining table along with the wine and glasses, while Rose untied her hat and put it aside, and shoved back her deep lace cuffs with all the assurance of a practiced gamester. To Nick's amusement, she didn't even blink at the sailor's board, the checkered squares framed by lovingly inked, bare-breasted mermaids frolicking with Neptune. And this from a lass who'd nearly wept from modesty when he'd seen the torn hem of her shift!

"I assume you'll wish to be black, on account of being Black Nick," she said briskly as she shoved the round black pieces across the table to his side. "Which leaves me the white."

"For White Rose?"

She grinned, oddly pleased that he'd thought of it too. "It doesn't have the same fearsome ring as Black Nick."

"A good thing, too, for a lady," he said. "Though I've never quite determined whether the black referred to my hair, my temper or my soul, or if some wag attached it to my name simply because it sounded well."

She deepened her voice to the register of a bullfrog. "Black *Nick,*" she intoned dramatically. "*Black* Nick!"

"Don't try me too far, White Rose," he warned as she tried not to laugh. "I have hung men for less."

"But not a lady."

"Only because I haven't had the opportunity." He dropped a small leather bag onto the table with a thump. "I've a mind to make this more interesting than playing for pennies. That should be two score of gold pistoles. My stake, Miss White Rose."

His smile was charming as he considered the possibilities. He'd accept a small forfeit to begin, a garter perhaps, and proceed from there. To find her willing to gamble like this made his goal almost pathetically easy, and when she laughed like this, her face as rosy as her name, he learned how very much he wanted to win. "And what, my dear, shall you wager?"

"Oh, I won't need a stake," she said blithely. "I'm sure to win from you."

"So certain?" he teased. "Luck's a part of any gaming."

"Not for me." She stacked her pieces on the first two rows of the board, then looked up expectantly. "Where is your watch? We'll need it for keeping time."

He drew his heavy old captain's watch from his pocket and set in on the table. "I'll admit I haven't played draughts for years," he said, though in truth he'd never played the game at all, "but I don't recall there being time kept."

"Oh, the way Papa and I played there is," she said easily, turning the watch so she could see the face as well as he. "Ten seconds per play, else you must forfeit your turn. It keeps the game moving most wondrously fast."

And fast it was. In eight lightning moves, Rose managed to capture all of Nick's pieces but one boxed hopelessly in a corner, and to make kings of half of hers. Eight moves, and, he reckoned by his own traitorous watch, less than three minutes.

"I warned you," she said with a note of pity as she tapped the first of his lost pistoles on the edge of the table before her.

"Opening luck," he said, still smiling though he'd determined not to let it happen again as he refilled her wineglass. "But at least you've earned your stake, just as you promised."

Two games later, and she'd tripled it.

Certain by then that he'd learned the rhythm of her leapfrogging moves, Nick raised the stakes for the next game, and she beat him in two minutes flat. She smiled sympathetically and offered to go back to a single coin, and he irritably insisted on raising again. Another two games, and Nick was certain she'd been weaned in White's; three games after that, and he swore it must have been Newgate, for her to learn to take a man's purse with such ease.

"I'm very sorry," she said as she added the last pistole to the neat pyramid of gold coins before her. "But I did warn you."

Before Nick was forced to admit defeat, the steward and two boys appeared at the cabin door with the trays bearing dinner. Thoroughly pleased with herself, Rose scooped her winnings into the bag, leaned back in her chair and drank her wine while the cloth was laid and the dishes set out. Braised onions, sauced potatoes, a pair of roast chickens, and some sort of savory stew besides—Rose hadn't seen, or smelled, such a deliciously bounteous meal since clearing Portsmouth, and her mouth watered with anticipation.

"I hope you pay your cook well," she said as she began to help herself to the vegetables. "From this he looks to be worth every last ha'penny."

Nick only shrugged with a noncommittal sound in the back of his throat, still too furious with himself for losing to venture much more.

But Rose's heart sank. She'd been wrong to win every game, selfishly and foolishly wrong. One or two would have let him save his pride, but she'd been too caught up in the play to consider the consequences.

Another small way, then, that Lily would have succeeded where she'd failed. Lily might not have won as many games, but she would have known when and how to lose to soothe her male opponent's dignity. Rose had only to look at the rigid set of Captain Sparhawk's mouth and the way he was savaging the roast chicken instead of carving it to see the damage she'd done. Her gaze dropped to the plate before her, her pleasure in winning shrinking and fading with every second.

"You're thinking of Lily again, aren't you?" he demanded fiercely. "It wasn't enough that you've proved you're the sharpest gamester I've ever sat down with. Somehow, someway, that blasted sister of yours always seems better."

"But I should have let you win," she said in a tiny voice. "Lily would have."

"And why in blazes should you have done that?" He set down his knife and fork with an emphatic clatter. "I love to win and I hate to lose, and it doesn't matter whether I'm fighting for my life against another ship or fumbling my way through a wretched game of draughts. Why should it be any different for you?"

"Because I—"

"Nay, Rose, you'll hear me out this time," he said firmly, resting his arms on the table to lean across it toward her. "You made a good start there at being your own person and leaving Lily's shadow behind. Now you've got to keep on. I know how hard it is. I've done it. I was cursed and blessed with a father who was pretty near next to God in Newport, and my older brother Jon's a close second. Sparhawks are like that. I heard about 'em from the cradle onward. Nothing I did would ever be as good, let alone better."

With painful clarity he remembered the first time he'd realized his place in his family. He couldn't have been more than four, which would have made Jon six. As a special treat Father had taken them to the dock- yard to see a new ship of his still on the ways.

He and Jon had spent the morning climbing in and around the unfinished ship, balancing on timbers, poking sticks into half-set tar and bellowing com- mands back and forth to hear their voices echo in the great empty hull. He could still recall the fresh, sharp scent of the newly planed pine and oak and how the clanking sound of the mallets against the hawsing irons rang out across the waterfront in the chilly March air, even the new pair of red mittens that he'd stained with tar.

"Jon?" roared Father. "Where are you, lad?"

In a flash Jon had raced to the quarterdeck to their father, and unsure of what else to do, Nick had fol- lowed breathlessly. Father stood near the wheel, his height and commanding presence making him tower over the circle of men around him, and with a smile he'd bent and welcomed Jon into the group.

"Here's the next Sparhawk captain," he said as he'd lifted Jon up to try the carved spokes of the ship's wheel. "Mark my words now, Jon here will be master of his own vessel before his seventeenth birthday!"

The men had all laughed and cheered and clapped Jon on the shoulders while Nick had hung back, lost in the forest of knee breeches and mud-covered boots. At last the men had moved away, returning to their tasks, and Nick was able to push his way forward. Jon was wearing Father's black beaver cocked hat with the gold braid, grinning proudly as he held it back from his eyes. Father was laughing, his green eyes as full of pride as Jon's, his black hair tossing in the wind as he rested his hand across his eldest son's shoulders.

"Look at me, Nick," said Jon importantly, one hand still clasped on the wheel. "Father says that when I'm a captain, I'll have a ship that's twice as fine as this one!"

"True enough, lad, true enough!" Father had laughed again, his eyes still warm as his gaze lingered on Jon. Then he'd sighed, and turned at last to Nick.

"Well now, there you are," Father had said. He was smiling still, his handsome face pleasant enough, but the special warmth he'd showered on Jon was gone from his eyes, and Nick had felt the difference like a knife in his stomach. "I suppose you'll want to try, too?"

But Nick had only shaken his head, and told himself he was too old to cry. Then, at least, he was; but later that night, alone in his bed in the dark, he had wept with all the grief in his four-year-old soul.

"I cannot believe that you were ever second to anyone," said Rose, frowning.

"Ah, trust me, I was. Most likely still am, in Father's eyes." He refilled their glasses, wondering why the devil he was sharing this with her now. He couldn't remember telling anyone else, not even Gideon. It must be Lily that was making him urge Rose to rise up and rebel like this. It couldn't possibly be that the misery and dejection he'd seen in those silver eyes across the table had so closely echoed the way he himself had felt times beyond counting.

She cradled the wineglass in both her hands. "So what did you do?" she asked in an excited conspirator's whisper.

"The only thing I could. I ran away." He smiled at her open amazement. He'd tell the short version, the tidy, romantic one that played so well in taverns, and spare her the bitter details of his homecoming. "Not directly, mind. I suffered along for a good long spell, trying to be what Father wanted, but when I was fifteen, I jumped ship—one of *his* ships—in London, and signed on with an Indiaman outward bound for Bombay the same night. I didn't go back to Newport until I could go on my own terms, master of my own ship without a lick of help from the old man."

"Bombay," she marveled softly. "Lord, but it's different for men."

"Not so different," he said with a shrug. "Look at you, bound clear across the ocean to marry this navy captain. I can't imagine a better way to turn your back on Lily and your old way of life."

She made an odd little sound in the back of her throat that could have broken into a sob if she'd let it. "It's far more complicated than that," she said, and gulped the rest of her wine. "Far more."

"Then tell me, Rosie," he said gently. He refilled her glass, trying to remember what Lily had told him about Rose's betrothal and wondering how much of that to believe. The truth—or at least the complete truth—

didn't seem to be Lily's strongest point. "It can't be as complicated as all that."

Troubled, she hesitated, not sure if it was even her story to tell. She didn't wish to be disloyal to Papa or to Lord Eliot, either, and she certainly didn't wish to shame Lily's memory by complaining. And as Aunt Lucretia had said, Lord Eliot's offer was likely to be the best she'd ever entertain on her own merits.

Yet when she looked across her plate at Captain Sparhawk, her same Black Nick of the draughts game with his mouth curved in a half smile as he waited for her to begin, the temptation to confess her fears to his handsome, sympathetic ear was more than she could resist.

She sighed and looked down, tracing her finger along the rim of the glass.

"Lord Eliot Graham had come to Portsmouth to join his new ship," she began. "Though he was there but a fortnight, he met and fell in love with Lily, like so many other gentlemen. But unlike the rest, when he asked Papa for her hand, Papa agreed, and what was more, so did Lily. Their betrothal was announced the night before he sailed again."

Nick listened, his irritation with Lily growing. No wonder she'd been so convinced that Rose was to be unhappily wed; Rose had claimed Lily's sweetheart for herself.

"Then Lily went frolicking in the snowflakes, took ill and died," he said. "So Eliot took to wooing you instead?"

Startled, Rose wondered how he could have known the details of Lily's final illness. "Not exactly, no." Fearfully she glanced around the cabin. "Lily's not here now, is she? I don't have the same feeling I did last night, but you did say you can see her and I can't."

Nick sat back in his chair, his palms flat on the tablecloth as he looked to all of Lily's favorite perches to be sure. "She's not here. She wouldn't be able to keep her mouth shut if she were."

Rose smiled weakly. "That would be Lily, yes." She took another breath, tracing her finger more and more slowly around the heavy glass. "When Lord Eliot learned she'd died, he wrote to Papa that grieved though he was to learn of Lily's death, he still wished to wed, and that he'd accept me in her place."

"He'd *accept* you?" demanded Nick, appalled. Blast Lily for only telling him half the truth! "As coldhearted as that? He'd trade one bride for another, like a new coat or hat? Didn't he give a damn whether *you* accepted *him?*"

"To marry Lord Eliot is a very great honor," said Rose mechanically, her aunt's repetitious arguments now echoing from her own lips. "He is second in line to be marquis of Danbury, and they say his brother's not even wed, let alone sired any heirs. He has excellent connections in the Admiralty to ensure that his career prospers. He has a small estate of his own in Hampshire. He is by all reports a most comely and agreeable gentleman and officer."

"You don't know the man at all, do you?" thundered Nick in disbelief. "Damnation, I'd wager you've never even met the bastard!"

"Once," said Rose, her voice shaking. "Once, when I was with Lily in a shop, he bowed and asked our health, but I don't recall—that is, I cannot remember the details of his person, but I—"

She broke off abruptly, her trembling fingers leaving the glass to touch the blue stone of Lord Eliot's ring. "If I can't recall him, then I'm certain he has no memory of me except as Lily's younger sister, and he expects me to be like her, I know it, else he wouldn't have asked for me at all! He'll expect me to be beautiful like her, and to laugh and sing and dance and captivate all his friends among the other officers, when I can do none of those things to please him that Lily could, *none!*"

For Nick, who had never found any woman he'd consider spending more than a few weeks with, let alone a lifetime, the marriage that she was describing was inconceivable. "For God's sake, Rose, you cannot marry the man!"

"I can, because I must," she said, her voice brittle. "To break with Lord Eliot now would bring shame to my family and disgrace to me, and that, *that,* is what I cannot do."

"But to shackle yourself for life to a man who—"

"No." Swiftly she rose to her feet, the chair scraping over the deck behind her. With a single sweep of her hand she shoved aside the plate with her untouched dinner. Strange how the idea had come to her so suddenly, but now that it had, it made perfect sense. A man as unprincipled as this one must be would surely agree to her offer. Once her ransom was paid, she'd never see him again, and it was most unlikely he'd ever be on speaking terms with Lord Eliot. And of course he would be capable of what she'd ask; he was so breathtakingly beautiful that women likely tossed themselves in his path wherever he went.

"You say I must free myself of Lily, and perhaps it is time I did," she said with a careful, calm deliberation. Thank heavens she'd drunk so freely of the wine. Without it, she'd never have had the courage she needed now. "Instead of fearing and fussing that I won't be acceptable to Lord Eliot, I must make him forget my sister entirely. I may not be as beautiful as she was, but there must be other ways for a wife to please her husband. Lily told me that—but no, I won't speak of her again."

Her heart pounding, she grabbed the leather bag with her winnings, dumped the pistoles out in a pile onto the cloth, and with both hands pushed them across the table toward Nick. Then she slapped the draughts board down where her plate had been and with shaking fingers began setting the pieces on the checkered board for a new game.

Rapidly Nick rose to his feet and reached out to seize her hand. "Nay, lass, stop. Stop!"

"Why should I?" Her eyes wild, she jerked her hand free. "I'm only offering you the chance to regain your losses. One game, Captain Sparhawk, that is all. If you win, all the gold is yours again.''

He turned his head to one side, eyeing her uneasily. ''And if you win?''

She lifted her chin defiantly, but Nick didn't miss the tremor that vibrated through her small body.

''If I win,'' she said, ''then you will teach me how to please my husband.''

Chapter Eight

"You want me to teach you how to please Lord Eliot?" repeated Nick, completely, totally stunned. "Oh, Rose, you don't know what you ask."

"Yes, I do." Her chin rose another fraction higher. Now that she'd begun, it wasn't as difficult as she'd feared, the same as bargaining for any other commodity. Of course taking him by surprise like this again certainly helped, too. "I know all about what husbands and wives do together. Lily explained some of it, and Aunt Lucretia told me the rest."

"Did they now?" He could not believe he was having this conversation with her, her earnest little mouth only inches away from his. Earnest and unbelievably enticing, and slowly he lowered himself back into his chair and marginally farther from temptation.

"Of course they did," she said with wounded indignation. "I may be inexperienced, Captain, but I am not ignorant. While the whole arrangement sounds rather foolish, it doesn't sound particularly difficult, especially for the wives. Much easier, say, than riding a horse.''

Nick gulped. Lord help him, she was imagining herself riding a blessed *horse*. How much wine had she had to drink, anyway? He'd hoped to relax her defenses, true enough, but he'd never dreamed things would come to this.

''Therefore,'' she continued, ''if Lord Eliot honors me by giving me his name and his protection, then I should try to be as agreeable to him as I can. Which is where I believe you can help me. That is, if you lose the next game.''

Nick groaned. ''Which you bloody well know I'll do.''

''Well, yes.'' She shrugged, not in the least contrite. ''I was rather counting on it.''

Nick swore under his breath, drumming his fingers on the edge of the table and trying not to stare too obviously at how her shrug had made the coral silk slide delectably down her white shoulders.

He told himself he should be rejoicing, that things were progressing with her even better than he'd expected, but he couldn't. There was something about Rose that made the coolheaded seduction he'd planned impossible. It wasn't only that she'd neatly managed to turn the tables on him again, just as she had with the draughts game. It went deeper than that, beginning with her description of her hideously wrong betrothal and followed by this ridiculous proposition of hers. He felt *sorry* for her, for heaven's sake, which had to be the worst possible emotion for unentangled debauchery.

Damnation, next he'd be considering himself too nice to fire anything bigger than a green pea at the British. At this rate he'd have Lily with him forever.

"Rose," he began, "Rose. I know you've given this all some thought, but—"

"Hardly any, really." She smiled proudly, refilling her wineglass yet again. "The notion came to me only a moment or two ago, yet it does make sense. I may not be beautiful, but I am more clever than most women—cleverer than most men, says Papa—and I learn very quickly. I believe it won't take more than a lesson or two for me to be sufficiently skillful to impress Lord Eliot."

As she gazed across the table at him, her smile turned dreamy, the wine casting everything in the cabin with a golden haze. Not that Captain Sparhawk needed any further polishing in her eyes. When the servants had brought dinner they had also lit the two brass lanterns hanging overhead, and the warm light swung gently back and forth over him, highlighting first one side of his perfect face and then the other. She might have forgotten Lord Eliot's face, but she'd always remember Black Nick's.

Especially if he kissed her now. Dear, sweet, merciful heaven, she prayed silently, this once in my life let me kiss a man of my own choosing!

But he, for his part, seemed in turn to be having an inordinately difficult time meeting her eye, and as she wondered why, the first tiny uneasiness began to creep around the edges of her well-being.

He cleared his throat with a rumble. "Miss Everard, this may come as a surprise to you, being so clever, but most men prefer brides that aren't skillful. Prize it, in fact. That's why virgin brides are generally the rule, or at least they are where I was born."

"Oh, my, I never meant for us to proceed so far!" Amazed he'd believe that of her, Rose felt her face grow hot. And here she thought she'd been explaining it all wonderfully well! "That is, I believed the preliminaries should be sufficient. Kissing and that sort of thing."

Her smile wobbled. "I shouldn't expect more, you know. Not for a single game, even with forty pistoles in the balance."

That unsteady smile nearly did him in. That, and the flush that began on her cheeks and went clear down to the tops of her breasts above the gown.

"The devil take your game," he said gruffly. "I don't like the stakes, and I don't kiss women in exchange for gold."

Her smile vanished as she struggled to read his expression. His face was set and rigid, his green eyes intense with some sort of inner fury. What had she done? she wondered miserably, and all the old inadequacies that had made her a perennial wallflower wilting in Lily's shadow came rushing back.

With a sigh she pushed her chair away from the table and slowly stepped around it, trailing her fingers along the edge of the cloth. She stopped directly before him, studying the sharp line of his chin and not daring to meet his eye.

"It has nothing to do with the game, does it," she said sadly, "and everything to do with the woman. I understand perfectly if you do not wish to kiss me. No gentleman ever has. I am small and scraggly and too pale and—"

"Don't," he ordered, his hands reaching out to take her lightly by her narrow shoulders. "You're Rose, and that's enough."

"Captain Sparhawk—"

"Nick," he said. "You can't ask me to kiss you and not call me by my right name."

"Nick, then." Bewildered, Rose forgot to breathe as his hands glided from her shoulders along the curve of her throat to the pulse that throbbed below her ear. How was it possible, she marveled, how could hands so large, so strong, touch her as lightly as a feather upon her skin? She shivered, still staring at his chin and no more, and his hands slid around the curves of her face, his palms cradling her cheeks as his fingers threaded deep into her hair. Under his spell she swayed forward, pliant as a willow, as he drew her face closer to his. Sensation overwhelmed her, and her eyes fluttered shut.

"Look at me, lass," he murmured, his voice dark as night and his breath like another caress upon her cheek as his fingers moved restlessly through the heavy waves of her hair. "Don't hide from me now."

"I can't," she whispered, afraid not of what he'd do but that he would stop before he'd done it.

But he didn't, and in the next instant she felt his lips brush against hers, gently, so gently. She gasped, not so much with surprise as with wonder, that he above all men would wish to kiss her. Uncertainly she began to answer him, her lips moving across his, and her wonder grew as he responded, deepening and melding his kiss with hers. Wonder, and a joy rare to her, for with him she wasn't awkward or plain. His touch made her miraculously beautiful, flooding her entire body with a warmth she'd never dreamed existed.

Instinctively she looped her hands over his shoulders, and as she did he curled his arm around her waist and drew her onto his lap with a rustle of petticoats and silk. Even beneath the layers of her skirts she was aware of the hard, corded muscles of his thighs as she slid across them, moving closer to his body as his arm tightened around her waist. She heard him groan, deep in his chest, and she, inexperienced though she was, knew it was a sound of pleasure, an animal-like growl that somehow she'd managed to bring to him. She knew because she felt the same, and with a shy eagerness she parted his lips further.

But to her surprise, he broke away, easing his mouth free of hers.

"Sweet little Rose," he said raggedly, his voice at once both rough and gentle. "What are we doing, eh?"

He brushed his fingers across her lower lip, still sensitive from his kiss, and she shivered. Her breath felt tight in her chest, and the warmth he'd brought to her body remained, deep in her belly, lingering though the kiss had ended.

He shifted slightly so the lantern light played full across his face, and she saw how his green eyes had gone cloudy while his face seemed oddly tense. A heavy lock of his black hair had fallen across his forehead, over the scar, and watching her, waiting for her to answer, he hadn't bothered to shake it back. Self-consciously she took her hands from his shoulders, and held them curled into tight little knots in her lap.

Maybe she'd been mistaken. Maybe all of this was no more than drinking too much of the sweet wine. Maybe he'd felt nothing, and she was the only one left giddy with the world singing and spinning around her heart.

"What are we doing? I cannot answer for you," she said in a small voice, "though I'd rather thought you were kissing me. And I—I'm but collecting a wager for a game I never played."

"Then you're just as clever as you claim, and I'm the greatest cully you've ever cozened." He didn't try to hide the disgust he felt for himself. One more time she'd turned the tables on him, her ingenious young girl's kiss making him as weak-kneed as any green-horn boy. In his life he'd dandled more women than he could count on his lap before he'd followed them into his bed. Why should this one be any different?

Because *she* was, different from any other woman he'd met. It was as deceptively simple as that. With her silver-gray eyes and her odd mixture of confidence and insecurity and her coltish legs sprawled over his and her little pink mouth, the devil take him, the fire she'd started in him with that little mouth—no, he couldn't begin to explain it. All he knew was that he wanted her, wanted her so badly that his whole body ached, and yet something deep inside of him, even deeper than the desire, forbade him to do anything about it.

"Oh, Rosie," he said, sighing with frustration as she shifted her plump little bottom across his thighs. "You truly are as innocent as you pretend, aren't you?"

She ducked her chin, certain he was ridiculing her. "I told you before that no man had ever wished to kiss me, or had done so," she said, both wounded and defensive. "You are the first. If I've done it so poorly that I've offended you, I am sorry, but I did give you warning that—"

"That's enough, lass." He touched his fingers again to her lips, this time to silence her. "Don't tempt me to make hackneyed jests about roses with thorns. You were fine, sweetheart. More than fine, in fact. If you kiss your lord of a husband like that, you'll make him happier than he's any right to be."

"Really?" she asked breathlessly.

"Really," he said. Unable to help himself, he had begun to run his open hand up and down her back, gently stroking her as if she were a cat, and like a cat, she stretched and arched against his hand. Through her dress he could feel the stiff, stitched linen and whalebone of her stays, stays he knew she didn't need, and imagining the feel of her lithe young body without the fashionable armor shot another bolt of desire ricocheting through his body.

"I am glad of that." She shut her eyes for a moment, trying to focus on Lord Eliot instead of the lazy, seductive way Nick's hand was gliding along her spine. "I want him to be happy, you see. Aunt Lucretia says that most gentlemen—and Lord Eliot most assuredly is a gentleman, even though he's in the navy—most gentlemen keep mistresses after they're wed and I must be understanding and turn a blind eye, but I'm not sure I could. It's selfish of me, I know, but I'd much rather he stayed happy with only me."

"He'd be a fool not to," said Nick. Effortlessly he tipped her into the crook of his arm, bringing her to rest against his chest. Lord help them both, why did she have to trust him like this? It was that trust that was his undoing. How could he tumble her when she had simultaneously asked him to and trusted him to do otherwise? Desperately he hoped Lily wasn't within hearing, that she was off instead on some other sort of angel's business or another. Otherwise she must be laughing herself ill at his expense.

"Besides," he said as evenly as he was able, "you could always play draughts."

"I suppose we could." She sighed, nestling against his shoulder. She liked the way he smelled, salty like the sea and something more elusive and intensely masculine, and cradled in his arms like this she felt warm and protected. "But I believe I'd rather kiss."

"Well, hell, so would I." He'd like to do that with her and a good deal more besides. He smoothed her hair away from her ear, brushing his fingertips tenderly over the downy curve of her flushed cheek as he wondered what the devil was happening to him.

"I meant what I'd be doing with Lord Eliot." She chuckled drowsily, at last succumbing to the wine and the warm circle of well-being. "Though you were very nice to kiss, Captain. I mean Nick. I don't see how he'll be able to improve upon it."

"Thank you," said Nick. "He won't."

But Rose was too sleepy to hear the bitterness in his voice, and with a contented sigh she let her eyes drift shut, her last wistful thought of her sister. How much she wished she could have told Lily how she'd been finally, wonderfully, perfectly kissed!

Nick, too, thought of Lily, but without her sister's wistfulness. For a long time he sat with Rose in his arms, watching her sleep and drinking by himself with the uneaten dinner cold on the table before him. She was soft and warm against his chest, and when he'd gently smooth her hair or brush her cheek with his fingers she would stir and smile in her sleep, private little smiles that made him smile, too, since they were given to him alone.

Yet still he wasn't happy. Last night, thanks to Rose, he'd finally been convinced he wasn't mad. Tonight, again because of her, he'd begun doubting anew. No woman had ever had this effect on him before, and it worried him.

He listened to the bells from the deck above that marked the hours of the watch, and the shadows in the corners of his cabin beyond the lanterns' light deepened as the day faded into dusk, then night. No one disturbed him; his orders had been explicit, though that, he thought wryly, had been when he'd been confident of a far different outcome for the meal.

Finally, when the bells marked the end of one watch and the beginning of another, he knew it was time he, too, returned to the *Angel Lily*'s deck. There'd been more than a little truth to Gideon's accusation that lately he'd been too busy chasing ghosts and petticoats, and if he ever wanted to capture another ship, he'd do well to be back at the helm where he belonged.

Carefully he carried Rose to his own bunk. She stretched against the pillows, mumbled something he didn't understand and once again sank deeply asleep. Before Nick drew the coverlet over her, he unbuckled her shoes and set them neatly side by side on the deck. Next he unhooked the front of her bodice far enough to loosen her stays to make her more comfortable; every woman he knew complained of how stiff and unyielding fashionable clothing could be, and the hooks, tapes and laces that held a lady's gown together offered no challenge to him.

Yet as unmoved as he tried to be, he still swore softly to himself in frustrated admiration at how her small, high breasts swelled above her stays, the darker nipples clear through the sheer linen of her shift.

"So this is how you treat my poor sister, is it?" demanded Lily imperiously. "Make her insensible with strong drink, then tumble her onto her back while she's incapable of protesting? Or is this what passes for lovemaking among the wenches in the lower sort of dockside taverns and brothels you frequent?"

"I was waiting for you to appear." Nick wheeled around to find her sitting on the back of his chair, her fluttering wings providing the necessary balance. Her arms were folded and her blue eyes were narrowed, and he knew he was in for a fight. "I've been expecting you all afternoon."

"Not enough, apparently, to restrain you from this sorry performance!" Sweeping her arm toward her sleeping sister, Lily dramatically brought her angled wrist to rest on her forehead. "To think that I am the cause of dear little Rose being used so!"

"Oh, stow it, sweetheart," said Nick, disgusted by her histrionics. "You're not exactly blameless yourself. Why the hell didn't you tell me the whole story? Why did you leave it to 'dear little Rose' to air your family's shabby linen?"

Her painted brows arched higher. "What, about Papa? How I was to be his powdered and perfumed calling card to genteel society? The dutiful daughter who'd bring him a titled son-in-law?"

Nick was surprised by her cynicism. It wasn't exactly something he'd expect from an angel, but then Lily herself in her white-and-gold gown with the cherry-colored stockings wasn't too ordinary, either.

"Why should your father care about titles? He already has one himself, doesn't he?"

"Not a real one." She sighed and flicked open her fan. "I suppose you wouldn't know, being an American given to vile democratic tendencies, but a knighthood's only granted for services rendered. It expires with him. Papa's made vast piles of money, you see—he's a merchant and a shipbuilder and goodness knows what else, which is how he earned the knighthood, fitting out navy ships in record time during the last war. But in the eyes of the real lords and ladies, Sir Edmund Everard's only a jumped-up tradesman, and he hates that with a vengeance. That's what he planned, too, I suppose—vengeance, with me to do the venging."

Nick sighed and dropped into the chair where Rose had sat. As annoyed as he was with Lily, he could understand all too well the power that strong-willed patriarchs wielded. "And that's when you fell in love with Captain Lord High-and-Mighty Eliot."

"Love Lord Eliot?" Her blue eyes flashed. "Oh, pish, I never could abide the man, let alone *love* him! He's vile and mean-spirited and puffed up with his own imagined self-worth, but he has the bluest blood that Papa could lure into our house, and he was the one with the deepest debts. When Papa promised to clear those plus stuff his pockets deep with more gold, of course Lord Eliot offered for me."

Her bitterness was unmistakable, and there were lines furrowed in the powder around her mouth that

Nick didn't remember seeing before. "Rose and I both had our proper roles, you see. I was to be the great belle launched among the aristocrats with Papa's money, while poor Rose was to stay home and be his nursemaid in old age. We never had the chance to be anything else. Papa saw to that."

She looked down, away from Nick, and concentrated instead on straightening the blades of her fan. "Wonderfully sordid, isn't it? Too bad for Papa I'd have none of it."

"But Rose said—"

"Rose didn't know." She sighed, and looked fondly toward her sleeping sister. "She's always been much more dutiful, while I wasn't nearly as amenable as Papa wished. Oh, I agreed to wed Lord Eliot to stop his nagging, but I'd no intention of actually marrying him. I'd set my cap for Thomas Carville, really, and he'd nearly come round to proposing an elopement when I died."

She smiled wickedly at Nick, tapping her closed fan to the dimple on her cheek. "Tom's father owns some sort of mills to the north, which makes him even more tawdry and common than Papa, though Tom himself is quite wonderful, tall and comely with a laugh, la, that fair made me swoon. He's rather like you, actually."

"Pity you didn't come back to meddle in his life instead of mine," grumbled Nick, propping his long legs on the edge of the table. "So now on account of all your flirtations, your poor sister's going to have to marry this bastard of a lord?''

For a moment Nick thought he saw something like remorse, even guilt, flicker across her lovely face. But before he could be certain, her expression swiftly regained its usual assurance, her chin imperiously high.

"I can assure you, my dear captain," she said indignantly, "that I'd no intention of dying when I did. I know it seems as if I were being abominably selfish, but it wasn't like that. Well, not really. If I'd lived and run off with Tom, then I would have made sure, *quite* sure, to rescue Rose from Papa. But I've told you before that I can do nothing to help her now."

Nick's sympathy promptly evaporated. "Except to toss me into her path."

"*That* was before I knew you meant to treat her so dreadfully!" she exclaimed huffily. "A right model Yankee Don Juan, you are!"

"Don Juan, ha!" Nick's feet dropped down from the table to the deck with a thump. "If you'd been here earlier, you'd have seen how your sweet little sister practically ravished *me!*"

"Oh, hush." Lily sniffed above her fan. "I won't hear you say ill of Rose, especially when the proof's here asleep in your own bed. In matters such as this it's always the man who's at fault. Once in Portsmouth I saw a play by Mr. Rowe called *The Fair Penitent,* and in it was a low character who much resembles you at present. Perhaps, my dear captain, I shall take to calling you after him—Lothario Sparhawk."

Nick had heard of neither Mr. Rowe nor this low character Lothario, but from Lily's tone he was certain it was no compliment.

"Hold there now!" he said warmly. "Your sister was the one who proposed that infernal game in the first place, setting kisses for wagers!"

Lily frowned and shook her head as she clucked her tongue. "Oh, dear, Nick, now that was a mistake. You must never, ever play draughts with Rose."

"Well, I did," declared Nick, "and I'm damned lucky she left me my breeches. But I swear I didn't touch her, not beyond that one kiss."

"You didn't?"

"I did not," he said flatly. "And don't go looking at me like I don't know the difference. All this is your fault, anyway. If you'd disappeared like you were supposed to, I would have left Rose alone. Instead I coaxed her down here with every wicked intention in the world, and kept her glass filled to addle her wits just like you said. But then she started winking those big silver eyes of hers and telling me how sorrowful her life has been, and I couldn't do it. Hell, I was the one who put an end to that single blessed marvelous kiss!"

"Oh, my, my," said Lily archly. "Next all cats will walk on water and dogs will fly."

"Why the devil not?" he asked glumly. "They gave *you* a pair of wings. But the worst of it's what's happened to me."

Nick bowed his head with disgust as he ran his fingers through his hair. "Look at me. You save my miserable life, and now I've turned too bloody noble to toss a pretty girl's petticoats. What's gone wrong with me, eh?"

"Not a single thing, my darling captain," said Lily softly, her smile for once genuine, even sweet. "For this time you've listened to your conscience, and though a weak, feeble little conscience it is for someone of your size and years, 'tis better than having none at all. For a bit there, you know, I'd rather feared you didn't."

He lifted his head sharply to stare suspiciously at her. "You knew it all along, didn't you? The draughts game and Rose's silver eyes and why I didn't—damnation, why I *couldn't*—tumble her here tonight?"

"Of course I did," she said gently, her pale form already fading away. "But I wanted to hear you say it yourself. Sweet dreams, my dear, darling captain!"

Rose was sure, quite sure, that she was going to die.

Or at least, right now, that was what she prayed would happen. Her head ached and throbbed, and her empty stomach roiled with such an ominous uncertainty that all she wanted to do was lie as still as she possibly could until this slow, certain death ended her suffering.

But even that seemed impossible, for the ship and the bunk in which she lay were surely in the middle of the worst storm they'd seen since they'd cleared the Channel. Yes, that would explain it all, the aching head and the wobbly stomach and the cabin that refused to stay level. With a groan she didn't bother to stifle, she pressed her face to the pillow slip and wished again for the end to come.

But something wasn't right. Sick as she felt, her senses were still working, and the linen beneath her cheek smelled not of her own perfume but of some deep, masculine scent that was disturbingly familiar. With great care and growing dread she forced herself to open her eyes. The cabin was filled with morning sunlight, the polished brass lanterns swaying gently with the most moderate of seas instead of the storm she'd imagined, and Captain Sparhawk's blue coat draped carelessly across the back of his chair where he'd left it last night.

Last night. Oh, dear heaven deliver her, she was in Captain Sparhawk's cabin, worse yet in his bunk, and with dreadful, humiliating clarity the night before came rushing back. Or most of it did: she remembered her nervousness and drinking far too much wine because of it; she remembered the game of draughts and kissing him and sitting on his lap like the most wanton hussy; she remembered his hands stroking her back and curling familiarly around her waist, and then—then nothing more.

Nothing.

Her dread growing by the minute, she threw back the coverlet, running her fingers through the tangles of her hair. Her shoes were on the deck and her garters half-untied, her skirts rucked up around her waist and her bodice shamelessly unfastened, even the laces on her stays loosened. With shaking hands she shoved her skirts down over her bare legs and pulled the front of her bodice together.

She had been lonely, and he had understood. She had felt lost, and he had been kind and generous. She had smiled with giddy pleasure and dressed in coral silk, and he had smiled, too, and worn a waistcoat embroidered with forget-me-nots. And with a magic that she couldn't explain, he had made her feel beautiful and cherished and safe. She bowed her head, and saw how the bright sunlight glanced off the betrothal ring on her finger.

Swiftly she closed her eyes, fighting the sick feeling in both her stomach and her soul. If she had let herself be so easily... *dishonored,* then she had shamed not only herself but her father and her sister's memory as well. Papa had made it clear enough that her duty as his daughter was to marry Lord Eliot, and that she would not be welcomed home again except as Lady Eliot.

But now she'd given Lord Eliot ample reason to refuse to marry her, and to her sorrow she would not be able to fault him. Not even Lily herself would have dared to do what she had done. What gentleman wanted a wife who had first become one more conquest of a notorious rebel privateer? Nick Sparhawk was exactly the kind of rogue her future husband had been sent to the Caribbean to hunt down and hang.

Nick Sparhawk. Dear Lord, when had she started to think of him by his given name? When had her very thoughts begun to betray her with the same eagerness as her willing body? Two short days ago, she had not even known he existed. Better she had never known; better she had never learned how firm yet gentle his mouth could be upon hers, or how something as seemingly simple as a single kiss could flare and scorch her to the quick. And, oh, merciful heaven, how much else she might have done that now, in the clear, harsh light of morning, she hadn't even the decency to remember!

Her fingers still clumsy, she rushed to finish dressing. She could not undo the past, but she could try to reclaim her tattered future. She was the American's prisoner, not his guest, and she must be nothing else. She would keep to her cabin, avoid his company on the deck, refuse his invitations and ignore his smiles. She must always remember that she was the daughter of Sir Edmund Everard and the betrothed of Captain Lord Eliot Graham, and she must forget every single, sinful thing she'd learned from Nickerson Sparhawk.

And if her heart broke, too, it would be no more than she deserved.

Chapter Nine

Nick stared down at the folded letter in the boy's hand, and saw that the seal—his seal—remained unbroken.

"Th' lady said I'd best bring it back t' you, Cap'n," said the boy, Johnny, with more sympathy than judgment. "Miss Everard, she said your compliments was all well an' good, but she was of no more mind t' read this letter than any o' the others."

Without a word, Nick took the letter from the boy, who did know well enough to duck his head and scurry away from the quarterdeck when the captain's face had that particular ominous look to it.

Nick didn't notice. Lightly he ran his finger across Rose's name, written in his best penmanship across the front of the folded sheet, and then with a muttered oath he stalked to the stern and tossed the unopened letter over the taffrail and into the *Angel Lily*'s white-churned wake.

Every morning for the past nine days he had written to her, and every morning she had returned his letters unread. She wouldn't even deign to take them from the boy's hand.

He gripped the rail, oblivious of how the wind whipped at his hair. She had kept to her own cabin since that single night she'd spent in his. She'd insisted on taking her meals alone, and turned down all invitations to come topside at all, let alone with him. She hadn't been rude about it; she'd been quite polite, really, refusing everything with the most genteel and ladylike regrets. But still she had refused his offers, and so in her genteel way had refused him.

He couldn't begin to make sense of it. The first time in his memory that he'd behaved honorably with a woman, and she did this. How could she blame him when for once he'd done nothing? It hurt his pride, but worse than that, it simply hurt because he missed her.

He tried to tell himself it was because he hadn't bedded her, that it was the incompleteness of the thing that made him feel so foolishly on edge, endlessly replaying in his mind every word she'd spoken to him, and writing those damned notes over breakfast. Deep, deep down he knew it was more than that; but exactly what he couldn't say, because he didn't know the words for the desperate need he felt for Rose Everard.

It was Lily's fault, he was certain of that. But each time he'd tried to tell her, she'd only laughed and disappeared in her usual, maddening way that always let her have the last word. But in this he was determined to win. The next time he was alone with Rose, he wouldn't turn sentimental and respectful. Instead he'd shower her with the full force of his considerable charm, and he wouldn't stop with one kiss. Next time when she woke in his bunk, she'd be wearing a contented smile and nothing else, and she wouldn't be so damned eager to run away. And then he'd see if Lily laughed!

If, that is, there ever was a next time.

Nine blasted *days*.

And as if Rose's closed, latched cabin door and the rejection it represented weren't enough to infuriate him, his famous luck as a privateer seemed to have turned tail and vanished, too. No matter that he'd set a course to cruise through the busiest merchant lanes in the Atlantic, or that the weather had been flawless, with the favorable winds and cloudless skies of early summer. Not once since the *Angel Lily* had captured the *Commerce* nearly two weeks earlier had the cry come down from the lookout in the foretop. It wasn't just that they hadn't made chase or taken a prize; they hadn't even seen another sail on the horizon. Nick couldn't remember a spell this dry since the war began, and uneasily he wondered if this, too, could be laid at Lily's doorstep.

"You want to blame everything on me, don't you?" she asked, her voice raised to be heard over the wind. She was standing against the rail beside him, leaning back on her elbows. The ribbons in her hair streamed back from her face in the wind, and random feathers in her wings bent backward, like those of a gull trying to fly in a gale. "Everything that goes wrong is my fault."

"Well, hell, it is, isn't it?" He scowled, then self-consciously looked away from her, out over the water, so the man at the helm wouldn't see or hear him talking to the air. "Look at everything that's gone wrong since you decided to bless me with your care."

"Oh, my, yes, it's quite a list." She tipped her chin as she ticked off her fingers. "First of all, I kept you from dying. Then I saved your ship when by every right it should have sunk, and gave you a newer, better one in the bargain. I also arranged for you to regain your crew's confidence by capturing the *Commerce*. Though really you were the one who was doubting, not them. They still seem determined cheerfully to follow you to Hades and back, the greater fools they."

"Aye, as if they—"

"Hush, now, dear captain," she said evenly, her fingers still spread for counting. "I'm not finished."

"Oh, yes, you are," ordered Nick. "You're becoming a damned bore."

"Boring?" She stiffened. "No one has ever dared to call me boring!"

"You're a bore because you're so bloody predictable," repeated Nick wearily. "I know I could sail straight into Carenage Bay on St. Lucia, haul alongside the admiral's flagship and order every man to drop his breeches and salute the English flag, and you'd still find a way to get me clear. Almost makes me want to try it. Things are getting blessed boring for me, too."

She cleared her throat with a harrumph of disgust. "What has become of your great plot upon my sister? Or is that too boring to contemplate as well?"

"Absolutely nothing is happening between your sister and myself," he said, bristling at what she implied. "As you know damned well."

"Not surprising when the best you can do is send a scrap of paper every morning. Highly resistible, that, even by a girl as inexperienced as Rose."

"Lily, I have had other more pressing demands upon my time. You might recall that I am captain of this ship—"

"Oh, pish, that's not it at all." She glanced at him sidelong, her eyes gleeful. "You're afraid she'll say no to your face."

Nick took a deep breath, struggling to control his temper. "I am the captain, Lily. The captain, mind? I have nearly two hundred men under me. I cannot and will not go below to beg outside your sister's door like some tomcat."

"That's because you're not nearly the hardened rakehell you fancy you are, my dear Nick," she said shrewdly. "If you were, you wouldn't give a fig about being a captain. You'd go down there directly, break down her door and toss her on her own bunk, never mind how much she screamed or fought. If you truly wished to upset me, that is. But I don't believe such barbarous behavior's in your blood, thank the heavens."

It took every last shred of Nick's self-control not to roar his outrage. Where Rose was concerned, Lily was right, blast her, but she'd never get him to admit it.

"Damnation, woman," he said, his usual roar half-strangled, "did I ask for your advice?"

"Not yet, no," said Lily mildly. "But if you do, I can tell you that Rose—"

"Rose will do whatever she pleases." Nick's eyes gleamed with triumph. A new idea had come to him while they'd spoken, one that was guaranteed to end boredom for all parties. "You can't control her or what she does. That's up to her, not you. Or have you forgotten?"

"I'd rather thought you had, Captain Sparhawk." She smiled, and with a graceful sweep of her arm rose in the air to hover before him, the same wind that filled the ship's sails holding her wings steady. "But don't underestimate my little sister, Nick. She doesn't need my help to deal with you."

Nick shaded his eyes with his hand as he looked up at her. "Don't cash your bets yet, Lily. I told you before I play to win."

"Doubtless the same way you played draughts." Her smile remained bright even as her outline faded into the sunshine. "Next time I hope she *will* take your breeches."

"There you be, Miss Everard." Carefully Johnny set the tray with the battered teapot, cup and now-cold toast on top of the trunk that Rose used as a table in her tiny cabin. "I'll be back in a bit to collect th' tray when you're done."

Standing by the door with her hand still on the latch, Rose nodded, exactly the same way she'd done on the seventeen other mornings. She'd learned early in her self-imposed isolation that Johnny would never say more than he needed to, whether from orders or inclination, and now she didn't even try to begin conversations with him. But this morning, she couldn't keep still.

"There's no letter?" she asked, curiously disappointed. "Captain Sparhawk didn't give you one today?"

"Nay, Miss Everard, th' cap'n didn't," said the boy, his jaw jutting forward with undisguised disapproval. "Not that I'd expect you t' care, seeing as you couldn't never be bothered to read th' others. Too fine a lady *you* is, I 'spect, for th' likes o' good free men like us an' th' cap'n."

"It's not like that at all," said Rose swiftly. "It's not Captain Sparhawk who is to blame, but myself. I'm the one who acted wrongly, not he, and that is why I couldn't accept his letters."

Lord, how could she explain what she'd done to the boy when she could scarcely understand it herself? She had only meant to be loyal to her father's wishes and her own country, as well as respect the promise she'd made to marry Lord Eliot for Lily. She knew she'd been right to refuse Nick's—no, Captain Sparhawk's—letters, to salvage what remained of her honor and to punish herself for her weakness by keeping here alone in her cabin.

But even that punishment had turned into a bittersweet agony, for not a minute passed that she didn't recall the way his green eyes watched her, the warmth that had streaked through her blood at the touch of his lips on hers, the unsettling possibility that somehow fate had brought her here to him before she wed another and it was too late, too late for everything....

She gave a small, shuddering sigh as she jerked her thoughts back to the boy before her. "It must seem capricious of me, I know," she said sadly, "but it's how things must be between Captain Sparhawk and myself."

"Just blessed peculiar to me." The boy sniffed and wiped his nose on the cuff of his gingham shirtsleeve. "But I 'spect th' cap'n's got himself other plans for merriment now than botherin' with fine lady prisoners like you. We'll be back in Charles Town by nightfall, to refit an' take on our mates from the *Liberty*'s prize crew."

"Charles Town?" asked Rose. Her eyes widened with surprise. Charles Town, any town, meant land instead of the endless ocean, and the chance to free herself that she hadn't dared hope for. She'd had hours alone these past weeks to plan an escape in case she found the opportunity, and now that, miraculously, she did, she remembered every carefully worked-out detail. "That's in one of the American colonies, isn't it?"

"One of th' free American states, miss. South Carolina, t' put the nail on it." He squeezed past her to reach the door. "Like I said, miss, I'll come round in a bit for th' tray."

"Wait!" Rose scrambled to her bunk and thrust her hand beneath the pillow, pulling out a little needle-worked pocketbook that clinked dully with coins inside. "I would ask a favor of you, Johnny. Two favors, really. And of course I'm quite willing to compensate you for obliging me."

He paused at the doorway, drawn back by the sound of the coins. "What kind o' favor?" he asked suspiciously. "I won't do nothing that's traitorous nor cowardly against Cap'n Sparhawk, not for all th' gold in London."

"I swear to you what I ask is neither." She clutched the pocketbook in both hands, praying for the right words to convince the boy. "I should like to buy a suit of your clothes—breeches, shirt, coat and a hat."

The boy sniffed scornfully. "I only have but th' two Mam saw me off with."

"I'll pay you enough so you can buy yourself five new shirts in Charles Town, plus a new bonnet for your mother, too, if you please!"

She knew from the expression on his freckled face, trying so hard to be as distant and aloof as a grown man, that he was tempted.

"What be th' second favor, then?"

Rose licked her lips nervously, knowing better than to smile. "Simply that you ask Mr. Hobb to come speak to me. He's new to your crew, so if—"

"Th' Englishman that fair talks your ear from your head. O' course I knows him." He rubbed at his nose again. "Do you be plotting some mischief with him? 'Cause if you is, then I want no part o' it."

"I swear I'll never mention your name to a soul," she promised, shifting the little pocketbook in her fingers so the coins jingled again. "And if anyone finds your clothes in my keeping, then you can say I stole them."

"They'll believe it o' you, no mistake." But he thrust out his open palm for the money, and at last Rose dared to smile.

It was after supper and almost dusk when Hobb scratched at the door, and in an instant Rose opened it to let him slip inside.

"You're sure of this now, lass?" he asked, his long, earnest face lined with concern. "Cap'n Sparhawk, he does mean to give you back, just as quick as your pa's people pay down your ransom. But if the cap'n catches you trying to escape, well, who knows what a man with a wicked temper like his will do?"

"I don't intend to find out." Restlessly Rose tugged Johnny's worn knit hat lower across her forehead, hoping the rolled rib brim would shade her face from the other crewmen in the dark. "And you're not to protect me, either. If anyone suspects that you've helped me, you're to deny every word. I don't want Captain Sparhawk taking out that 'wicked temper' on you for my sins."

"Ah, miss, 'tis no great sin," said Hobb gruffly, wiping his palms nervously on the thighs of his loose-fitting trousers. "How can I fault a bride what wants t' join her bridegroom?"

Rose blushed, not from modesty but from shame for the lie she'd told. "This is only the first step, you know. I still must find passage from Charles Town to St. Lucia."

"And so you shall, Miss Everard, on account o' wanting it so bad." He beamed at her. "Myself, I'm promised to wed a sweet, dear lass at home, an' I'd expect my Annie t' do same for me. Leastways I hope she would."

"I'm sure of it, Mr. Hobb," said Rose wistfully, wishing now she hadn't used Lord Eliot as her reason for escape. Oh, it had seemed plausible enough when she'd concocted it, but that was before she'd asked Hobb, who truly did miss his intended, to risk himself for her and the sake of her own pale, passionless betrothal. Hearing him speak of his Annie made what she was doing seem far worse, and even more of a lie. "Look at what you're doing for her sake."

Hobb shrugged. "Eh, a spell o' privateering seemed th' only honest way I'd have to give the darling th' pretty things she craves." His face turned grave. "Now swear you have that navy cap'n o' yours leave Cap'n Sparhawk alone, like you said. If'n he catches th' *An-*

gel Lily, why, he'll string me up for a traitor for changin' sides, an' I don't want my Annie left t' mourn an' marry some blunderhead from th' village.''

"Of course you don't," said Rose unhappily. "I told you I would speak to my—my husband, and I meant it. I swear I shall do my best.''

She'd swear to try, even though she'd no idea how much, if any, influence she'd have over Lord Eliot, particularly in regards to his command. Begging him to spare the Americans who'd captured her didn't seem like a very wise way to begin their marriage. She knew she should instead be pleading with him to recapture the *Angel Lily* both for her father's sake and for her country's honor, yet even the thought of Hobb and the other men being hung on her account sickened her.

And as for Captain Sparhawk, the wild Yankee who'd caught twenty-two English ships and taught her the passion to be found in a single kiss; the infamous Black Nick caught and hung because of her avenging bridegroom—Lord help her, she'd perish herself from the shame and dreadful guilt of it!

Unaware of her doubts, Hobb nodded with satisfaction. "You be a grand lass, Miss Everard. You'll bring that man o' yours a wealth o' happiness. Now come along, we'd best be joinin' th' others topsides 'fore th' shore-goin' boat gets too crowded.''

Her head bowed, Rose followed him into the companionway. Dressed as she was, with her face and hands grimed with soot and her hair twisted up under her cap, she prayed no one would recognize her in the twilight. The boy's clothing felt odd on her body, the shirt and coat too loose after a lifetime of close-fitting bodices, while the breeches seemed shamelessly tight over her hips and legs. Below the knee she wore rough knitted stockings and thick-soled shoes that tied with leather thongs instead of buckles, the toes stuffed full of handkerchiefs that made her walk stiff and ungainly.

Adding to her discomfort was the sheer weight of the coat, for she'd spent all afternoon picking apart the lining and replacing it with as many of the gold guineas from her dowry sewn inside as she could manage.

But the guineas weren't all that she carried. Around her neck and beneath the rough gingham homespun of her shirt she wore her mother's pearl and sapphire necklaces, and on each wrist, hidden beneath the shirt's cuffs, were the matching bracelets, plus two others with pearls and another with opals. And finally, on a double-knotted ribbon around her neck, was her betrothal ring, hanging between her breasts with all the weight of her secret misery.

After so many days in the cabin, Rose almost gasped aloud with pleasure as the sea breeze ruffled across her face, cool and fresh with the scent of the saltwater. Moonlight washed the deck, just as it had the first night when, with Nick's arms around her, she'd felt Lily's presence so strongly. The memory was so vivid, so strong, that she could almost believe her sister was here again, and with a sudden pang of doubt she wondered if she should be trying to escape after all. Perhaps, in her way, Lily was warning her to remain here on the *Angel Lily*. Rose hung back near the hatch with her heart racing, torn between fleeing and staying.

"Come along, lad, no dawdling," warned Hobb loudly for the benefit of the other men already gathered near the side. He took Rose by the shoulders and gave her a gentle shove across the deck. "Cap'n, he says he don't mean t' tarry here more'n two nights, an' I don't aim to spend 'em here waiting on you."

Rose had a fleeting image of the harbor, of the tall black silhouettes of other ships moored around them and the dark, irregular line of the city—the first land she'd seen since leaving Portsmouth months ago—punctuated by faint pinpricks of lantern light beneath the star-filled sky.

Then abruptly Hobb was pushing her around and over the side, guiding her fingers to the tarred lines on the ladder as her turn came to climb down to the waiting longboat. Clumsy in their borrowed shoes, her feet fumbled for a toehold on the swinging ladder, and her fingers went white as she clung desperately to the rungs. She had always used a bos'n's chair before, or walked aboard a plank from a wharf, but never had she hung on a swinging, swaying ladder like this. Her coat with its heavy golden lining thumped against her back as the ship rocked. If she fell into the black water now she'd sink like a stone, and as the panic swallowed her she closed her eyes.

Lily, oh, Lily, if you're here somewhere, please, please help me now!

"There now, lad, no need to whimper," said Nick as he helped the frightened boy take the last step from the ladder to the boat. "You've done well enough."

The boy tumbled into the boat with a surprisingly heavy thump that made the men at the oars guffaw, and though Nick smiled, too, he couldn't help but feel sorry for the lad, scurrying shamefaced to the bow to sit beside Hobb. Probably another of the English turncoats, like Hobb himself, for Nick didn't recognize him as one of the Rhode Island boys. No wonder he'd been so clumsy dropping into the boat; it might well have been his first time, considering this was the *Angel Lily*'s maiden voyage.

But as Nick settled in the stern sheets of the boat himself, he soon forgot the boy and lost himself in his own thoughts. He had spent the day seeing to his affairs here in Charles Town, calling on his bankers, lawyers and the officials of the prize court. As a whole, they were neither more nor less corrupt than most, and with a few judicious bribes, Nick had managed to have the *Angel Lily* simultaneously condemned and transferred to his name. The *Commerce,* too, had been knocked down and sold the previous week without a single protest, and in the dockyard, the much-damaged *Liberty*'s repairs were nearly done.

And he'd even managed to keep his surprise to himself when he learned that everything belonging to Rose taken with the *Commerce* had been set aside in a warehouse, exactly as he'd ordered. His orders, ha. Lily might not be able to watch over her sister directly, but she'd certainly mastered the ways of doing it through him.

With an impatient sigh he brushed a bit of spray from the sleeve of his dark green dress coat. He'd agreed to make an appearance this evening at a collection given by the governor's wife and then, tomorrow, the day would be all his to squander as he wished.

His, that is, and Rose's. He'd planned it to the finest detail, from gallantly bringing her breakfast tray himself to carrying her off for a day's driving through the lush countryside around the city, the carriage's hamper filled with fresh fruit and pastries and wine and, of course, the most elegant draughts set he'd been able to find in the Charles Town shops. He wanted to make her smile and hear her laugh, and he wanted those silver-gray eyes to gaze only at him.

At last he'd take her to a favorite lodging house of his, very genteel and very, very private, where after a suitably seductive meal, he meant to spend the night making extravagant love to Miss Rose Everard and call Miss Lily Everard's bluff once and for all. No wonder he was smiling as the boat cut smoothly across the water toward land.

Smoothly, evenly, and then without warning, the boat lurched wildly to starboard with a turn so sharp that it nearly capsized. The men at the oars toppled from their benches, oars swinging and crashing like jackstraws and oaths filling the air.

Grasping the side, Nick swung around to glare furiously at Stark, the man at the rudder.

"I—I don't know what's happened, Cap'n," he said miserably as he struggled to move the tiller, throwing all his weight behind it. "It's like she's froze solid in one place."

Unperturbed, Lily sat on the tiller, holding the rudder immobile with one slippered foot. "Forgive me for being so dramatic, my dear captain," she said, "but you did say your life was plagued by tedium."

"Not like that, you little fool!" sputtered Nick. "You could have dumped us all over the side!"

"Aye, aye, Cap'n." Stark hung his head with shame. He wasn't the largest man in the crew, true, but for the captain to call him a "little fool" proved how badly he'd erred. Once again he fought to move the frozen tiller.

"For God's sake, Stark, I didn't mean you," began Nick, then stopped when he realized too late that every eye in the boat was watching him expectantly. "That is, it's not your fault, it's—it's—oh, hell!"

Lily smiled indulgently at his frustration and wiggled her toe against the tiller. "You've been so inattentive this evening, that you left me no choice. If I hadn't acted when I did, you would have let my sister slip entirely through your fingers, and as bad as *you* are, heaven only knows what would become of her alone in this wild place."

He didn't answer. With this much of an audience, he didn't dare.

"She's running away, in this very boat," Lily continued, "and I couldn't let her do that. Rather, I couldn't let *you* let her. There, the boy up front, the same one you were so kind as to help. The one in the cap ducking his head so you won't notice him. That's Rose."

Nick looked to where she pointed, and wondered why he hadn't seen it before. Even by moonlight alone there should have been no mistaking the delicacy of Rose's face beneath the coarse knitted cap or of the fine-boned hands clasped anxiously before her.

He couldn't believe she'd do this to him. He thought of all the pretty, foolish plans he'd made for tomorrow to please her, from the wild strawberries he'd ordered to the imported draughts board inlaid with ivory and silver wire, while the only ones she'd been making were to flee him as soon as she could. It wasn't the loss of the ransom money that concerned him. It was Rose herself, so eager to run away without another word to him.

Hadn't she felt the same magic in the kiss they'd shared? Had it meant that little to her when inexplicably it had seemed the world to him?

"There we are, Cap'n," said Stark with a final oath of sheer relief. "She's workin' right at last."

"Very well, Stark." Nick settled back on the bench as the men began to pull at the oars again. He didn't bother looking for Lily again. She'd done her mischief for the evening, and now he was left to settle it.

He looked again at Rose. She had turned in her seat to gaze at Charles Town, her face in profile and her lips parted in eager wonder. Without friends or family in a city where she was the enemy, where did she plan to go? The reality of what could happen to a small, young and very pretty woman alone amid the taverns and brothels that crowded the waterfront appalled him. But for her, apparently, it was a better fate than remaining with him, and the truth of her rejection cut cleanly through his pride and anger straight to his soul.

He wouldn't let her go. He couldn't. Lily had been right enough there. But now there would be no wild strawberries in fresh cream, no riding beneath ancient oaks in dappled summer sunlight, no elegant private chamber filled with the flowers that bore her name. Thank God at least he'd been spared making a fool of himself that way. Now instead he'd be the rough, ruthless Yankee pirate she'd expected from the first.

He stared unseeing at the nearing wharves, his face impassive while his emotions roiled within him. Strange how one sister believed he was so much better than he was, and the other so much worse. Tonight he would prove one of them wrong, and it wasn't going to be Lily.

The boat glided alongside the wharf, and as the oarsmen tipped the oars upward, the blades dripping silver droplets, two of the others caught the rings with boat hooks to hold them steady for mooring. Though Nick as captain was first to climb ashore, he waited on the end of the wharf while the crewmen followed, in laughing jostling groups or pairs. Last ashore came Hobb and Rose, her head bowed and her shoulders

hunched as she tried to hide herself on the far side of
the Englishman.

"Where are you bound, Hobb?" asked Nick mildly.
"I heard there's a red-haired wench at Mrs. Smedley's
tavern who juggles flaming candles for sport, all the
while singing songs in praise of General Washington.
Could make for pretty tales for the village."

Hobb shrugged nervously, tugging at the red shore-
going kerchief around his neck. "Aye, sir, thank'ee, me
an' th' boy will consider it."

"Oh, aye, the boy." His arms folded over his chest,
Nick leaned forward to see Rose, who shrank even
farther behind Hobb. "He must have come with your
people, for I don't recall having seen him before myself. What's your name, lad?"

Rose's mind went blank. Why, why, did he have to
have stopped them at all?

Nick cleared his throat ominously. "Speak up, boy.
I like to know the names of those that serve with me.
Your mother must have called you by something."

"Henry, sir," she muttered at last, the first name she
could think of. "It's Henry."

"Henry, eh?" Nick chuckled. "A king's name, boy,
a tyrant's name! Why, a whole slew of Henrys have sat
on the English throne! Not the best of names for a boy
on a Yankee vessel, but since your mama chose it, I'll
let it stand."

"Thank'ee, sir," said Hobb with a quick duck of a
bow. "We won't trouble you further, Cap'n, nay, we
won't. Come along, Henry."

Rose had already turned to scurry away when she felt the wide, heavy hand on her shoulder and her heart plummeted. She didn't have to look to know the hand belonged to Nick, not Hobb.

"Not so hasty, Henry," he said softly. "Considering this is your first time in my country, I warrant you deserve something finer than that wench with her tumbling candlesticks. I've a fancy to take you with me, so you can have a taste of how the gentlemen entertain themselves here in Carolina."

Speechless, Rose's mind whirled with all the dreadful possibilities—drinking and gaming and cockfighting and consorting with low women—that he might propose. She'd never been to the Carolinas, but somehow she doubted that the gentlemen in America entertained themselves in any more decent fashion than they had in Portsmouth.

And clearly Hobb feared the same, his mouth dropping open with dismay. "Oh, Cap'n Sparhawk, sir, don't you think th' boy's a sight too young for them things?"

"I think not, Hobb." Nick smiled. "Henry comes with me."

Chapter Ten

The more Rose struggled to keep pace with Nick, the more convinced she became that she loathed him, despised him, hated him, for doing this to her. It didn't matter that he believed she was merely another of the ship's boys. He'd no right to treat any human being under his command the way he was treating her now.

Given the differences in their height, she would have had trouble matching her shorter legs to his long stride under the best of circumstances. But after months at sea, her legs felt wobbly and weak beneath her, and the land seemed to pitch and heave beneath her feet the same way as the deck had before she'd adjusted to it. She could feel blisters growing with every step in her heavy borrowed shoes, her heels slipping and rubbing in the coarse stockings. On the wharf she'd planned to run away from him as soon as she could, but if he'd hobbled her with leg irons she couldn't have been more bound to follow him.

Even the climate conspired against her. Away from the breezes off the water, the night air in the city streets was thick and muggy, and her wool jacket, made by Johnny's mother in far-off and much cooler Rhode Island and weighed down still further by the coins Rose herself had sewn inside, prickled against her neck and back.

And oblivious to it all, Nick walked onward, a slight smile on his lips as he led them heaven only knew where. The only mark of the heat that showed on him was a faint gleam of perspiration on his well-shaven upper lip and a few damp, wayward curls that escaped from the black silk bow at the back of his neck. His soft linen shirt remained immaculate, his light superfine coat unwrinkled, and Rose didn't need to see the admiring looks of every woman they passed to remind her that he was the most handsome man she'd ever known.

The most handsome, and the most loathsome.

"You'll be my excuse for the evening, Henry," he said cheerfully. "I've been invited by the governor to one of his wife's collections, and they're always tedious as hell. But since you're not included in the invitation, we'll have to find some other entertainment, eh, Henry?"

Glumly Rose nodded, not sure she could disguise her voice enough to answer. It seemed odd to her, this companionable side of him. On board the *Angel Lily*, he was always curt and captainish with the crew. But maybe on land he wasn't as concerned with discipline.

"Now don't fall behind, Henry," he warned. "I wouldn't want to lose you here in the dark."

Mutinous as Rose was, she had to agree, and she struggled as best she could to keep close to him. They had left the waterfront with its crowded, noisy taverns and were now in what she guessed must be a business district by day. The street was narrower here, scarcely better than a lane, and flanked on either side by brick warehouses shuttered for the night. The only light came from the moon overhead, slanting between the buildings, and the sound of their footsteps on the paving stones was a lonely echo.

It was the footsteps she heard first, the ones that didn't belong to her or Nick, footsteps running behind them. Startled, she turned, and saw the three men coming toward them, two with pistols in their hands and one with a knife. With a gasp of panic she looked for Nick. He stood beside her with his legs spread and slightly bent and his back turned to a wall, every muscle tensed and ready to fight, the moonlight glinting off the blade of the knife that had somehow instantly appeared in his own hand.

Her fingers flew to touch her mother's necklaces beneath her shirt. There were three men and only one of Nick; as brave as he was, how could he win against odds like that?

"Get behind me," he ordered curtly. "Damn it, *now!*"

But instead, Rose turned and fled. Her legs were so weak and her coat and shoes so heavy that she felt as if she were running in molasses, yet still she forced herself to plunge on as fast and as hard as she could.

There was a rush of wind that she realized was her own breath, and over the racing thump of her heart she could hear the sounds of a fight, scuffling feet and grunts and the sickening dull thuds of blows.

Oh, dear God, not Nick, oh, please, please, as arrogant as he is, please, not Nick!

Yet still she ran, driven now by terror. She was almost to the corner, even with a pile of bricks and sand left by workmen, and she knew if she could reach the other street she could hide and be safe and they wouldn't find her and—

"Got you, you little weasel!"

And with a sharp cry Rose pitched forward, the man's weight heavy on the backs of her legs as she fell into the pile of sand.

"Lord, but you be a cunning little beggar!" The man breathed hard from running after her, and his hands tightened around her knees as she struggled to break free. "But not bloody fast enough, eh?"

If his hands moved any higher, he'd discover she was a woman, not a boy, and he would take her mother's jewelry and her father's gold and dear heaven deliver her, what he could do, what he would do to her as a female!

With a broken sob of fear, she lunged forward and seized one of the bricks with both hands just as the man flipped her onto her back. She had a fleeting image of his face over hers—stubbled whiskers, a bent, scarred nose, the stale stench of rum—as she raised the brick into the air to strike him.

And then he was gone, torn away from her as suddenly as he'd come. Her heart racing still, she scrambled to her feet, swaying unsteadily with the brick clutched tight in her hands. The man was facedown now the way she had been, and Nick was standing over him, his hand curled in a fist and his hair torn free from its neat black bow.

"Thank God," she said shakily. "I thought they'd killed you."

Nick glanced up, and the rush of excitement he'd felt from the fight melted away in an instant. He'd known cutting through this street was dangerous; he'd done it willfully to provoke Lily, and it had. But because he wasn't accustomed to thinking of anyone other than himself, he'd overlooked what a common little street brawl such as this would do to Rose. With her eyes enormous with fear and her face smudged with dirt beneath that ridiculous cap, she looked small and painfully vulnerable, and he hated himself for putting her at risk. Three to one were odds he liked, but she didn't know that. Instead she'd worried that he'd been killed, and he began to hold his arms out to her, intending to reassure her.

But something in her face that he couldn't describe stopped him, and in the last instant he let his arms slip empty to his sides. He risked his life without a thought, but to risk her rejection a second time took courage he didn't have. Of course she didn't want comfort from him. If she had, she wouldn't be here now at all.

"You're not hurt?" he demanded. "Not harmed?"

"No." She was holding the brick to her chest, cradling it like an infant, with the shapeless knitted cap still pulled tight over her brow. "But you—"

"They can't hurt me," he said flatly. His fingers tensed and relaxed restlessly at his sides, nearly overwhelmed by the desire to hold her. "Not even if I wanted them to."

Lily. Rose swallowed hard. Lord, why hadn't she thought of her sister before this? He'd told her before that Lily was bound to keep him safe, and here was the proof. He'd fought three men here in this street, and the worst he had to show for it was a tear in the sleeve of his coat and his queue undone. All she'd been able to do was run like a frightened, ineffectual rabbit, but Lily—Lily could keep him safe. But why, she wondered forlornly, couldn't Lily spare a little of that same care for her?

"Aye, aye, Captain," she said at last, her voice steadying through sheer will. "Whatever you say."

Nick looked at her hard. So she still wished to play at being a ship's boy. In spite of himself she rose another notch in his estimation. Most women, especially ones as gently bred as she'd been, would be wailing and swooning after what she'd just been through.

He bent to retrieve his hat from the pavement where it had fallen and poked his shoe at the unconscious man lying beside her. "Best to be on our way, Henry, before the watch comes to ask questions I've no mind to answer."

She shuddered and looked down the street for the two other men, now little more than crumpled black shadows on the street. "Are they—are they quite dead?"

"I doubt they're dead at all." He shrugged carelessly. Thanks to Lily's assistance, scolding away as she'd lifted the pistols right out of their hands, it hadn't been much of a fight. "Bastards like that don't kill easily."

She nodded and touched the front of her shirt, feeling for something beneath the rough cloth, and he noticed how her hand was bare. It didn't take much for Nick to guess it was the betrothal ring she was searching for, slung in secret around her neck, and a fresh wave of loneliness swept over him. Despite the bleakness of her betrothal to a man she didn't know, that same man was the one she turned to for comfort, to the reassurance offered by his ring because he was the one destined to be her husband.

Not that it mattered to him, he told himself fiercely. After tonight, the British captain could have her. Why should he care what some lord's little daughter thought?

Because the woman was Rose, and he couldn't help caring.

Blast Lily for having done this to him!

"No more dallying, Henry," he said with more sharpness than he realized as he turned away. "Come along."

She dropped the brick and blinked back the tears that suddenly stung her eyes. Somehow Nick still believed her to be a boy; that was why he'd been so brusque. A boy on a privateer's crew would have seen far worse than this. She should consider herself fortunate that he hadn't railed at her as a coward for running instead of staying to fight beside him.

But for a moment, just a moment, she'd thought otherwise. She'd thought he'd begun to raise his hands to her, that she'd seen the warmth of compassion and more flare in his eyes. But the next instant those eyes were cool and emotionless, and she realized to her sorrow that she'd only imagined them otherwise. Even if he'd seen through her disguise, how could she expect comfort from him now after she'd scorned him this past week? She had made her decision, and now she must stick by it.

And, oh, Lily, if you have a moment to spare from him for me, please help me now to do what is truly right!

She stuffed her trembling hands into her pockets, trying to remember how she could have thought escaping—escaping *him*—could be so easy. With her head bent and her heart heavy, she hurried her steps after Nick.

They walked in silence another three blocks, the neighborhood changing again to town houses with white-painted porches and walled gardens. Finally Nick stopped at the last house on the corner, the grandest and most elegant on the street, set back behind a tall stone wall with a wrought-iron gate. With classical piazzas on both floors, the house was unlike any Rose had seen in England, and the sounds of uninhibited revelry and laughter that drifted through the tall, open windows didn't remind her of Portsmouth society, either.

"The house of an old friend," Nick explained offhandedly as he lifted the brass knocker cast in the shape of a woman's face. "She's sure to welcome you, too, Henry, because you're with me."

The door opened as soon as the knocker struck, and an enormous African in pale blue livery and a white peruke bowed them into the hall. Rose looked curiously around her. The wallpaper painted with antique scenes must have come clear from Italy or France, and the gilt-framed looking glasses were costly imports as well. Candles blazed from a dozen bracketed sconces as well as the chandelier overhead, and except for the laughter and music in the parlors on either side of the hall, muffled by closed doors, she could have imagined herself in any of the better homes in Portsmouth after all. Whatever Nick's friends did to earn their living, there was no doubt they'd been successful.

"Good evening, Pompey," said Nick as he handed the African his hat. "'Tis good to seeing you look so well. I trust your mistress—ah, Cassie, sweetheart, here you are yourself!"

"Nickerson Sparhawk, by all that's holy!" cried the woman as she swept down the stairs, her ruffled skirts drifting around her. She was tall and handsome, her

hair fashionably powdered and her gown an extravagant fantasy of yellow silk overlaid with black lace that
barely covered her lush breasts. On the bottom step she
waited, her arms raised in welcome, until Nick caught
her around the waist and spun her in a swirl of black
silk petticoats and emerald-colored stockings while she
laughed with delight. She kissed him with a bawdy
smack as he set her down at last, her laugh fading to a
throaty chuckle.

Oh, yes, thought Rose wretchedly, this friend of
Nick's was most successful at her business, and from
the way she was treating him he was one of her best
customers.

"You've kept away too long, Captain," she said as
she ran her hand along his arm with an easy familiarity that made Rose wince. "This wicked war, you
know, it makes us all so sad when you gentlemen don't
come to cheer us. And such tales I've heard of you,
Nick! They say you've taken to kidnapping English
ladies along with their ships!"

So her plight was common enough knowledge,
thought Rose as her dismay grew by the moment. If
even this—this *woman* knew she'd been taken along
with the *Commerce,* then by now every other person in
town must have heard it, too. Being worth a sizable
ransom was the same as having a price on her head,
and even if she could escape from Nick's company
there'd be no way she could quietly slip away from
Charles Town to the Caribbean the way she'd hoped.

Nick grinned. "You should know better than to believe every story you hear, Cassie," he teased, curving his hand around the back of her waist—the same way, thought Rose unhappily, as he'd held her. "You only wish some handsome privateer would kidnap you."

"Don't make me beg, you black-hearted rogue." Cassie thumped his chest and laughed again, her gaze at last landing on Rose. "And who is this little fellow, Nick? Stars, he's scarce more than a babe!"

"Henry's one of my lads, and I won't hear you say ill of him." Fondly Nick chucked Cassie beneath her chin as Rose wished she could disappear into the wallpaper. "I told him you welcomed strangers."

"Whatever you please, Nick." Cassie pursed her lips, accented by three tiny black patches at one corner. "The usual, then?"

But Rose didn't want to know what was usual for him. She'd seen more than enough already. "I'll wait in the garden, Captain," she said as she edged toward the door. "You can—"

"Nonsense, lad." Nick seized Rose by the shoulder and propelled her up the stairs before him. "I won't hear of it. Cassandra Morton's hospitality is the finest in Charles Town, and you'd be a fool to miss it."

It was on the stairs that Rose saw the wallpaper more closely, and noted exactly what the antique satyrs and nymphs were doing before their little painted temples. With a gasp of shame she jerked backward into Nick, nearly toppling them both down the stairs. "Truly, Ni—I mean Captain Sparhawk, I do not wish—"

"Don't be shy, Henry, not here." He guided Rose into the chamber he always favored, the one at the back of the house. "Cassie won't hear of it."

Leaving Cassie smiling on the landing, he closed the door gently after him, shutting himself inside alone with the girl, and wondered what the devil he was doing. He'd seen the alarm in Rose's eyes on the stairs, and the repulsion she hadn't been able to hide. In a way, this would be worse for her than the thieves in the street, a sheltered young lady who'd blushed when he'd seen the torn hem of her petticoat. If he'd any decency at all, he'd end this now and take her back to the ship.

But he wasn't decent and he wasn't a gentleman, and besides, because of Lily, it was already too late to turn back.

The candles in the room had already been lit, the tall windows to the piazza thrown open to catch whatever breeze might rise from the water. Rose stood before the window, her back to him until she heard the click of the lock. Then she spun round to face him, her eyes flashing with a fury he hadn't expected.

"You knew, didn't you?" she cried, her voice rising as she tore the cap from her head and shook her hair loose over her shoulders. "From the very beginning, in the boat, you knew who I was and yet you kept silent, determined to let me humiliate myself! You *knew!*"

"Then that makes us quite the knowledgeable pair, sweetheart." Nick jerked his arms free of his coat and threw it across the back of a chair. Despite the open windows, the air in the room was still and hot, and already vibrating with the tension between them. "I knew you weren't a boy, and you knew you were going to run away. Where the devil did you think you were going to go, anyway?"

"Certainly not here!" She waved her arm, encompassing the room and all its furnishings. She might have been too innocent to understand the true nature of Cassie's house when they'd stood in the front hall, but there'd be no such mistakes here. The chamber was small, only large enough to contain two chairs, a table and washstand, and an enormous bed with hangings and pillows of a brilliant scarlet. Looking glasses were placed strategically on either side of the bed, and the single decoration hung over the mantelpiece, a colored engraving of Leda and an exceptionally amorous swan. "Here in a—a bagnio!"

Nick's expression hardened. "Don't be so certain, sweetheart. The world, and all the bagnios in it, are filled with little girls who thought the same."

There was a light scratching at the door and Cassie slipped inside, followed by a maidservant bearing a wide silver tray with food and drink to set on the table. As she did, Cassie leaned over Nick, her breasts perilously close to slipping free from her bodice.

"Another of my guests this evening has told me of a certain neighbor of his north on the Santee River," she said archly, "a certain Tory braggart who vows his ship full of indigo can outrun all piddling Yankee privateers to London. Perhaps you would like to greet him when he sails tomorrow, and convince him of his error.''

"I'd like nothing better," said Nick with a chuckle. "How else will the rascal learn to respect the cause of freedom?"

"How else indeed, my pet?" Cassie smiled wickedly. "'Tis all in the name of liberty, you know. Not every battle's won on the field, eh?"

Her knowing glance slid from Nick to Rose and back again, and her smile turned sly as she shooed the maid from the room.

"So much for your pretty cabin boy, Nick," she said, pausing at the door. "I didn't think your tastes had changed so vastly. *Bonsoir et bonne chance, mon cher capitaine!*"

"Forgive me for not being as beautiful as your customary guests," said Rose, her voice brittle with anger and hurt. He belonged with a woman like Cassie, a woman as tall and beautiful and wicked as he was himself, and one who didn't need foolish wagers to make a man kiss her. "I'm sorry to have lowered your estimation in Madam Morton's eyes."

Nick stared at her. In her boy's clothes with her cheeks flushed with defiance and her dark hair tumbled over her shoulders, she was one of the most desirable women he'd ever seen. "What the devil are you talking about, Rose?"

"I'm no fool, Captain Sparhawk. I heard what she said." Rose tossed her hair back, hating him for making her spell it out. "She said she didn't think your tastes had changed so vastly, by which of course she meant they'd sunk to include me."

His sudden smile, rich and lazy and for her alone, made the temperature of the room rise another ten degrees for Rose.

"Cassie didn't mean you at all. There are some men who prefer the company of boys to women, and she was merely relieved for her own selfish reasons that I wasn't one of them." Carefully he filled one of the tumblers from the bottle the maid had brought, tasted it and smiled again over the glass at Rose. "Relieved, and likely a bit jealous. Cassie's too clever a business-woman not to know competition when she sees it."

"Don't be ridiculous," snapped Rose, though her cheeks flushed just the same. He was teasing her, nothing more. How could she ever compete with a woman as undeniably lovely as Cassie Morton? "And how charming that she's willing to betray her—her *guests'* confidences to assist you."

"Oh, I've never been above listening to the ladies," said Nick easily, and he thought fleetingly of Lily's assistance. At least she seemed to be blessedly absent now. "All's fair in war and love."

Unconvinced, Rose watched as he filled a second glass and held it out to her. With a contemptuous sniff she shook her head. "Thank you, no."

"Are you sure?" He cocked one brow, blatantly tempting her with more than the rum alone. "Rhode Island rum, the best there is. Cassie always sees to the niceties."

Rose ducked her chin and scowled, wishing he hadn't pointed out one more way in which the other woman was superior. "I told you no. I'm never drinking with you again."

"And I'm not playing draughts with you." He leaned against the armchair, crossing his long legs as he sipped the rum. "I've learned my lesson."

"So have I," she said tartly. "Though I very much doubt it's the same one."

"Don't be so sure," he said easily. "We're not really as different as you like to think."

"I don't 'think,' Captain Sparhawk. I know." To see him so perfectly at ease here in a hired room of a brothel with lewd pictures on the wall and his favorite rum in his hand only served to prove to her how different they were. "Night and day, oil and water, black and white, you and I. Pick whichever you choose, for it's all as one to me."

"All as one, or one from two. Your ciphering pleases me, Miss Rose." This kind of seductive bantering came as second nature to him, as much a game of give-and-take as chasing and capturing enemy ships, and he'd always been good at it. At least he was when Lily didn't interfere, and for now, thank the Lord, she was nowhere to be seen. "But then you'd warned me before that you were clever."

Rose eyed him suspiciously. He was clever, too, and she wasn't accustomed to anyone who could match her like this, especially not anyone with green eyes and black hair that fell so carelessly over his brow and a smile that was whiter than the linen of his shirt.

"One from two leaves one, Captain, by my ciphering or any other's, and so it shall be with us," she said. "Now if you're done guzzling your fine Rhode Island rum, you might as well march me back to your prison ship, for I've no wish to remain here any longer than I must."

"All in good time, lass," he said, intrigued by how deftly she tossed his words back at him. She'd done it from the first time she'd appeared on his deck, and it was one of the things he liked best about her. She was a challenge, no mistake. Even fully dressed, she'd never be boring. "All in good time."

In response she grumbled to herself and began pacing restlessly back and forth before the open window, holding the heavy weight of her hair off her neck and to the side with one hand, and as Nick watched her move, his eyes narrowed with careful, practiced appraisal. Now this, he thought, was interesting; he hadn't dreamed she'd such initiative.

"How much have you sewn into that coat of yours?" he asked gently. "Nay, don't deny it. I've done it myself on occasion in an unfriendly port, often enough to recognize how that plain Yankee homespun doesn't sit quite right. Dollares, is it, or pistoles?"

Sharply she drew in her breath and stopped her pacing, her eyes full of reproach. "It's guineas," she said. "One hundred *English* guineas, each marked with the heads of King William and Queen Mary. You might recall them as two more of your royal tyrants, but now, I suppose, you'd rather wish to add them to the rest of your plunder at my expense.''

She yanked off the coat and hurled it at him, and he caught it easily in one hand. But then he would, she thought unhappily. Everything came easy to him, even her gold.

He tested the weight of the coat, shaking his head, and then tossed it onto the second chair. "I don't want it, Rose," he said softly. "Any more than I want the rest of your things. You'll find them all, even the pianoforte, safe in a warehouse here in Charles Town, and none of it, I trust, the worse for my men's removal from the *Commerce*.''

Strange how even to his own ears he sounded so frighteningly earnest. He'd thought to turn that bit about her goods being safe in the warehouse to his own advantage and not just Lily's, but somehow instead it sounded as if he really had ordered Rose's belongings saved from auction.

Maybe, heaven help him, because now he wished he had.

She stared at him, not sure whether to believe him or not. "That might have worked once with the gown and the hat," she said slowly, "but not again."

He sighed, the broad expanse of his chest swelling beneath the embroidered waistcoat. "We're not discussing some broken timepiece, Rose, or why 'that' does or doesn't work. I meant only to show my goodwill and respect toward you, to prove that things don't have to be so blessed disagreeable between us.''

"But they do, Nick," she said in a small, weary voice. "It's better this way."

She turned a little away from him, and with her face bathed in the light of a candle he saw how her anger had faded away, her profile as impassive as a cameo against her dark hair. By the candlelight, too, he could see the outlines of her body, soft and curved with now only the worn gingham shirt over her round, high breasts. He couldn't recall having seen a woman in breeches before, and he liked how the fabric pulled taut over her thighs and hips, surprisingly full hips, considering how slight the rest of her was. He liked how she looked. He liked it a great deal, and there wasn't any way now he'd mistake her for a boy.

"Forgive me if I'm being thickheaded, sweetheart," he said, his voice low as he raised his gaze back to her face, "but I'll be damned if I can see why it's better."

"Why not?" she asked, her breath suddenly tight in her chest. By a trick of the candlelight his green eyes had turned dark to match the night, the spiky shadows of his lashes impossibly long as they crossed his cheekbones, and she shivered as she realized how intently he was watching her. No one had ever looked at her like that before, as if she were so special that he found great pleasure in the sight. It took all her strength to remember why it was wrong that he should.

"Aye," he said. "Isn't it bad enough that our countries are at war without us turning on each other, too?"

"But that's exactly the reason why!" she cried, hugging her arms to herself as if that were enough to protect her from her own weakness. "You're an American who has robbed my father in the name of this foolish war, and I am betrothed to an officer of my king, a man whose duty is to destroy Yankee privateers like you. What kind of future does that make for either of us?"

For once he had no ready answer. What, he wondered, had happened to the blithe, bantering game of cat and mouse that had begun this conversation? He couldn't even remember the reasons why he'd brought her here in the first place, they mattered so little now. Now he found himself drawn into something deeper and darker, with currents swirling between them that he didn't begin to understand. And for the first time in his life he wanted to. Lord help him, he *needed* to, almost as much as he needed her, and the realization shocked him.

She turned her face toward the open window, her hand curled beneath her chin, and the graceful line of her cheek and throat in the moonlight was something he'd never forget.

"No matter how much you might wish it otherwise, Nick," she said, so sadly, so softly, that if he weren't as keenly aware of everything to do with her, he would have missed it, "you cannot change the truth."

Rose heard him set the tumbler down on the tray, and when she turned to look she wasn't startled to find him standing behind her. Not by that, no; some part of her had almost expected him to be there, drawn to her by the same force that had made it so impossible for her to leave him. The expression in his eyes reminded her of the night they'd stood on the *Angel Lily*'s deck, and she remembered how she'd felt close to him then, drawn to him in a way that was at once irrational and inevitable. Then she'd thought it was Lily's doing. What other explanation could there be?

But in this narrow room tonight there'd be no Lily to guide her. Only a bed hung in crimson, Black Nick and White Rose. Any other time and Rose would have laughed from the sheer overblown spectacle of it.

She wasn't laughing now. Not when Nick was sliding his hands into her hair, lifting her face toward his so her lips fell open, shamelessly waiting to welcome him. Not now that she realized he needed her, maybe as much as she needed him.

"Ah, little Rosie," he breathed hoarsely, his words warm as they spilled across her skin. "You make me think I've lost my wits all over again."

Beyond caring for anything but him, she arched up to brush her lips against his. "If you are mad, Nick Sparhawk," she whispered, "then so, Lord help me, am I."

Chapter Eleven

Madness.

There could be no other word for what was happening to him. She was small and perfect, and if she trembled as his hands reached out to draw her close, he did, too. He was as much beyond caution as he was past reason, and far, far beyond caring for the consequences. Nothing mattered now except the girl in his arms, and his whole world, mad or sane, had narrowed to the featherweight touch of her body against his.

She was kissing him with the same untried eagerness she'd shown before, her mouth sweet and soft as velvet, and when he hungrily deepened the kiss, unwilling to hold back, she yielded and met him, her slender fingers reaching up to thread restlessly through his hair. He was drunk with the taste of her, dizzy with her scent. She smelled of flowers, violets and her own womanliness, a scent he remembered with stunning clarity from his sheets; after the night she'd spent alone in his bed, her fragrance had clung to the linen, an unintentional reminder so vivid that he'd been unable to sleep there himself without imagining her.

Except that nothing he'd imagined had been as wildly breathtaking as the reality of Rose. His Rose, his for this single night. Tomorrow she would go to wed another, tomorrow he could be killed by the enemy's gunpowder, but tonight—tonight would be theirs.

He drew her closer, painfully aware of how fragile the bond between them was. The silk of her hair, still crimped from the hat, rippled over his arm as he slid his hands along her back, lifting her against him. He marveled at her delicacy, at how easily his spread fingers could span the narrowness of her waist as she arched against him, and his heart pounded at the knowledge of what she was offering, her urgency a match for his own. Clumsy with inexperience, her blind fingers fumbled at the first of the long row of buttons on his waistcoat until she broke away from his kiss long enough to look down at her hands.

Her dark brows drawn together with concentration, she scowled as her fingers worked to slip the buttons free, one by one by one, until impatiently he pulled her face and his lips back to hers. She dug her fingers into the front of his half-open waistcoat and yanked, the last buttons giving way and flying from their broken threads. She circled her arms around his waist, tugging his shirt free from his breeches as she slipped her hands up along his bare back.

"That time I saw you while you were shaving—day and night, I haven't been able to put it from my thoughts," she confessed shyly. The warmth of her kiss made her voice dusky with promise as she looked up at him through the veil of her lashes. "If I could, Black Nick, I would play you again for your shirt and win, too, so that I might gaze my fill of you once more."

"I told you, lass, I'll never play against you again," he said as in his haste he pulled his shirt and his unbuttoned waistcoat together over his head. "But I'll give you what you wish anyway, with neither dice nor a card in sight. I can, you know, be powerfully obliging."

Gently he took her by the wrists and placed her palms on his bare chest. Her face turned serious as she tentatively touched him, her fingers brushing over the dark, curling hair.

"You've been hurt, haven't you," she said softly, "and often, too, from the look of it." She was running her fingertips across his lean, muscled torso with a tenderness that was exquisite torture to him, and hesitating over the paler ridges of old scars. "How lucky you must be to have survived so much!"

He remembered her concern for him earlier, her fear that he'd been killed. No one had feared for him like that for a long, long time. "Luckier still to be here with you."

But she didn't rise to the blatant compliment, her silver eyes still solemn as she explored his body, learning it, until he could bear no more and pulled her back into his arms. He didn't wish to frighten her, but his whole body was hot and ready for her, the tension growing tighter and tighter with every unabashed touch of her hands.

"You *will* drive me mad, Rosie," he whispered hoarsely as he swept his lips across her cheek to the soft, sensitive place below her ear. "Wicked, clever, little creature."

She shuddered with pleasure, her eyes closed and her head tipped back, the pulse throbbing in her pale throat. "It's you, Nick," she breathed. "You make me wanton. Bold and wanton and not at all like me. You and the moonlight and—and, oh, my, what you do..."

"Then go ahead and blame the moon, sweetheart," he whispered raggedly, "for it's never been like this for me, either."

Swiftly he eased the gingham shirt free from her breeches. Made for a boy, the breeches hung low on her hips, accentuating the flaring curve below her waist. The contrast was unexpectedly provocative, and the novelty wildly exciting because she wasn't shrouded in the endless layers of women's dress.

Gently his hand glided beneath the rough homespun to find her silky bare skin, and he felt her shiver as he traced the arcs of her ribs. At last he reached the high swell of her breast and she gasped as his hand caught and caressed the taut flesh, the crest tightening in an instant beneath his touch. With the same untutored boldness she arched against his hand, pressing her aching flesh into his palm as again she gasped, her breath harsh and uneven.

"Sweet Rose," he murmured, shoving the shirt higher as he caressed her. "My sweet, perfect Rose."

She moaned softly and twisted beneath the sensual fire he was fanning in her body, and as she did, something hard and jagged bumped against the back of his hand. He paused and frowned, puzzled.

"Oh, please, Nick, don't stop," she begged in a hoarse whisper as she twisted back toward him. "Please don't."

The thing swung into his hand again, and this time Nick caught it in his fingers. A hard, faceted oval, still warm where it had lain against her skin. Swearing softly to himself, he swept the loose-fitting shirt over her head, and she gasped again, this time from surprise, not pleasure, backing away and fanning her fingers to cover her bare breasts.

"Hell and damnation, Rose," he murmured, nearly speechless as he stared at her. "I'd no idea."

Framed by the scarlet hangings of the bed, her skin glowed ivory pale in the candlelight, her tangled hair midnight around her bare shoulders and the dark breeches hanging low on her hips. Like some sultan's houri, her nakedness was draped in jewels, blue sapphires in star-shaped gold settings and heavy strands of pearls that glowed against her flawless skin. Her fingers couldn't hide her breasts completely, soft and ripe and waiting again for his touch. Her silver eyes were clouded with passion, her small pink mouth swollen and stained darker by his kisses, and he had never seen anything more exotically, seductively beautiful in his life.

"My mother's jewels," she said. She shifted her hands higher over her breasts and the twin rows of bracelets cascaded, shimmering, down her wrists. "I couldn't leave them behind."

She couldn't leave the jewels, but she would have left him, without a parting word or regret, and the truth sliced at his heart before he could guard himself. He had always been the first to run away; he was never the one abandoned. She raised her chin, a small defiance he'd come to associate with her, and the candlelight caught the aquamarine ring on the ribbon around her neck. Her lord's ring, right where Nick had guessed it would be, the mark of the man she had chosen over him.

He would always be second, he would never be good enough for the ones he cared for most....

"Was it that easy to decide, then?" he demanded, his pride lost in the raw, aching need to know for certain. "Are you so eager for that bastard's bed?"

Her cheeks flushed dark. "I—I have to marry him, Nick. My father—"

"The devil take your father!" His body was still hard as granite for her, frustration rising into anger. "If you're so hell-bent on leaving, then why are you here now? Why stay to torment me like this?"

"Don't make this out to be my fault, Nick!" she shot back at him, her own temper flaring to match his. Swiftly she retrieved her cast-off shirt from the floor, clutching it to her breasts. "You're the one who brought me to this dreadful place, stinking of tobacco and rum and harlot's scent! How could I be the one tormenting you?"

"Because, damnation, you are!" he thundered. "*You* are! Is that answer enough?"

Even as he spoke, he knew the words made no sense. From the look on her face he was sure she knew it too, and likely didn't care, either, and the angry silence between them stretched longer and longer.

From another room in the house came the high-pitched, giddy laugh of a woman who'd had too much to drink, and almost in answer a dog in the street barked a sleepy response. Slowly Nick realized that the other sound, the dull, heavy thud, was the racing of his own heart.

With a groan he closed his eyes. He couldn't seem to make his mind run straight, as it jumbled the black-and-white board of the draughts game with the rustle of coral-colored silk and the scents of violets and woman on linen sheets and her husky little laugh and the way her silver eyes would suddenly turn serious and solemn when she looked at him and the muffled flutter of an angel's wings as she lifted him clear of a sinking ship to save him for this. For this: rejection and despair and longing so sharp that he wondered how he'd bear it.

Lord help him, maybe he truly *was* mad.

He shook his head and looked to Rose, waiting, the shirt still crushed in her hands before her. Her shoulders drooped forlornly and her hair hung down on either side of her face.

"You made me feel different, Nick," she whispered, the tears there on the edge of her words. "That was all. Can you believe it? You never looked at me and saw Lily, the way Lord Eliot will. You saw only me."

She twisted and balled the crumpled shirt in her hands as she struggled not to weep. "I've no excuse for being here at all now, not after I swore I wouldn't be caught alone with you again. I'm weak, Nick, vastly, horribly weak. This time I cannot claim I'm tipsy, or that you've somehow forced me against my will because you haven't. All you did was make me feel beautiful, beautiful and clever and special, and for this one time—likely the only time—in my life, I wanted to believe it."

"Oh, Rosie," he murmured, touched to the quick by the depths of her misery. "Believe it, my dear, sweet lass, believe it because it's true."

And for him it was. This, then, he could give her, even if she'd take nothing else from him. What did his own wretched faults and weaknesses matter beside her sorrow? With rare tenderness he took her by the hand and drew her once again into his arms, her back to his chest and his arm possessively around her narrow waist as he turned her toward the mirror.

"Look, Rosie, and trust your eyes," he said as he pulled the shirt from her hands and dropped it to the floor. Gently he eased her hands from her breasts, letting her see her own beauty without shame. Her nipples were already pink and tight with longing, and he guided her hips back against his so she could feel his own arousal, hard and ready. Standing before him like this she scarcely reached his shoulder, and Nick was struck again by how small and delicately made she was, how pale and untouched she looked against the dark hair and old scars on his chest. "You're a beautiful woman, sweetheart, finer, rarer, more precious than any of those jewels."

But instead of looking at her own image, her gaze was raised higher, to his face, her eyes filled with wonder. "I'd rather see you," she said breathlessly. "You're as good as you are handsome, Black Nick. No wonder Lily wishes to keep you safe."

She twisted gracefully against him, raising her arms around his neck to draw his mouth to hers, and as she did he caught her around the waist and pulled her with him onto the bed. She kissed him feverishly as he rolled her beneath him, the fire that had burned between them earlier now sparking even hotter. Impatiently he swept the necklaces aside, bending his head to kiss the eager, pink crests of her breasts as she twined her restless fingers into his hair and arched her aching flesh against his mouth. He slid his hand along her flat little belly, unfastening the fall of her breeches and shoving them down over her hips, her skin damp and glowing against the scarlet coverlet.

"Little Rose," he murmured. "Sweet, perfect little White Rose."

He kissed her again, taking her first gasp of wonder into his mouth as his fingers slipped through the black curls to her womanly center. Already she was wet and swollen, her body easing the way for his touch, and she shuddered, writhing beneath him as he urged her fire brighter. He wanted, needed, nothing more than to bury himself in her, to find himself in all she offered and forget what he would lose. Desperately he tore at the buttons on his breeches, only half aware of the flutter of white at the head of the bed before them.

"This isn't right, Nick," said Lily softly. "You know in your heart it isn't."

His head whipped up, his fingers stilled in midcaress. Lily was sitting cross-legged like a Turk on the pillows at the top of the bed, her wings behind her echoing the curved headboard and her hands draped across her bent knees. She sighed sadly and shook her head.

"I've kept my distance," she continued, "hoping you would see the error of this path yourself, but you are still in too many ways a hugely stubborn man, determined to trot directly to the very gates of Hades and pound on the door to be let in."

Why now? he thought wildly. Why in blazes did Lily have to come to him now? His blood was pounding in his veins, his body primed and poised for release, and from the little cries that tore from Rose's throat and the flushed sheen of passion that colored her breasts, he doubted she'd any more wish to be interrupted than he himself.

"Damnation," he rasped as he glared at Lily, "I thought you wished to make me happy."

Beneath him Rose's eyes flew open, wounded and uncomprehending. "I thought I was making you happy, Nick, truly," she whispered uncertainly, breathing hard. "But if somehow I've done something wrong—"

"Nay, sweetheart, not a blessed thing," murmured Nick quickly, sweeping his mouth down on hers to reassure her. Once again his fingers found her rhythm, and he took her soft, startled cry of pleasure.

Double blast Lily for doing that to her own sister!

"Of course I wish you to be happy, my dear captain," said Lily, unperturbed and unrepentant. "That is the point of this whole exercise between us, isn't it? Though I'll vow you're doing a remarkably fine job at present of making my sister quite, quite gladful. La, who would have guessed she'd blossom so!"

Nick lifted his head from Rose to glower at Lily, counting on that fearsome, unspoken warning that had sent so many sailors scurrying and quivering to obey to do the same with her.

Of course, Lily being Lily, it made no impression at all.

"It's not this foolish trick to blackmail me, if that's what you're thinking," she said mildly. "I told you before that the only thing you can do to make me leave is to improve yourself, and Lord knows you've still a way to go. And I told you, too, that I've no control over Rose's life in the slightest. As her sister I'm not overpleased with her losing her maidenhead to you in a brothel bedchamber, but I can't stop her. At least I suppose it's better you than Lord Eliot, though she'll be in for pots and pots of trouble if he ever finds out.''

Nick shut his eyes and tried to concentrate on Rose, not Lily. If he tried hard enough to ignore her, he reasoned as he ground his teeth, perhaps she'd give up and go away.

But Lily only clucked her tongue. ''You can be as rude as you please, my dear Nick, but you won't shed me until I've said my piece. I don't care how you do this to my sister. It's the *why* that worries me, because you don't know why yourself. Randy and virile you doubtless are—most wondrously virile!—but lust alone isn't making you do this. And until you can sort out your reasons, you truly must not be on this bed with my sister wriggling beneath you.''

In another room, a woman screamed, then another, and the frightened, urgent voices of men urging calm. ''For God's sake, it's a fire!'' shouted someone at last, his voice cracking with fear. ''Fire, here!''

Lily beamed proudly. ''Why, I do believe someone's been careless with a candle,'' she said. ''Fancy being so distracted as not to notice when the bedclothes are on fire! I hope your friend Cassie pays her jolly hussies what they're worth.''

Nick groaned. He could smell the smoke himself now, and the confusion of screams, running footsteps and conflicting, shouted orders was growing louder by the minute.

"I shouldn't tarry if I were you," advised Lily, already fading away herself. "As warm as you've made things here for yourselves, I'll wager they'll get too hot even for you if you remain much longer."

"What's wrong?" asked Rose as she reached up to lightly stroke his cheek, sensing rather than understanding the change in Nick. "Something's happening, isn't it?"

All too aware of what he was giving up, Nick turned his mouth to kiss her fingers, then swore and rolled to one side, reaching for his breeches. "I'm sorry, sweetheart, but we're going to have to leave."

"I'd rather not," she said wistfully as she watched him dress, curling herself tight to hold on to the fading warmth his body had brought to hers. Instinctively she knew she'd come close, so close, to understanding one of her life's greatest mysteries, and her body quivered and ached with unfulfillment. "That is, I wish to stay if you do, too."

"There's no wishing about it, Rose." Lily had been right, the devil take her cursed wings. They didn't have much time left to escape, for now he could hear the muffled crackle of flames. "Dress yourself, lass, quickly now. This whole bloody place's on fire."

"On *fire?*" How could she have been so besotted that she hadn't noticed the terrified wails and the smoke that was beginning to drift into the room under the door? With a frightened yelp she grabbed for her clothes, struggling into them as quickly as she could. Shrugging on her coat, she ran to the door.

"Nay, Rose, leave it!" shouted Nick as he tore down the last of the bed's hangings. "There's too much smoke to try the stairs. We'll do better over the rail. Come now, hurry!"

The smoke stung her eyes and burned at her lungs. Coughing, she turned in time to see Nick tying one edge of the bed curtains to one of the white-painted columns of the piazza. He tested the knot with a quick jerk, tossed the bundled fabric over the railing, and held his hand out to her.

Coughing and wheezing, she peered over the edge. They were at least twenty feet above the gravel garden walk, and the knotted bed curtains swaying gently from the railing seemed to her even less substantial than the rope ladder on board the *Angel Lily*. She didn't want to do this, and she wasn't sure she could. But now she realized that the dull roar she'd been hearing was the fire itself, and the sharp, brittle pops were the sound of the house's windows exploding with the heat. Shoving her hair back from her face, she bravely swung one leg over the rail.

But then Nick's hands were around her waist, pulling her back and into his arms. "Put your hands around my shoulders," he ordered. "Hang on tight, sweetheart."

Without pausing to think she did as she was told, clinging to him with her legs around his waist as well for good measure. She gasped when he took them over the rail, swinging out easily to brace his feet against the white pillar as he held the knotted red curtain, and then she made the mistake of looking down at the ground spinning dizzily so far beneath them.

"For God's sake, Rose," rasped Nick, "don't throttle me!"

"But I don't—"

"Don't argue!" he ordered, his voice strained. "I've run through rigging my whole blessed life, but I've got to have some air to do it!"

"Aye, aye," she said miserably as she tried to shift her grasp to please him. She squeezed her eyes shut and buried her face against Nick's hair for good measure, still hanging on to him for dear life—a life that seemed to become more and more dear by the moment. At last, she heard the gravel crunch beneath his feet.

"Oh, Nick," she began as she slid down his body to stand on her own shaky legs. "How can I—"

"Damnation, Rose, not yet," he ordered, and seizing her hand he guided her through the garden to the gate in the wall and to the safety of the street.

Once outside, he stopped, taking both her hands as he anxiously searched her face. "You're not hurt, are you?" he demanded hoarsely. "Not too much smoke?"

She shook her head. Bits of cinder and ash drifted in the air like gray-and-black snow, and all around them people were shouting and running with more buckets to fight the fire, but to her there was no one else than this tall, soot-covered man gently rubbing his thumbs into the underside of her wrists.

"Oh, Nick, you know I'm fine," she said. She coughed again and lifted her shoulder to wipe her face with her sleeve. "Look at me. How could I be better, considering?"

He frowned. "'Tis my fault. I should never have taken you there in the first place."

"True enough. You shouldn't have." She smiled shyly. "But I'm vastly glad you did."

"Vastly?"

"*Vastly* vastly." Her smile wavered a fraction. She wasn't quite as fine as she might wish—she'd been too frightened for that—but she wasn't about to tell him that. "You took very good care of me, you know, saving me like that. You're the one who did all the work."

"Not quite all, Rosie." He grinned wickedly, his teeth white in his black-streaked face, his eyes brilliantly green. "I promise you'll have the rest soon enough."

Before she could answer he swept her into his arms and kissed her hard, lifting her feet from the ground as he took away what little breath she had left. He laughed when he set her back down and the best she could do was to grin stupidly in return.

She tried to remember back to that morning, when all she thought lay before her was another endless day in the little cabin with only herself for company. Instead she'd been saved from toppling overboard, attacked by street thieves, brought close to losing her virginity in a brothel and carried down the wall of a burning building. Yet to Nick it seemed to be normal enough, nothing to remark, and as he took her hand to lead her to the street in front of the burning house, she wondered if every day for him was as exciting as this. Her heart still pounding, she tightened her fingers around his and prayed she'd have the chance to find out.

Cassie was standing beneath a palmetto tree, forlornly clutching a dark green dressing gown about her shoulders as she watched the fire with her girls weeping and sobbing in a circle around her. Standing with his arm around Cassie was a stout man who'd lost his wig, shoes and neck cloth, a gentleman whom Nick recognized as a Carolina delegate to the Continental Congress. Not that Nick would be so tactless as to greet the man, but it pleased him that Cassie's friends stayed by her no matter the circumstances. Needless to say, he intended to do the same, especially since he was, through Lily, responsible for the fire in the first place.

"Nick, my love," she said sadly as he bent to kiss her cheek. "It was that addlepate Adele, of course, the foolish little drab. How could she not notice when her own bed's in flames?"

Grimly Nick thought of Lily's interference, and sympathized with poor Adele. "If I come across a certain London-bound vessel tomorrow, I'll see that you get a share of the profits to help rebuild."

"You're a gallant, generous rogue, Nick Sparhawk, and I thank you for it." Cassie's gaze wandered back to the house, where the line of men handing buckets of water from the pump in the street to the fire had finally managed to douse the last of the flames. "We all thought 'twas much worse, but they say now 'twas really only the one room damaged. Strange to have a fire come up so sudden like, then burn out with so little damage. Not that I'm complaining, mind you. At least no one was hurt."

Nick shook his head sympathetically. Where Lily was concerned nothing was strange. He'd wager that just as the fire had begun when he'd refused to listen to Lily, the flames had begun to die down the moment he and Rose were once again safely dressed, and he resolved to send Cassie a handsome gift to help pay the carpenters, whether he captured the Tory planter's ship or not.

"And I'm sorry your own evening had to end so soon." Cassie leaned around Nick to find Rose and winked broadly. "But you tell that pretty cabin boy of yours that when she tires of the sea, there'll be a place waiting for her here if she wishes it. She's got the spirit I like in my girls, and she must be fair enough beneath the grime, else you wouldn't bother with her."

Nick laughed, as much at the shocked look on Rose's face as at Cassie's offer to reform his unkempt cabin boy into a high-priced tart.

"Oh, I don't think she's ready to give up sailing just yet," he said, still chuckling. "You have my word of honor that I'll see to that."

And Lily, and all her hows and whys, could just go to the devil where she belonged.

Chapter Twelve

"So you really will try to capture the ship that Madam Morton told you of?" asked Rose excitedly as she stood beside Nick on the quarterdeck of the *Angel Lily*. Once they'd left Cassie's house and returned to the wharf, Nick had ordered the boat to return to the ship immediately, preferring to leave behind the handful of crewmen who'd dawdled too long in the taverns than waste even a minute of time. He'd begun calling orders before he'd even clambered on board, and to Rose's amazement the men had jumped to obey with the same eagerness to be under way and gone.

He swept back his untied hair with one hand—his hat, just like Rose's cap, had been casualties of their swift escape from the fire—and grinned down at her. Somehow he'd shed his coat and acquired the sword she'd tried herself and a pair of flintlock pistols were thrust into his belt. In the moonlight he looked like every idea of what a pirate should be: his billowing shirt still open at the throat with the sleeves shoved up over his forearms, his patterned waistcoat unbuttoned and tossed by the wind, his expression rakishly confident, his broad-shouldered body radiating energy and, decided Rose, dangerous excitement that she wanted very much to share.

"Of course I'm going after them," he said, clearly amused that she'd even ask such a question. "That is, you know, the whole reason I'm here. 'To attack, subdue and take all vessels belonging to the inhabitants of Great Britain.' That's what Congress tells me, anyway. Besides, I wouldn't wish to let Cassie down, would I?"

A tiny flicker of jealousy rippled through Rose. Given Cassie's occupation, her "old friendship" with Nick doubtless had gone further than was usual for most friends, and Rose, her imagination now considerably more informed, tried not to picture the details. She'd no real right to be jealous, anyway. After all, Cassie might have told him about the merchant ship from the Santee River, but *she* was the one he'd taken with him to capture it.

But she did wish he'd kiss her again. Now, here before all his crew bustling about to guide the *Angel Lily* through the entrance of the bay to the deep water. She wouldn't mind at all.

Oh, he'd been charming enough since they'd returned to the ship, but then he did that as easily as he breathed. What she'd hoped for was something a bit, well, a bit more, considering all that they'd said and done in that red-draped room. Surely it had meant something to him, hadn't it? She smiled to herself as she remembered how tenderly he'd held her, the magic she'd found in his kiss, the way he called her Rosie. Inexperienced she might be, but she didn't think of herself as being foolish or overtrusting. She'd never been changeable and impulsive like Lily, falling in love with a different man every day of the week. At least, she thought wistfully, she hadn't until she'd met Nick.

"If what Cassie said proves true," he was saying, as much to himself, thinking out loud, as to her, "then we'll most likely fall in with this brash-mouthed Tory by dawn. Not my favorite time for a fight, on account of the sun, but if we can catch him on his lee, then 'twill save us all the fuss and wear of a long chase."

He sighed, gazing up at how the topsails caught the wind, then looked back to her with a careless shrug of his broad shoulders. "Here I am prattling on about chases and fighting, without a thought for you. You're Tory yourself, or at least English, and likely you've no wish to hear me say such—"

But suddenly he broke off, and as he reached out to brush his fingers against her cheek, his whole face seemed to light from within, and Rose felt her heart race in anticipation.

"Cassie said you had spirit, sweetheart, and you do, more than most women can muster in a whole life of trying." His hand slipped from her cheek to her shoulder and he drew her to him, close enough for her to hear the conspirator's confidence that now colored his words. "Before we start out after this Tory planter's ship, I'll make you the same offer I make all the Englishmen before I take them as prisoners. Join up with me, and I'll grant you shares same as everyone else. I won't ask you to fight, of course, but if you wish to stay here by me, then it seems only fair to offer you a part of the prize money."

She stared at him, not sure she'd really heard him aright. "You wish me to swear loyalty to your country when you attack a ship from mine, and in return you're offering me prize money?" she asked incredulously. "Change sides just like that? Captain Sparhawk, you've worried before that you've lost your wits, and now I truly know you have."

"Nay, not over this," he scoffed. "This planter's really more one of my countrymen than yours, anyway. You don't have to look when they strike the king's flag if you don't want to."

"Then why should I agree at all?" she demanded indignantly. "Isn't it bad enough that you've taken my father's ship to use against the English without making me party to it, too? What sane reason could you possibly offer?"

His grin widened wickedly as his hand strayed beneath her jacket and around her waist. "Because, sweetheart, I thought you'd want to," he said, his voice low and seductive but teasing, too. "Lord knows you're brave enough. Stay beside me and prove it to yourself. You'll never have a better chance to see that you're not your papa's little gingamabob of a girl wrapped up in cotton wool."

She hesitated, strangely tempted by his argument. She'd told him before how he made her feel unlike herself, but she hadn't confessed how much she enjoyed being this other Rose, the one who left off her stays to wear boy's breeches and practically threw herself on her back before a man she scarcely knew. Silently this other Rose pleaded with her conscience. How much could this last adventure cost her? As Nick had said, this wasn't really an English ship they'd be chasing, and besides, neither her father nor Lord Eliot need ever know. She glanced down at the battered sword at his side, remembering the weight of it in her hand, and how much easier it was to imagine herself as a wild pirate queen than Lady Eliot Graham.

"Say aye, Rosie," urged Nick, his breath warm on her ear. "Say it for yourself, and for me as well."

He didn't know why it seemed to matter so much that she agree, but it did. Any lass that had come this far with him would find a chase like this one after a Carolina merchantman dull work indeed, but the truth was that he didn't want her away from his side. He wanted her here to smile at him and laugh with him and say all the outrageous things to him that no one else would ever dare. With her he felt younger and happier than he had in years. And here on deck, she couldn't expect him to play draughts. His dear, conniving White Rose. Perhaps he'd give her the fancy draughts set anyway. He couldn't help smiling at her again as she stood nestled beneath his arm, frowning her indecision as she looked up at him from beneath her lashes.

No one would mistake her for a lady now, and especially not for the prim little wren who'd landed squawking on his deck that first day. How she'd blossomed, his pretty little Rosie. He slid his hand back and forth along the flaring curve from her waist to her hips, remembering again how she'd looked sprawled across the scarlet bed wearing nothing except her mother's jewelry, and feeling, too, just how quickly his body responded to the memory. How the devil he could have thought her plain was beyond him. After this chase, after this capture, he'd show her exactly how desirable he found her now, and this time not even Lily would stop him.

"I won't let you go until you agree, Rosie," he said, considering what she'd do if he kissed her here on the deck before all the men. "If this planter's as rich as Cassie promised, then even your mean old papa wouldn't fault you for claiming your share. All I ask is that you don't tell that grand lordling of yours. I'd hate to see him hang you for a traitor."

At that her eyes flashed with defiance, not so much luminous silver by this moonlight as pure English steel.

"I'm not his wife yet," she said, lifting her chin stubbornly, "and until I am, I've no obligation to tell him anything. I'll come with you, Nick, and I promise—I *swear*—that Lord Eliot won't hang a single one of us."

"Oh, he'd have to catch us first, lass," said Nick, delighted by her rebellion, "and I've no mind to let him do that. Over here, Gideon, and learn the news."

"What now, Nick?" asked Gideon dryly as he joined them.

Earlier Rose had noticed how the lieutenant had been one of the few men of the crew who'd been able to look at her in breeches without open amazement. She'd overheard from someone on board that the captain and his lieutenant had been friends since boyhood, which most likely explained Gideon's world-weary air. All those years in Nick's company would leave few surprises. Now Gideon stood with his hands behind his back, his neat and orderly dress, even in the middle of the night, the complete opposite of Nick's.

"So what is it this time, Nick?" he asked blandly. "Don't tell me you two are ready to cry the banns?"

"Nay, nay, better than that," declared Nick. "Miss Everard's agreed to join our company, at least for this day."

Gideon sighed patiently. "You can't read in a lady. It isn't done, and it's probably against your commission, too."

"Since when has that bothered us?" Nick swept his hand through the air as if to wave away all objections. "I'm captain, and I say we'll take her. The only question is how to rate her."

Gideon sighed again, and let his gaze wander slowly over Rose, slowly enough that she self-consciously tugged the front of her coat closed over her breasts. She hadn't really intended to agree, but now that Nick had taken her part against Gideon's misgivings, she found she wanted nothing more.

"Since she's wearing Johnny Hinson's clothing," said Gideon at last, "I'd rank her a boy, same as Johnny. Half a share."

"You can't call me a boy," protested Rose, drawing herself up as tall as she could. "I'm far too old. I'll be twenty-one next May."

Nick raised his brows in feigned wonder. "Twenty-one? Goodness, Miss Everard, I'd no notion you were so advanced an ancient. We'll have to put you down on the books as a gentleman volunteer. That way you'll earn a full share."

"As it should be," she said, "considering whose father built this ship and whose sister it's named for. A whole share seems entirely proper."

She smiled up at Nick, and as he winked his hand slid lower beneath her coat, no longer quite on her hip. But she didn't stop him or move away, though at least she did feel her cheeks grow warm as she tried not to gasp with pleasure. Oh, bad, wicked Rosie was here, all right, she thought, and having such a grand time that Miss Rose Everard's meek little warnings could scarcely be heard at all.

"Aye, aye, Captain Sparhawk, we'll add another gentleman volunteer to the books." Dutifully Gideon touched the brim of his hat before leaving them, but the glint in his eyes was more from bemusement than respect. "And my compliments on your splendid recovery, Captain. Better these 'gentleman volunteers' than angels any day."

"What did he mean by angels, Nick?" asked Rose curiously as the lieutenant made his way forward. "Has he seen Lily, too?"

"Nay, I told you, she only shows herself to me," said Nick as lightly as he could, "and she hasn't even done that lately. Maybe she's gone to her peace at last."

But the mention of Lily doused Nick's playfulness, and he disentangled himself from Rose to take up his spyglass again. He didn't want to lie to Rose, but he didn't want to discuss her meddling, ethereal sister with her, either, especially not after what had happened earlier at Cassie Morton's house.

Instead he handed the heavy glass to Rose. "Take your last look at Charles Town, sweetheart. With any luck we won't be back again for a good long spell."

With any luck, he thought grimly, she wouldn't be back at all. By now her father's agents on St. Lucia would have received the letter Gideon had sent on his behalf, and were likely arranging her ransom in plenty of time for her wedding. Another fortnight, maybe three weeks, and he'd have to give her up.

And then, God help him, he'd be alone again.

Unaware of his thoughts, Rose took the glass from him and tried to focus on the city fading on the horizon. But in the dark all she could make out in the distance were a few church spires, and with a sigh she lowered the glass. Inexplicably his mood had changed, his face set and his eyes shuttered against her. The coming chase and fight for the other ship, she thought; for all his foolish teasing about her becoming a volunteer, any battle when lives would be at risk would concern a captain.

"Charles Town seemed a pretty city, from what I saw of it," she said, striving for empty talk to fill the silence. "I'd never dreamed that the American colonies—I mean the American states—had anything half so fine."

"What, you thought we still lived in Indian huts made of bark and twigs?" His smile was empty, his thoughts patently turned inward. "Charles Town is fine enough in its way, but it can't begin to compare with Newport. When I was a boy, we already had a colony house and a market house, both handsome buildings made of brick, and enough wharves and warehouses and shipyards to make Charles Town here look like a muddy puddle. In Newport there was at least a score of churches and meetinghouses, with all faiths—Friends, Congregationalists, Baptists, Anglicans and Jews—content to live side by side without squabbling. There were shops as well stocked as those in London, and gentlemen's houses by the dozen. My own father built one house in town, on the point near the water, and kept a second as a country seat, high on a hill near Middletown, both grander than any other in the colonies."

"In the states," said Rose with a smile, unable to resist correcting him as he'd so often done her. "You said colonies, and you meant states."

"Oh, aye, I suppose I did." But he didn't smile in return as he absently fingered the hilt of the sword at his waist. "Of course by now Rhode Island's as much a state as any of the others."

What the hell had made him babble on so about his home to her? Nay, it wasn't even his home, only the town where he'd been born and grown as a boy. He'd been eager enough to leave Newport behind, hadn't he? Even now he didn't think of himself as having a home at all, at least not the way other men did, a home port with a house and bed ashore that were his alone. But that was the price of the freedom he'd earned for himself, the hard-won cost of independence that had let him become his own man on his own terms, and had taken him to lands most people never dreamed existed. And from his fifteenth birthday, he'd never doubted that he'd done the right thing.

So why the devil was he speaking of Newport like this now?

Why was he remembering the scent of the roses in his mother's garden that overlooked the harbor, and the singsong voices of his sisters, playing with their dolls beneath the table in the kitchen to keep out of their bustling mother's way, and the fat-cheeked cherubs carved into the paneling in the front parlor that he'd reach up and rub for luck when no one was looking, and the secret place he'd made his own in the attic, high up under the eaves, where he'd go with a fistful of gingerbread to dream of all the places he'd sail to when he was old enough, while the rain drummed a drowsy rhythm on the shingles overhead?

"Perhaps one day I'll be able to visit Newport," Rose was saying, her face no more than a blur through the haze of his lost past. "I should like to see the town that's your home."

"You can't," he said, turning to stare out at the black water. "It's gone. The British saw to that last year. Everything the way I remember is gone."

And when he looked again for Rose, he found instead he was alone. Not that he'd expected her to stay, or deserved her to, either, considering how he'd been rambling on like some doddering graybeard in his chimney corner, not—

"Oh, stop feeling so curst sorry for yourself!" said Lily impatiently. "Melancholia doesn't become you. It doesn't become anyone, really, except perhaps consumptive poets in moldering garrets."

"Perhaps that's what you should make of me next." He barely bothered to glance to where she sat, perched on the rail, swaying gently with the ship's motion.

"You are dressed for it, I'll grant you that," she said, hugging her skirts over her knees in the wind. "The unshaven jaw, the filthy shirt, your hair blowing every which way like a madman's. Which, you should know by now, you most certainly aren't, so you can stop feeling morose over that, too."

"Why, thank you, Lily," he said wearily. "That's most reassuring. I'm certainly not a madman, but I do talk to meddlesome angels that no one but I can see."

"So you do," she said promptly, "but you also have another ship to chase and capture, don't you? I vow at first I didn't care for you taking advice from another woman, and a powdered and patched strumpet such as Cassandra Morton at that, but I've come to rather like your friend Cassie. Besides, you've offered to give her a share of your profits, something you wouldn't have done for anyone a year ago, so of course you must go take this prize for her."

His expression was skeptical. "You're not going to split all my canvas when I come within range?" he asked. "Or block up my carriage guns so they misfire?"

She tipped her head and pursed her lips with an arch little moue. "I wouldn't do such things to *you,* my dear captain. I told you, I favor this particular venture of yours."

"None of your parlor tricks?"

Her mouth curled into a smile. "Not a one. But while I heartily approve of your generosity toward Madam Morton, I am not nearly as pleased by your doing the same with my sister." The smile flattened into something less agreeable. "Whatever were you thinking of? Treating Rose like some common sailor, telling her you'd give her a share of your profits if she stood by your side!"

"I wanted her there," he said, surprised by his own defensiveness. "I still do. The business about the shares was only a jest, that was all. I'll take it from my own earnings as owner and captain, not from the pockets of the men. Where's the harm in that?"

"Because of the harm that could come to her," said Lily firmly, all traces of good humor gone. "Nick, how many times must I remind you that I watch over you, not Rose? I'll keep you from any ill today, but who's going to see that she's safe if this other ship turns out to have more teeth than you've been led to believe? Remember, dear captain, how we first met. Gunfire and explosions and heaven knows what else. Do you care so little for Rose that you'd put her into danger like that?"

Nick scowled, looking down to rub away a smudge on the polished brass of his spyglass. "Ah, she won't come on deck if there's an out-and-out battle. Rosie knew I never meant for her to do that. Besides, she's a lady, gently bred, and I expect that with the first broadside she'll be cowering in the hold where she'll be safe."

"Then your expectations are most barbarously wrong," declared Lily. "Maybe she would have behaved that way when she was still pinched under our father's thumb, but not now. And since when has her *gentility* been of any concern to you? You, who took this 'gently bred lady' to the most notoriously low house in Charles Town with the express purpose of seducing her, letting her be mauled and terrified in a common street brawl in the process?"

Nick's scowl deepened. He couldn't deny what she said because, hell, it was true. "Rosie wasn't hurt," he said, knowing his defense was a lame one. "You've seen her. I'd wager she even enjoyed herself."

"My point exactly, my dear, darling captain." Despite the wind that tugged at Lily's hair—the ship had the wind at her heels, and was racing fast as the thoroughbred she was—she still managed to sweep open her fan with practiced grace.

"Rosie, Rosie," she mused. "Did you know no one else has ever called her that? Yet still you haven't answered my question. Is it because you care so little for her that you continue to risk her life?"

"Damnation, Lily, it's not like that! It's not like that at all!" He shook his head in fierce denial. "Well, perhaps in the beginning it was, but not now. She's not like any other woman I've ever known. You wouldn't know, being her sister, but kissing her—only kissing her, mind—was better than a whole week with Cassie's girls. I swear the room spun clear around my ears."

"Clear around?" Lily's brows arched higher. "I should like to see that."

"Nay, Lily, that's but the half of it!" He struck his fist on the rail for emphasis. "Your little sister likes to gamble, same as I do, and not just over draughts, either, and she speaks her mind plain and makes me laugh, and she has more courage than a good many men I could name, and—and she needs me, Lily. Strong as she is, she needs me, and even when she had the chance, she didn't leave."

"My, my, goodness." Lily clicked her tongue as she snapped her fan shut. "And here I thought all Rose was worth to you was six hundred of Papa's hard-earned guineas!''

Even as he smiled, he swore softly under his breath. She laid a good snare, he'd grant her that. "You've caught me up again, haven't you, Lily?"

"Perhaps I have," she admitted, already fading into the pale light of the coming dawn, "but I'd rather believe you've caught yourself."

She was a coward, a hopeless, weak, appalling coward.

Furiously Rose ripped the hairbrush through the tangles in her hair, wishing for all the world she could relive her parting with Nick. She wasn't greedy; the last two minutes would make difference enough, and, oh, what she would say and do instead!

So much for her cleverness and understanding. Here poor Nick had showed her a part of his soul that she hadn't even suspected was there, and when he'd come to the worst, how the English had destroyed the home he clearly loved so much, she'd run away. Turned tail and fled, exactly as she had when the thieves had attacked him in the street, running with all the haste and speed that's granted to true cowards.

She groaned and bent her head over the hairbrush clasped in her hand. What could she have said to comfort him? She was one of the enemy, and what her countrymen had done to him was unimaginable to her. Safe as she'd been in Portsmouth, this colonial war was so far removed from her world that, before the *Com-*

merce had been captured, she'd scarcely been aware of its occurring. For all she knew, Nick's own home had been destroyed, his family murdered, perhaps even a wife and children. She remembered how he'd spoken of his father and an older brother with a certain reluctant affection, but it had always been carefully worded to stay in the past.

She thought of how he'd returned her belongings to her, how he'd chosen not to keep what was by the rights of war his to sell. Nothing remained of his beloved Newport, yet instead of retaliating against the bride of a British officer, he'd ordered her things kept separate. He'd returned her clothes and left her her mother's jewels untouched.

And then there had been the other gifts he'd shared with her, gifts of himself that no one else would ever see and infinitely more precious to her than all the cold, hard gold sewn into her coat. She smiled to herself when she thought of how his green eyes lit when he called her his Rosie, and she shivered when she remembered the fire his dark caresses had brought to her blood. For her the legendary, ruthless Captain Black Nick Sparhawk was only her Black Nick, hers as long as she'd be his White Rose.

And Lord help her, how she had repaid his kindness! The first time he had turned to her, when in despair he'd asked her to believe in Lily's spirit, she had hidden her feelings in denial. Then this night, when the bleak, empty look in his eyes had shouted his suffering to her, begging her to listen, she'd been too frightened of what she might learn that she'd slipped away before he could tell her. To listen would be to admit to caring, and to care would be to admit to feelings that would make her sham of a wedding impossible.

Coward, coward, *coward!*

With a loud sniff she sat upright on the bunk, squaring her shoulders in her boy's clothes. Twice was enough. She wouldn't fail him again. This time she'd be as brave as he needed her to be.

She listened to the noise from the deck, the subtle, excited change in the men's voices and footsteps overhead. They'd cleared for action an hour ago, but now, at last, they must have sighted the other ship.

Swiftly she finished brushing the tangles from her hair and braided it into a single, tight plait that she tossed over her shoulder. Since she'd lost Johnny's cap, she tied a scarf across her head to keep her hair from her eyes. Finally she reached inside her shirt, feeling the heavy weight of the necklaces still against her skin. She hadn't taken them off, remembering how Nick had liked the wanton display of the gold and sapphires against her bare skin, but one piece she'd do without. She lifted the loop of ribbon with Lord Eliot's ring from around her neck and stuffed it unceremoniously into her trunk. Heaven knows it was wrong of her to do it, but as soon as she had, she couldn't help but smile, her neck and her soul feeling instantly, endlessly lighter.

Her hand was already on the latch of the door when she heard the knock on the other side. Instantly her heartbeat raced, as she hoped irrationally that it might be Nick, but when she threw open the door she found instead Gideon Cole.

"Don't look so downhearted, lass," he said wryly, offering his arm crooked out for her to take. "The great man has his hands full topside, and so he sent me with his regrets and to shepherd you down to the hold."

"Nick's unharmed, isn't he?" she asked quickly. "I haven't heard any gunfire, but still he could—"

"He's never been in better health, Miss Everard. We're scarce in firing range, and if our fortunes hold, they'll strike their flag to us without our firing a single shot." He nodded sagely, though his eyes kept their wry twinkle. "And don't waste your worry on Black Nick, Miss Everard. By rights the man should have died a score of times already, but I tell you his life is charmed. The devil watching out for his own, eh?"

The devil, thought Rose uneasily, or someone even more unpredictable, someone who favored white silk taffeta and pearls with a Roman cameo.

"Now come, lass," said Gideon patiently. "You've just time to gather any little trinkets you'd like to keep with you, then I must take you below."

Rose smiled sweetly. "That's most kind of you, Mr. Cole," she said, beginning to sidle past him, "but quite unnecessary, for I'm going on deck to be with Nick, the way he wished."

Deftly Gideon shifted to block her way, reaching out again to take her by the arm, though now with less gallantry than determination. "He didn't mean that, Miss Everard. Oh, he'll likely grant you the gold if you make a fuss for it, but now he wants you below, where he won't have to worry over you.''

Undaunted, Rose swung her hips gently from side to side the way that Lily always had when she wished for a gentleman's attention. Her hips weren't as lushly provocative as Lily's, but the snug-fitting breeches more than made up the difference, and automatically Gideon's gaze dropped away from her face. Instantly Rose darted past him and up the companionway steps to the deck, and didn't stop until she'd skidded to a halt before Nick, standing beside the helmsman at the wheel.

''I'm here, Nick,'' she announced breathlessly. ''Just as you wished me to be.''

But the ominous look on his face was far from welcoming. Since she'd left him earlier he'd changed into a dark gray coat and a black hat pulled low over his brow that made him look grim as a preacher, forbidding as the devil and, to Rose, achingly handsome as sin.

''You don't belong here, Rose,'' he said sharply. ''I told Gideon to take you down into the hold, below the waterline, where you'd be safe.''

Her gleeful grin wobbled and faded. She shouldn't have left him alone before; now he wasn't going to forgive her. She'd waited too long, and she was too late.

Lord, dear Lord, let him give me another chance!

''I'm rated a gentleman volunteer,'' she said, fighting to keep the panic from her voice. ''Don't you remember? You said you wished to keep me by your side, so you added me to the crew. You said you wanted me here, Nick, so I've come.''

Her timing, thought Nick dismally, could not have been worse. The Tory planter's ship had turned out to be every bit the prize that Cassie had promised, a heavily laden deep-water brig that looked close to new. But along with the cargo that made the brig sit so low in the water, the planter had outfitted his vessel with eight four-pounders that, with even a moderately capable gunner, would stave off most attackers. They meant that the captain had orders to fight rather than strike outright.

Nick hadn't counted on the guns, but he wasn't about to let the brig slip past him, either. He had the faster ship, the bigger guns and the crew to use them, and the wind was in his favor. If he kept close to the brig's weather quarter, he could worry her with a broadside or two to stop their guns, then board. He'd never been afraid of a fight, and the brig and her cargo would be worth it.

But seeing Rose made him want to forget everything else. She stood before him, smaller somehow in the pale, slanting light of dawn, her mouth working anxiously as her eyes pleaded with him in silence. She'd come back after all. He had asked her to join him and she had, and all he wanted to do was to sweep her up in his arms. It might have begun as a joke, but he most certainly wasn't laughing now.

Belatedly Gideon appeared behind Rose and grabbed her arm. "Come along, Miss Everard," he said irritably. "You've caused trouble enough for now."

"No, Mr. Cole, oh, please no!" As she tried to wriggle free, she turned back toward Nick, beseeching. "Don't make me go with him, Nick, please! I don't want to be locked away to think the worst. I know it's dangerous, but I want to be here with you!"

It took all of Nick's willpower not to smile and beam like a fool. She had come back because she wanted to be with him, and he thought of how fine it would be to have her here, nestled warm beneath his arm where he could explain to her all the finer points of the chase and capture.

Yet Lily's question echoed again as well: did he truly care so little for Rose that he'd continue to risk her life for a selfish whim like this one? He looked at her dear, pink-cheeked face, then forced himself to drag his gaze across the water to the enemy brig. Another minute, maybe two, and they'd be within range to try a warning shot, placed high through their rigging.

"Nick, please," she said one last time, her voice dropping low for his ears alone. "I came because I care what happens to you."

Something inside him lurched crazily. She cared, damnation, she *cared,* and before he could change his mind again he nodded to Gideon to let Rose go and held out his hand to draw her close. She curled close to him as he'd known she would, her clothes and hair still smoky from the fire and her body soft and warm against his.

"You're a wicked, evil hussy to do this to me," he said fondly. "Mind, now, that you stay out of mischief and close to me."

"Aye, aye, Captain." She smiled contentedly. "That's merely what I wished all along."

He called the order to fire to Gideon, who bawled it louder to reach the foremost gun crew. Lily had promised he'd be safe. If Rose stayed close to him like this, wouldn't her sister's protection spill over onto her as well? No harm could come to her. He wouldn't let it.

The shot splintered high in the brig's maintop, the topsails folding forward slowly as they tangled in the severed lines. With his glass Nick watched the panic of the brig's crew as they scurried back and forth across the deck. He smiled with satisfaction. Panic meant disorganization, and without discipline the brig's fancy guns were useless. He raised the glass higher, to their flag, expecting to see it drop in surrender.

Rose let out a little cry of surprise as, too late, she grabbed for the silk scarf that the wind had capriciously snatched from her head. The yellow scarf went twisting and bobbing over the deck only to snag on a belaying pin near the foremast. Before Nick noticed she ran after it, her hand outstretched to catch the scarf before the wind claimed it again.

Next came the bright flash from the side of the brig, then a half second later the sound of the gunfire. As Nick's mouth opened in horror to shout Rose's name, the *Angel Lily*'s foremast exploded into a deadly rain of sparks and splinters, canvas and shattered spars that plummeted to the deck with a thundering crash.

And somewhere, beneath it all, lay Rose.

Chapter Thirteen

Countless times Nick had imagined Rose in his bunk, lying here on his sheets and pillow, but never had he dreamed it would be like this. Small and too still, her magical silver eyes closed and the lids shadowed, her face as pale as the sheets she lay upon. Across the coverlet rested her left arm, her little hand like a doll's below the newly changed bandage. She had marveled so at all his scars; now she would have one of her own from the deep gash that ran nearly the length of her arm.

"She's doing admirably well, Captain," said Dr. Barker as he patted his waistcoat. "No fever to the wound, no putrefaction. Clean as they come. Damned fortunate I was able to save that pretty little arm, eh?"

Nick glared at him through bloodshot eyes. Three days of repairing the *Angel Lily* and the strain of sitting here helpless beside Rose had shredded what little patience he had.

"If you hadn't saved her arm, Barker," he growled, "I would have taken yours myself."

"Aye, saved the arm and that miraculous coat, too," continued Barker, unperturbed. "Cole told me there must have been at least sixty guineas sewn inside."

"One hundred," said Nick. "Not that it's any of your damned business. The gold's a wedding gift from her father."

He was all too aware of the excitement Rose's gold-lined coat and hidden jewelry had caused among the crew, even more than the capture of the brig *Cynthia* itself had. Barker might be the best surgeon afloat, but he was also one of the biggest gossips, and he'd barely washed poor Rose's blood from his fingers before he was recounting the coat he'd had to cut away to tend to her arm.

Barker rocked gently back on his heels. "One hundred guineas, you say! That, combined with her ransom, not to mention the sapphires and the pearls, makes the lady worth quite a tidy sum, doesn't it? A most tidy, interesting sum! No wonder, Captain, you were so very eager to save her, pulling her free with your own hands!"

"Barker," said Nick. "Shut up."

The surgeon bowed his apology as he took his bag from the table. "Rest assured, Captain, that I meant no insult to the young lady."

"And you rest assured, Barker, that it's still not too late for me to claim that arm of yours."

"I've never doubted your word, Captain, and I won't be so foolish as to begin now." Barker bowed again, this time in farewell, leaving Nick alone with Rose.

Tenderly Nick smoothed her hair back from her forehead, and she stirred in her sleep. No fever, as Barker had said, and already the ugly bruises that marked so much of her body were beginning to fade. His little Rose was a hardy blossom indeed.

But the horror of how close he'd come to losing her remained fresh. He'd clawed through the wreckage himself to find her, the successful attack on the other ship forgotten as he'd shouted her name with an open desperation that had stunned his crew. Until, that is, they'd learned from Barker about Rose's hidden value. Then doubtless he'd risen yet another notch in their mercenary estimation.

Only he knew the real value of what he'd nearly destroyed by his own selfishness. Lily's question haunted him still. Had he really cared so little that he'd shamelessly risked Rose's life, or was it because he'd cared so much that he hadn't wanted to part from her? Not that it mattered now. Either way she'd still suffered, suffered horribly, and it was all his fault.

"You are too hard on yourself, Nickerson," said Lily softly. "I thought you were quite heroic, considering. As wonderfully broad as those shoulders of yours are, they still can't bear all the blame."

He raised his gaze to where she hovered protectively above her sleeping sister, and for the first time saw the strong resemblance between the two. "Who the devil else can claim it?'' he demanded savagely. "My God, Lily, I saw what Barker had to do to save her arm!"

"So did I," said Lily. "And dreadful though it was, you'll recall that Rose had fainted dead away by that point. She won't remember a thing beyond that you were the one who rescued her."

"But she'll always have the scar to remind her." His eyes clouded, he lightly ran a fingertip across the back of Rose's hand. "I know how concerned you women are with how you look, Lily, so don't try to tell me otherwise. Rose was so flawless before this, and now every time she looks at her arm—nay, every time the weather changes, too, when she'll feel the pain again— she'll remember how bloody careless I was."

"Oh, pish, not Rose," she scoffed. "Or rather, not your *Rosie*. She'll have the sleeves of all her gowns fashioned to display the scar, just so she can brag about how she got it and how you saved her from worse. She'll dine on the tale for the rest of her life."

"Oh, aye, for however short a time that is, if she stays with me." He slumped back into his chair and rubbed wearily at his eyes. He couldn't remember the last time he'd slept longer than an hour at a time; was it really four nights ago, before Charles Town? "But I've considered what you said, Lily, considered it hard and long. And you're right. As much as I care for Rosie, I can't keep hauling her in and out of scrapes with me. I've no right to do it."

He smiled up at her bleakly. "You're always yammering about making me better than I am. Will you be happy if I give her up?"

Lily gasped. "Not to Lord Eliot!"

Nick sighed and let his head droop forward, unable any longer to meet her eye. "If that's what she wishes, aye, to Lord Eliot. I'm taking her to Martinique, to St. Pierre, and I'm leaving her there. As soon as your father's people on Barbados pay her ransom, she'll be free to go wherever she pleases."

Lily's mouth rounded in a perfect circle of dismay. "But you can't do that to her, Nick!" she wailed. "She'll marry him and be utterly miserable!"

He looked up at her from under his brows. "I thought I was the only one you were protecting."

"You are, of course," she said, fluttering her fan anxiously. "Of course you are, Nickerson."

"Then rejoice, Lily, for I've reformed." He'd never believed he'd catch her like this in her own kind of trap, but now that he had, he found little satisfaction in it. "You've won."

"But this isn't at all what I wished!" she cried.

"Nor I, Lily," he said heavily, "but there's no other way. I'm taking Rose to St. Pierre where she'll be safe. And nothing either one of you say will change my mind."

"I don't want to be here, Nick," said Rose, her chin low against her chest like a stubborn child's. "This is worse than being sent down into the hold with the rats and mice. Far, far worse.''

''Well, thank you, too.'' Nick scowled, equally stubborn. ''I'd appreciate it if you didn't share that opinion with my sister.''

He knew this would all go much better if he could smile, but he was too much on edge to even try. The little two-wheeled cart jostled and bounced its way behind the pair of white mules, up the steep, angled streets of St. Pierre. He felt foolishly conspicuous in the pink-painted cart, his knees drawn up beneath his chin in the narrow space behind the driver and Rose's huge piebald trunk lashed behind them. And as always the sun here on land seemed to beat down on them with ten times the intensity that it did at sea. Since when, he wondered irritably, had the way to his sister's house become so damnably far?

''You'll be much better off here with Jerusa and Michel,'' he said, striving to sound reasonable. ''A ship is not a fit place for a woman.''

''So *you* say,'' said Rose mutinously. ''*I* would have vastly preferred to stay aboard the *Angel Lily* than to be an unwilling inmate in your sister's house. Will she lock me in my chamber each night, I wonder?''

He sighed. ''Don't be ridiculous, Rose. You'll be Jerusa's guest, not her prisoner. You might even come to like her.''

''I won't if she's anything like you.'' Pointedly she turned her shoulder to him and stared out at the pastel houses lining the street. She wore the hat with the curving feather again and held a parasol tipped over her head for extra measure against the sun. Still swaddled in bandages, her wounded arm rested gingerly in a sling improvised from a sheer lawn fichu, elegant but also necessary. Perhaps it was the wound that was making her so disagreeable.

Perhaps. Nick knew better. She'd been prickly like this from the moment last night when he'd told her he was bringing her here. He couldn't blame her; he felt exactly the same way. But because they might never be alone together again, he was willing to try one more time to make her understand.

Gently his hand crept across to cover hers. "Forgive me, sweetheart," he said softly, keeping his voice low so the driver wouldn't overhear, even though he likely wouldn't understand. "Forgive me for everything."

She turned back to face him, sorrow filling her eyes. "But Nick, there's nothing—"

"Hush, Rosie, and hear me out. I know this isn't what you wanted. The devil knows it's not how I'd want things to end, either. But there's no other way, not for us, not now."

"In Charles Town and after, I thought there was," she said wistfully. "What you've given me, how you made me feel—no one else ever did that for me, or will again. I would have done anything to stay with you, Nick, anything at all."

"No, Rose, don't say that." He looked down at her hand, groping desperately for the right words to make her accept what had to be. The sacrifice she wanted to make was so much greater than she realized, and as much as he wanted her, he couldn't let her do it because he had so little to offer in return. He would never forget finding her small, battered body nearly crushed beneath the rubble of the fallen mast, and he would never forgive himself for letting it happen. "You can't mean it."

"But I do," she said sadly. "God help me for a fool, I do, and I think I always will."

"Nous sommes arrivés, m'sieur," said the driver in his thick Pierrotin patois, grinning as he hopped down from the cart to tie the mules to the post before the house. *"Ici la résidence de M'sieur et Madame Géricault. Très belle, très grande, non?"*

"Very grand, yes," murmured Rose. To her dismay Nick was already climbing down, too, patently relieved to be freed from her. She twisted the handle of her parasol, struggling to keep back the tears of disappointment and regret. She hadn't meant to make him run away. It had taken her so long to find the courage to tell him how she felt, and now—now it was too late. Not that he'd wanted to hear it, anyway. He couldn't have made that any more clear.

She looked up at the house before her, trying to concentrate on something other than the aching, empty place inside her chest. It was, as the driver had said, a grand house, one of the largest she'd seen, three stories tall and wide enough to seem square. The thick stone walls were painted a cheerful yellow and the shutters and door the same brilliant blue as the water in the bay, and the slanting roof was covered with orange clay tiles. Clumps of flowering vines—red, fuchsia, violet—climbed the front of the house, and towering behind it were the same top-heavy palmetto trees Rose had first seen in Charles Town. The windows on the upper floors appeared to have no glass in them at all, only thin grated bars to let in the breezes that came up the hill from the bay below, and white lawn curtains that fluttered in the summer air. Chattering birds and children's laughter drifted to them from beyond the garden wall, and from somewhere within the house came the sound of a woman's voice singing to herself in the lilting island French.

The whole effect was charmingly light and gay, so different from the dark, dank, brick houses of fog-ridden Portsmouth. How, thought Rose wistfully, could one be anything other than happy living in such a house? Though Martinique was a French island and St. Lucia English, the two were less than fifty miles apart by sea, so perhaps Lord Eliot's house would be like this. She prayed it was; then maybe she, too, could learn again to be happy.

Suddenly the blue door flew open, and a tall, black-haired woman came rushing down the steps to throw her arms around Nick. Spilling through the door after her came a tall blond boy and three smaller girls, giggling and jostling one another, and two terriers that raced circles around them all with noisy, yapping excitement.

The woman, of course, was Jerusa Sparhawk Géricault. Rose would have recognized Nick's sister anywhere, not just from the wide green eyes, high cheekbones and generous mouth that were a softer, feminine version of his, but from the energy that seemed to spin around them both, the supreme self-confidence that would always make them the center of any gathering.

In such company Rose knew she'd always be lost along the edges, just as she was now, sitting forgotten and forlorn in the little cart while the driver carried her trunk into the house and Jerusa and Nick laughed and the children shrieked and the dogs barked. She told herself it was her injured arm that kept her from joining them, that she was still so weak from lost blood and now the hot sun that she wasn't sure she could climb down and walk unassisted. That was true—she did feel appallingly light-headed—but even more than she feared fainting in the dust at Nick's feet was her dread that he'd frown or glower at her interference, or worst of all, simply ignore her. Lord help her, she couldn't bear that, and with her heartbeat throbbing in her head, she closed her eyes and bowed her head.

"And you must be Miss Everard!" The woman's voice was low and rich, her manner kind, and slowly Rose opened her eyes to find Nick's sister smiling up at her, shading her eyes against the sun with the back of her hand. "*Bonjour,* and welcome to my home! I'm Jerusa Géricault, and my brother is being his usual horrid self by abandoning you and not bothering to introduce us properly. *Venez,* this sun is wickedly hot, and I've both tea and chilled cider waiting inside. You see, even after all these years on Martinique I can't quite give up my Yankee tastes!''

Rose smiled weakly. "Either one would be most agreeable, madame.''

"Bien, bien! Now here, let me—oh, my, Nick didn't tell me you've suffered some sort of accident!''

"It wasn't exactly an accident," she began, unsure of how much Nick would wish her to explain. "Nick was busy attacking another ship, and I was foolish enough to be struck by a splinter from our mast."

Jerusa swung around to face her brother, her hands on her hips. "How *could* you, Nick?''

"But it was my fault, not his!" Rose dared to smile shyly at Nick, who was balancing his youngest niece on his shoulder while the other two swung on his coat-tails. "Nick was the one who rescued me."

But instead of the smile she'd hoped for in return, his expression grew dark as thunderclouds, his mouth stern and set. "If you hadn't been on deck during action in the first place, Rose," he said sharply, "you wouldn't have needed rescuing."

And Rose's heart plummeted. She knew it was her fault, but before this he hadn't been so cruel as to agree.

"En voilà assez!" Jerusa waved her hand at her brother in abrupt dismissal. "You can quarrel over this later in the house if you must, but I refuse to keep any

guest of mine waiting here in the hot sun. Come, Miss Everard, let me help you.''

Gratefully Rose took Jerusa's offered hand, but as soon as she stood she realized she'd need more than that. Her heartbeat was ringing like a bell in her ears, her forehead was hot and her hands like ice. She paused, struggling to stop Jerusa's face from spinning before her as she stepped from the cart, and instead crumpled unconscious to the paving stones in a soft sigh of silk.

Nick waited in the garden where Jerusa had banished him, and when at last she came to him, he rose instantly to his feet, his face lined with concern.

''She's sleeping now,'' said Jerusa to his unspoken question, ''and I'm certain she'll be well enough when she wakes, though I told her I'd send up a tray with her dinner. But *mordieu,* Nick, how you could have thought she'd be equal to parading about in the summer sun with you after what she's been through! Colette and I changed that bandage, and now it's all I can do not to thrash you for the selfish, pigheaded brute that you are.''

''She said she felt fine,'' muttered Nick defensively, unwilling to agree with his sister even though she was right. She was, after all, two years his junior, and had spent all of her speaking life trying to order his. ''Rose is stronger than she looks. She told me herself that she was much better.''

"Well, and what else was she supposed to say?" With an impatient sigh Jerusa dropped onto the teakwood bench shaded by lush tree ferns and pulled one of the loose cushions into her lap, thumping it with her fist as she wished she could do to Nick. "Especially if you've been as dreadful to her all along as you've been in my hearing. *Mordieu,* the way you snarled at her when she said you'd saved her! It's a wonder she didn't faint right then."

"I didn't snarl at her," he grumbled, fresh remorse sweeping over him. "I was ruddy furious with myself. If I'd half a brain, I would have insisted she go below before we'd even come into firing range. That's what I meant."

"Well, it certainly didn't sound that way." She looked at him curiously. "Just as I can't believe I've now heard you admit you were wrong. The first time I can recall, isn't it? Are you truly my bullheaded brother Nickerson, or has some otherworldly spirit carried you off and replaced you with another?"

Immediately he thought of Lily, and equally quickly thrust her from his thoughts. "Bloody amusing, you are," he said. "How is Michel able to survive each day without laughing himself silly?"

"He contrives to manage." She pushed a hairpin back in place. "Miss Everard's not at all what I expected from the note you sent with your man, you know. 'An English lady, taken with a prize and held now for ransom.' You can imagine what I thought."

The indignation in her voice came as permission for Nick to smile with relief. She wouldn't have let it show if Rose had been in real danger. "What, you thought I'd burden you with some ancient old dragon of a dowager, some sainted daughter of old Albion?"

"Of course not. It may have been over more than a year since you last showed your face here, Nick, but I doubted you've changed that much." She leaned back on the bench, crossing her ankles and hugging the pillow to her chest. She was past thirty now, the mother of four children, but Nick was willing to wager she still turned as many heads as when she'd been a belle in Newport. "I knew the lady would be young and beautiful, or at least agreeable, or else you would have left her with your agent in Charles Town instead of bringing her this much farther."

"Rose is all three, young, beautiful and infinitely agreeable," he said as he came to sit beside her on the bench. "Besides, she likes to wager. So what about her surprises you?"

"I didn't expect that she'd be in love with you," she said softly. "Not that you're unlovable—*mordieu,* other women have always found my wretched brothers irresistible—but this one, this girl, is different. It's writ in her eyes, plain as day, and she's miserable because she can't help it. She loves you, Nick."

"I don't believe it," he said flatly, even as his heart quickened with irrational longing. It was foolish, wrong, hopeless, but still he hoped. Could this be, then, what she'd been trying to tell him earlier? "She's bound to wed another man, an English officer with the fleet on St. Lucia, and even though she scarcely knows the bastard, she still hasn't changed her mind. How could she be in love with me?''

"Because she is, *stupide!*" said Jerusa with exasperation. "And even more appalling was realizing that you love her in return."

"Hell, Rusa, now you're just plain talking nonsense," he declared, stunned. Oh, he desired Rose, and he cared for her, and he liked her a great deal, more, in fact, than any other woman he could remember, but he wasn't in love with her. Damnation, no. "I've never been in love with anyone, not that I can help."

"You are now," said Jerusa serenely. "I suppose with this girl you couldn't help it, and about time, too."

Nick drew himself up with as much dignity as he could. "And I tell you it hasn't happened yet. Besides, even if I wished to, I wouldn't know how to begin."

"You don't have to *know* anything," she scoffed. "You feel, you dream, you sigh, you love. *Quelle bêtise!*"

"Stop insulting me in French," he ordered crossly. "You're still a Newport lass, for all that you tied yourself to that Frenchman."

"You'll recall I was promised to marry another man, too, before Michel stole me away." She sighed fondly, remembering. "Just as you've done to Miss Everard."

"It's not like that at all, Jerusa." But it was, and he wondered why he'd never thought of the similarities before. Michel Géricault had kidnapped his sister right out from under her priggish bridegroom's nose, and though Michel had taken her for complicated reasons of revenge, not ransom, he had brought her here to Martinique for safekeeping—just as Nick himself was doing with Rose.

But there the likeness would end, for he hadn't fallen in love with Rose the way Michel had with Jerusa, and he most certainly wasn't going to marry her in place of Lord Eliot, any more than Rose expected him to.

Jerusa smiled sadly. "It's only been eight years—you see how tall Alexandre and Louisa have grown!—yet it seems an eternity when I think of how much has changed since then." She hugged the pillow more tightly and looked up to him. She didn't need to say more; they were both the age that had suffered most from the war, and both had lost too many friends to the fighting. "Has Newport truly changed as much as they say? A friend of Michel's swore I wouldn't recognize it."

"You wouldn't," said Nick, the grim images rising fresh again before his eyes. "More than half the houses are burned or abandoned, the wharves deserted and shops shuttered, even the trees in the churchyards cut down by the Hessians for firewood."

"And our house?"

He leaned forward, his shoulders sagging beneath the weight of what he'd seen. "Our house still stands, aye, because the British officers claimed it for their own, and everything in it besides. What they didn't destroy they shipped back to their own firesides in Britain, the devil take their black, thieving souls. The porcelain and the plates and every stick of furniture, down to the brasses from the front door. Even Mama's roses are gone, torn up by the roots to feed their nags."

When he'd returned at last, he hadn't known the British had taken the town. He'd meant to play the prodigal, come home with a ship of his own and gold in his pocket to toss in his father's face, but the town and the family of his boyhood had been swallowed by the war and lost forever.

"What of Mama and Father?" asked Jerusa anxiously. "You saw them, didn't you?"

"Aye," said Nick heavily, the old antagonisms flaring again. "They fled through Middletown to Providence even as the British were landing in Newport, and all they could take was what they could carry. I swear they live on their pride now, in a mean little house with smoking fireplaces that must break Mama's heart. Yet when I offered to help, Father nigh tossed me into the street. Damnation, Jerusa, you know how he is."

"He's exactly like you," she said unhappily. "In how you look, how you act, even your temper and your stubbornness, you've always been alike."

Nick shook his head. "Nay, Rusa, you're wrong. It's always been Jon who's his favorite. Jon was the one who never erred, who always had the best that Father could offer."

"But you're the one he's most proud of," she insisted, leaning forward to loop her arm through his, "the one he'll praise to strangers in taverns, bragging of where you've sailed and what you've seen, even of how many years you managed to stay away and keep out from under his thumb."

"I don't believe it, Jerusa," he said, shaking his head. "Not Father. I don't believe it at all."

"Just the way you don't believe that Rose Everard loves you, either," she said sadly. "You've always done this to yourself, Nick. Whenever you fear you've cared too much, that you've let too much of yourself fall over the balance, you run away to keep from risking more. You've done it to Father and Mama, disappearing clear to the other side of the world, and to me, too, as if a year meant no more than a day. And now, *mon cher frère,* you're doing it to Rose."

But the sound Nick heard as he began to defend himself was wrong for a garden, sharp and repetitious, and swiftly he looked for its source. Lily was clapping her hands, applauding, as she sat in the child's swing that hung from the gnarled mahogany tree.

"Your sister is a wonder, my dear Nickerson," she said, swaying gently so her skirts floated over the grass. "In these short minutes she has been able to answer, oh, so many questions that have plagued me!"

"Why are you still here?" he demanded hoarsely, rising to his feet. Damnation, he'd done everything she could want, yet here she was again as if nothing at all had changed. Unless she never truly meant to leave him; unless he'd be cursed by her until he, too, was dead. "What happened to the promise that you'd be gone?"

"Nick?" asked Jerusa uneasily, coming to her feet beside him. "Nick, what is it?"

He closed his eyes and shook his head, realizing too late that he'd spoken aloud.

"Your sister seems both wise and intelligent, Nick," said Lily. "You could always tell her about me, the way you did with Rose."

He didn't answer beyond swearing under his breath, afraid to betray himself any more. His gaze swept across the walled garden, desperate to create some explanation that Jerusa would accept.

Jerusa was following his gaze, looking herself for an explanation. "Nick, is there something wrong?" she asked anxiously. "Michel is always warning me that I'm too careless of my safety, and if there's something amiss—*mordieu,* I must go to the children!"

"Nay, Jerusa, stay," he said, catching her arm before she ran into the house. "It's nothing, I swear. The children are fine."

Lily laughed. "I can make a real row if that will be easier to explain." She lifted her hand with a flourish and from somewhere in the house came a loud crash of breaking pottery.

Again Jerusa tried to pull away toward the house, and again Nick held her. "You're being skittish now, Rusa," he said softly as he glared over her head at Lily on the swing. "I told you there was nothing to fear, and there isn't. With your lively litter of brats, I'd wager something breaks once a day."

"Twice a day. And they're not brats, Nick, not really." She sighed and relaxed. "But what did you mean about the promise? What promise?"

"That blasted white bird over there." He pointed to the ancient molting parrot in a wire cage that hung from one of the trees. "Bit me last time I was here, and you swore to get rid of it by the time I returned."

"Oh, Père Blanc." Jerusa laughed. "I know I promised, but the horrid old thing is Aimée's pet, and for her sake I can't serve him the way he deserves. This time keep your fingers from his cage."

She patted his shoulder. "But I truly must go see what's been destroyed now. We dine at nine. Michel is looking forward to your news, I know. I'm glad you're here, Nick, alive and well. And I'm glad that the only ghosts you're seeing are unpleasant old parrots."

He laughed with her, albeit a bit uneasily, and stayed behind in the garden. She was barely through the door when he wheeled around to face Lily.

"That was a splendid recovery," she said merrily, kicking herself back in the swing so her wings nearly brushed the grass. "Fancy confusing *me* with a parrot!"

"What I fancy, Lily, is for you to be gone," said Nick, his temper rising. "You said you would leave once I'd improved myself, and blast and hell, I have. I've behaved as honorably with Rose as a mortal man could. I've brought her here to St. Pierre with her maidenhead intact, and she's Eliot's whenever he wants her. How much more honorable can I be? You heard my sister. I'm so blessed good now she thinks I'm a changeling. What more proof do you need?''

''I had considered you done,'' she confessed. ''Truly. You *are* vastly improved, there's no doubt of that. But then you began speaking of love and Rose in the same breath, and I simply had to return to ask your intentions. Which are, my dear Nickerson, exactly what?''

''Hell, not you, too.'' He shook his head with disgust. ''You wish to know my intentions, so here they are. I intend to leave *your* sister here in *my* sister's safekeeping, and wash my hands of whatever mischief they choose to find between themselves. I intend to bid Rose farewell, and wish her happiness in her marriage. I intend to sail in the morning, most likely back to the Carolina coast. I intend, in short, to return to my life as it was before you blundered into it.''

Frowning, Lily stopped the swing and clicked her tongue. ''Oh dear, Nick, that wasn't the answer I'd hoped for,'' she said with a sigh. ''I suppose we're not through with each other after all.''

''Damnation, Lily, *I'm* through! Doesn't that account for anything?''

''No, my dear captain, I fear it doesn't,'' she said sweetly. ''You'd do well to consider what your sister has told you, and mind you keep your fingers from the parrot's cage. He looks nearly as choleric at present as you do yourself.''

* * *

Slowly Nick climbed the stairs to his bedchamber, the light from the candlestick in his hand dancing shadows across the walls. Elsewhere in the house a clock chimed the hour, three deep, echoing *bongs*. Lord, had he really lingered that long with Michel?

His brother-in-law was excellent company, gracious and witty, as devoted a host as he was a husband and father. But beyond that, Nick wasn't certain exactly what Michel did. He went to no office, had no visible partners or associates, and while, according to Jerusa, he occasionally disappeared for days at a stretch with little warning, to the world he appeared to be no more than a charming gentleman of leisure and independent means.

But Nick wasn't fooled. Once Jerusa had left them, their talk had inevitably turned to the war. No idle gentleman could know as much as Michel did about the French and English naval forces gathered in the Caribbean or their leaders' strengths and weaknesses. Nick had listened carefully, storing away the information he could use and volunteering what he'd heard and learned in Charles Town, and though Michel had merely smiled and refilled their glasses, Nick was quite sure everything he said would be put to good use for the American—and of course the French—cause.

Yet as engrossing as their conversation had been, part of Nick's thoughts had continued to worry and tug at the idea that Jerusa had planted. He'd always thought he was immune to love, the way he was to smallpox, yet the more he thought about his feelings for Rose, the more he began to doubt. As he'd freely admitted to Jerusa, Rose was young, beautiful and agreeable.

But what he felt for her went a great deal beyond that, and the more he began to consider saying goodbye to her forever as he'd vowed, the more he realized he couldn't. Life without her in it had somehow become unimaginable, while the notion of blithely sending her off to marry a man who didn't care a whit for her had become the cruelest torture he'd ever conceive. Damnation, he couldn't let her do it.

But what followed was even worse: if he really did love Rose, then what the devil was he going to do about it?

Gently he turned the latch to his chamber door, careful not to wake the rest of the family. Lord knows they wouldn't return the same courtesy to him. If he didn't lock his door tonight, he'd have all four children bounding gleefully across his bed at daybreak, and likely the infernal dogs in the bargain. Love alone seemed terrifying enough to contemplate; how any sane man agreed to fatherhood was still far, far beyond him.

He set the candlestick on the chest of drawers and began to undress. The night was still warm, as it always was in St. Pierre, and the tall window overlooking the bay had been left unshuttered, open to the night breezes. Among the ships moored in the harbor, he could easily make out the sleek, elegant lines of the *Angel Lily* at anchor, and he smiled wryly to himself.

Whether Lily had brought the ship into his path or it had been fate alone, he was glad, infinitely glad, that things had happened as they had.

He pulled his shirt over his head, tossed it onto the chair with the rest of his clothes and snuffed out the candle's wick. Shrouded with gauze hangings against mosquitoes, the bed loomed ghostly pale, and with a yawn he shoved his way inside, grabbing a fistful of the coverlet to pull it back.

"Here you are at last," said Rose. "Faith, Nick, I thought you'd never come."

Chapter Fourteen

She had, once again, left him utterly speechless.

She had propped the pillows up against the headboard so that she was sitting as much as lying against them. Her hair was loose and full over her shoulders, her eyes shining silver, and she was wearing—dear Lord, what was she wearing?

"You shouldn't be here, Rose," he said as soon as he could force his mouth and brain to work together.

"I know that," she agreed promptly. "You shouldn't be here, and neither should I. We should both be back at sea, safe in your cabin on board the *Angel Lily*."

"Rose," he began, his voice strained, "Rose, that is not what I meant."

"Well, it's what *I* meant. The *Angel Lily*'s where we should be, but if we must end up somewhere else, this seems as pleasant a spot as any. Likely more comfortable, too, for there's no doubt your bunk was made for only one, while this bed—well, Martinique *is* French, so I suppose there's not a chaste, narrow bedstead on the whole island."

She shifted on the pillows so she could reach out with the hand of her uninjured arm to pat the sheets beside her. "Please, Nick. I vow I can't begin to guess what you and Monsieur Géricault found to rattle on about until now. Since I slept all afternoon long, I've been lying here awake forever waiting. And, of course, thinking of you."

She smiled, and by the silvery light of the moon slanting through the open window he saw the innocent eagerness that lit her eyes. So innocent, he thought, thoroughly wretched, his insides twisting with the desire to claim that innocence and make it his own. He still clutched the bunched coverlet in his hand, gratefully holding it to cover the most salient part of his naked male anatomy. The devil knows she wouldn't be prattling on so merrily herself if he hadn't. More likely she'd have run back screaming to her own bed.

"Rose," he said, his heated blood racing in his ears. "Rose, what in God's name are you wearing?"

"More than you, I'd say." She looked at him with such open, unfeigned admiration that he felt it as vividly as if her little hand had actually touched him. "You are a beautiful man, Nick."

"Not as beautiful as you, sweetheart."

Her grin turned into a shy smile as she awkwardly climbed up to her knees on the bed. "I wanted to wear the necklaces again since that had pleased you so before, but because of the way your sister tied the bandage around my hand, I couldn't work the clasps. And of course I couldn't very well ask the maidservant to help me dress like that. Can you fancy the look on her face, and on your sister's, too, when the girl told her? No.''

''No,'' he agreed. But he could imagine all too well how Rose would look, draped again in gold and pearls, and he shifted the coverlet in his hand a bit higher. ''You couldn't.''

''No, indeed. But then I found this in my trunk, directly on the top of my other things, where I'd no notion to expect it.''

She looked down at the gown she wore, her expression still faintly surprised at finding it on her body. Nick could understand that surprise. His own reaction was something close to shock.

The gown was some dark-colored silk, gleaming dully in the half-light as it slipped and fell over the soft curves of the body beneath. The bodice was cut without sleeves and so deep and low that only a handful of bows, fragile, straining little bits of ribbon, kept it clinging to her breasts at all. Through the fabric her nipples already showed hard as little pebbles, silently begging for his touch as his own rigid body ached in sympathy, and when she shifted her kneeling legs apart to find her balance on the yielding feather bed, the fabric pulled across her open thighs and dipped into the shadowy valley in between, and he barely held back a groan of frustration.

With artless pleasure, she slid her hand along the silk, unaware of how the simple gesture smoothed the fabric more provocatively over her hips. ''I found this among Lily's wedding clothes while I was deciding which to have remade for myself, but I thought I'd put it aside to leave behind as too wanton. One of the maids at home must have packed it anyway—there's no other explanation.''

Oh, yes, there was, thought Nick. What the hell was Lily plotting *now?* Honor and goodness were one thing, but was he supposed to become a candidate for sainthood and resist temptation like this? He would try, but he wasn't going to try with much enthusiasm.

''Be glad it wasn't left behind.'' He was, anyway. ''Your bridegroom will like it better than all your other wedding clothes combined.''

''Really?'' Her face lit happily. ''Then you like it, too?''

''Oh, aye, I like it,'' he said, his voice deep and hoarse, his gaze roaming over and enjoying what his hands didn't dare. ''I like it just fine. Unless he's dead—long dead, and buried, too—I'll wager Lord Eliot will as well.''

She ducked her chin, tucking her hair behind one ear. ''He won't because he's not going to see it.''

He hadn't expected the swift rush of happiness that particular news brought him. ''He'll be disappointed to know that.''

''No, he won't, because I'm not going to tell him.'' Without lifting her chin, she looked up at him, her smile tight. ''I'm not going to marry him, either.''

His happiness swelled into cautiously unbridled joy. "What happened to not dishonoring your father and shaming Lily's memory?"

She sighed, and sank back down to sit on her heels. "Papa will be furious. There's no overlooking that. He said he'd disown me if I disobeyed his wishes, and he very well might. If he does, I suppose I'll live with Aunt Lucretia, or find a position as a governess. And as for shaming Lily's memory—as soon as I saw this gown again, and thought of how much she was anticipating her marriage, I knew the real shame to her memory would be to wed without love."

She looked up at him then, her eyes bright with unshed tears. "You can't know how much I've changed, Nick," she said softly. "You've changed me. After all that I've done with you, I could no more become Lady Eliot, smiling docilely and pouring tea for the other officers' wives, than I could sprout wings and fly. You've made me different, Nick, and I wish—that is, I believe—oh, I practiced this over and over, and now it's coming out all wrong."

"No, it's not." He reached out to curve the hair more neatly around her ear, letting his fingers drift across her cheek. "It's not at all."

But Rose shook her head, determined to finish, and squeezed her eyes shut so she wouldn't be distracted. "I know you mean to sail tomorrow because I overheard your sister tell the children, and I know I'll be left behind," she said, her voice breathy and sad. "I don't know how long you'll remember me, Nick, or if you'll recall me as no more than that silly, undersize English virgin who won twenty pistoles from you playing draughts. I've heard how cavalier you seamen are. Maybe as soon as you sail from the harbor you'll forget I ever crossed your life. But I'll always remember you, Nick, *always,* as long as I live."

"Oh, Rosie," he murmured, reaching for her even as she eased herself away. "How you could ever believe—"

"I'm not quite done, Nick." She lifted her chin and opened her eyes steadfastly to meet his gaze. With the heel of her unbound hand she rubbed away the glaze of tears from her cheek, then lightly touched her fingers to his lips, begging his silence another few moments longer.

"That is why, you see, I'm here now," she said. "If I don't marry Lord Eliot, Papa will most likely reclaim my dowry, and without it I may never find anyone else to take me as a wife. I could bear that if I knew—if I knew the rest. I'm greedy and selfish, I know, but if all I'm to have for comfort are memories, then I want them to be grand enough to last my whole life."

She'd said too much, she thought with despair. The shadows masked his eyes and his feelings with them, but she knew, she *knew,* she had asked too much. She pulled her hand away, rubbing her bare arm instead.

"Ah, sweetheart," he said at last. "You know it doesn't have to be like that."

"How else could it be?" She tried to smile and couldn't. She'd rehearsed her speech this far, over and over as she had lain alone in the dark, but she'd never figured out what would come next. "I'm not so very clever now, am I? But I wish you'd treat me like you did at Cassie Morton's house. I wish that you'd touch me, and kiss me, and make me feel like that again, one last time. One time, that is all."

"Rosie, Rosie, what you ask," he said hoarsely. "As if one time with you would ever be enough."

This time when he reached for her she met him, his arm circling her shoulders to draw her across the bed to him. Kneeling as she was on the bed raised her to his height, and he slid his fingers into her hair to cup her head, pulling her mouth to his. Tonight she wouldn't wait for coaxing or gentle wooing, and at once she opened her lips to his, hungrily tasting him. She was greedy, greedy for him, and he knew it, grinding his mouth against hers with the same raw urgency that inflamed their kiss to a fever pitch in an instant.

She looped her arms around his shoulders, and he answered by fitting his hands around her waist, his fingers sliding restlessly across the slippery fabric to find the softer, fuller flesh below, kneading and lifting her hips against his. She broke away and gasped, instinctively moving her right hand lower along his back. His skin was smooth and hot beneath her fingers, and she reveled in the feel of him, the play of hard muscles and rough hair and the pounding of his heartbeat.

He was pulling at the ribbons on her gown, hooking his fingers into the bows one by one until they gave way, freeing her breasts to welcome his touch. He filled his palm with her softness, rubbing his callused thumb against the sensitive peak as the untied silken ribbons fluttered and teased against her skin. She moaned and arched against his hand, and then, as he lowered his lips to taste her, against his mouth, his tongue a gentle, flicking whip to urge her onward.

"Your arm," he gasped. "I don't want to hurt you."

She shook her head, too light-headed with passion to answer, as carefully, so carefully, he eased the thin straps of her gown down over her shoulders to puddle at her waist. She rubbed her breasts against his chest, shameless in her need to touch him, and kissed him again, melting into the heat of his mouth.

He was pulling up the hem of her gown and she shifted her legs to help him, the silk sliding across her skin another caress. She trembled with anticipation as his fingers traveled along the softest skin of her inner thigh, slowly tracing their way through the passion-damp curls to find the sweetest place of her desire.

She shuddered when he touched her there, clinging to him for support even as she blossomed and opened to him. This was what she remembered, this was what she wanted. Gently he stroked her, the same delicious torment from before, but this time he didn't stop, her body coiling and tensing tighter and tighter until she cried out his name as at last release came, and with it a sweet, delirious joy that left her panting and weak against him.

She was only half-conscious of him spreading her legs wider, lifting her, touching her again, and then the sudden shock of him thrusting deep within her body. She stiffened, the first pleasure gone before the sharp pain and the unfamiliar sensation of him within her.

Damnation, he'd hurt her. He had meant to go slowly, to be patient, but his body had wanted her too long. Even now she was so hot and tight around him that he could scarcely hold himself still.

"Rosie, sweet Rosie," he whispered hoarsely as he eased her onto her back, still sheathed within her. "Look at me, sweetheart."

Slowly she obeyed, her breath shallow and panting with confusion. Her eyes were heavy-lidded, her lips swollen and red from his kisses, her hair a tangled, fragrant cloud against the sheet. She curled her legs higher across his back and exhaled with a shuddering sigh, and he swore as he struggled to control himself. No other man would ever possess her like this; she was his, only his, and the realization fired his need even hotter.

"Rosie, I'm sorry," he gasped. "I—damnation, I can't. *Rose.*"

He kissed her again, hard, as he began to move within her. Somehow it didn't hurt as much now, her body stretching to take him, and tentatively she began to move with him. He groaned her name, driving in deeper, and she arched to match his rhythm. She hadn't expected to find the same pleasure, not now, but as she moved against him she began to feel it building again, more slowly but stronger, too.

"Please, Nick, oh, please," she begged, the words drawn out of her in a single long breath. "Oh, please don't stop!"

The pain forgotten now, she gave herself to their union, and when he slipped his hand between them to touch her where their bodies were joined, she cried out again as the waves of joy swept over her, over them both, carrying them together in its reckless path.

Shuddering and gasping, he kissed her again, brushing back the tangled hair that clung damply to her forehead. "I love you, Rose," he whispered raggedly against her cheek. "I love you."

Her eyes widened with wonder. "Oh, my," she whispered. "Oh, my, I never dared to dream...."

"You don't have to dream," he said with a tenderness he'd unknowingly been saving for a lifetime, just for her. "It's real."

"If you say so, Captain, then so it must be." She reached up to touch his face and laughed softly in delight. "I love you, too, Nickerson Sparhawk. I love *you,* mind?"

But he could only smile his joy, and hold her all the more tightly. So he had found love after all. The secret had been finding Rose.

And Lily, bless her white-feathered wings, had left him alone to do it.

* * *

"I trust your night was peaceful, brother dear?" asked Jerusa blandly as Nick joined her and Michel for breakfast. "Landlocked we may be, but I should think that every once and again you'd enjoy a bed that didn't plunge about beneath you."

"To tell the truth, it makes little difference at all," said Nick as he sat at the table. Instantly a maid set a plate filled with fried eggs and ham before him, and he smiled with anticipation. Lord knows this morning he was entitled to a lion's appetite. "I believe I can sleep anywhere."

"*When* you sleep," said Jerusa archly.

"Now what the hell is that supposed to mean?" Nick slapped down his fork with a clatter. He'd been careful to guard the hall this morning for Rose before she'd scurried back to her own room to wash and dress, just as he'd come down now before her to stave off the questions.

Jerusa shrugged elaborately, reaching for another roll. "The children reported that when they tried to come say good-morning, you wouldn't answer, though they were sure they heard you laughing in your bed. Quite put out, they were."

"I don't see what that's—"

"*Then,*" continued Jerusa, refusing to be interrupted, "then I had a tray sent up with tea for Miss Everard to spare her the trial of coming down for breakfast, only to have the maid tell me her bed was quite empty and cold, while your door, my dear brother, was still shut and locked against the world."

Nick snorted and picked up his fork again to attack his eggs. "No proof of anything at all, except that you're still as inquisitive and impertinent as you've always been."

"There now, *ma chérie,* I told you he would not be amused," said Michel indulgently, lolling back in his chair with his fingers arched together in a little tent before him. He wore a striped dressing gown over his shirt and breeches, his gold blond hair already perfectly tied back in a silk bow. "You cannot treat Nickerson like one of your little children. What he does behind his locked door is his own affair."

"At least it should be." Jerusa frowned as she buttered her roll, her teasing abruptly changed to concern. "You will tell him, won't you, Michel?"

"How can I not?" With a sigh Michel leaned forward across the table, his expression abruptly losing its indolent charm. "You have put your hand in a nest of vipers, *mon ami.* I have learned all this only this morning, from the letter of a, ah, friend. Did you not know that Miss Everard is betrothed to an officer in King George's navy, Captain Lord Eliot Graham?"

"Oh, aye, I knew," said Nick, his mouth full of egg. "She told me herself when I made her my prisoner."

"Then you would have been wise to listen," said Michel seriously. "The man is not pleased by what you've done. *Non, non.* Not only has he forbidden the ransom to be paid for her release, but he has also sworn to rescue her and capture you, not as a privateer, but as a pirate, and see you hung accordingly.''

"He can bluster all he wants," said Nick with the same supreme self-confidence that always served him so well in battles. "I have Rosie."

Impatiently Michel tapped his fingers on the table-cloth. "But you don't understand, *mon frère.* This man Graham—ah, *bonjour, mademoiselle!* I trust your health is much improved?''

At once Nick was at Rose's side, his arm protectively around her shoulder. He had never seen her look more radiantly lovely, dressed in a cream-colored gown embroidered with pink flowers and more flowers, real ones, tucked into her hair. Her cheeks glowed with happiness, and her eyes were bright with love for him alone.

God in heaven, *love,* love for him. No wonder he couldn't help smiling like a fool as he bent to kiss her lightly on the forehead.

But while he was oblivious to the others in the room, Rose was not, her cheeks now pink with discomfiture as well as pleasure. Nick's sister had been very kind to her, but how would she feel when she realized Rose's new relationship to Nick, begun under her own roof? Especially when they'd been discussing Lord Eliot, the man to whom she was still betrothed. Oh, what they must think of her!

With her fingers still twined in Nick's, she made a little curtsy of acknowledgment to Michel. "I am quite fine, thank you, *monsieur,*" she said carefully. "But pray continue what you were saying. I believe you were speaking of Lord Eliot."

"It was nothing, *mademoiselle,*" said Michel, sweeping his hand gallantly to welcome her to the table. "The gossip of men, eh?"

"If it pertains to Lord Eliot," said Rose, "then I would like to hear it." Michel could try to charm it all away, but she wasn't going to let him. He would have told her outright if it truly had been nothing but gossip.

Nick could feel her uneasiness, and he drew her closer. "She's right, Michel," he said. "If it has to do with Graham, then she—nay, we both should hear it."

Michel looked from Rose to Nick and back again, his fingertips drumming faster, and then once to Jerusa, who nodded. It was the look on his sister's face that put Nick on his guard that what was coming might be very bad indeed.

"Very well, *mademoiselle,* if you insist," said Michel, making it clear enough that he'd no wish of his own to speak. "Your fiancé has not taken the news of your capture well. He has sworn to save you from Captain Sparhawk, and hang him for a pirate."

Rose gasped, horrified. Less than an hour ago she had still been lying blissful and contented in Nick's arms, her happiness so complete she would have sworn nothing could disturb it.

"But Lord Eliot can't do that!" she cried. "Nick is a privateer, sailing for his country with all the proper papers! Lord Eliot has absolutely no grounds for—for wishing to hang him. My God, *hang* him!"

"Hush, love, hush," said Nick gently, holding her close. "He hasn't strung the rope over the yardarm just yet. He'll have to catch me before he can do anything. The Caribbean is a grand place for hiding, Rose, and I'd like to see the frigate fast enough to catch the *Angel Lily*."

"Not just one frigate, Nick," said Michel. "Four. Because of Graham's influence, and because soon the English fleet will leave these waters for the hurricane season, the admiral has granted leave to Graham plus three other captains to hunt you down. By stealing away this lady, you have become a great, bloodthirsty villain in their eyes."

"But Lord Eliot has no right to do that!" Desperately Rose clung to Nick, wishing there was something, anything she could do to keep him from suffering on her account. "I don't want to be rescued. I want to stay here, and so I shall. He can't recapture me if I don't wish to be retaken, any more than I wish any longer to marry him!"

Michel's drumming fingers stopped, his face turning dark with concern. "But you haven't told him your decision, *mademoiselle?*"

"Of course not," said Rose promptly, though her face grew warm again. "I only decided for certain last night. It's impossible now for me to marry Lord Eliot. I love Nick, and he loves me." Too much was at stake for her to be shy about admitting it now.

Again the looks shot back between husband and wife, silently saying more than words alone could express.

"*Ma chérie mademoiselle,*" said Michel gently. "I can sympathize with your new attachment to my wife's delightful brother, but you have perhaps acted more from your heart than your head. When the British learn you are here—which, *certainement,* they will, or may even know already—then those four fine frigates will come to crouch outside our harbor like lions on our doorstep."

"He wouldn't dare blockade St. Pierre," said Nick incredulously. "Not over this!"

"He would, and he will," said Michel. "There is nothing so dear to *l'Anglais* as his honor, and this man Graham feels his has been sorely mocked. No French or American vessels will be able to come or go from St. Pierre until you and the lady are given up to him. If we are not as prompt as he wishes, then he may choose to fire on our town. And as much as I cherish your friendship, Nickerson, I cannot allow that to happen."

"Blast and damnation, neither can I," thundered Nick. "I can clear the harbor within two hours. I'll take Rose along, too, and then those bloody English bastards will see what it means to chase me!"

"What, and play cat and mouse with him until eternity?" cried Rose, pulling free of his embrace. "How long before they catch you? A week, a month, as long as Christmas if you're monstrously lucky? Haven't you spent enough of your life running, Nick, to have it end like that, too?''

Running, always running. Her words echoed Jerusa's so closely that Nick almost stopped to think instead of shouting.

Almost, but not quite. "Hell, Rose, you heard Michel! There's no other way!''

"Oh, yes, there is, Nick,'' she said, her eyes flashing as she awkwardly tried to fold her arms before her breasts with her customary defiance. "I shall go immediately to St. Lucia—alone—and speak to Lord Eliot myself.''

"Non, ma chérie," protested Michel. "That is not what I intended at all.''

"Why not, when it is the obvious answer?'' she asked. "I shall tell Lord Eliot that any attachment between us is done, and that he must stop this foolishness at once. At once.''

Appalled, Nick stared at her. There was so much still unsaid between them, an entire future that she would put in jeopardy by this one impulsive act. "I can't let you do that. The danger of it, and your arm, and—and damnation, Rose, I love you! I love you, and I won't let you go!''

Though her jaw rose higher, he saw how her chin was trembling. "Yes, you will,'' she said. "I love you, too, Nick, but that gives you no more authority over me than Lord Eliot.''

"Don't be ridiculous, Rose!''

"I've never been more serious in my life," she said. But as she looked at him, her defiance crumpled, and she reached out to rest her hand on his arm, her worried gaze searching his face for understanding. "It's because I love you, because I wish you to be safe, I will go to St. Lucia."

"And for exactly the same reasons, sweetheart, I'm not about to let you go," he said, his anger tempered by the memory of the passionate lovemaking they'd so recently shared. He didn't want to quarrel with her now, and as stubborn as she could be, he refused to do it. "There's bound to be another way, and I'll be damned if I won't find it. And that, Rosie, is final."

He reached out to draw her back into his arms, and wearily she went to him, resting her head against the familiar hollow of his shoulder. She wished she could let him take care of everything. She wished they could go back to the big bed upstairs and kiss and talk and make love and sleep in each others' arms all through the hot summer day and night until they'd finally wake and find that all their problems had vanished like the morning mist.

But no matter what Nick promised, nothing was final.

And God help them both, especially not this.

It had seemed so obvious to Rose before, so rational, the only possible solution. And to her surprise, it had been appallingly easy as well.

Nick and Michel had left the house after breakfast, off to meet with friends of Michel's, and Jerusa had become so entangled in the usual chaos of her four children that no one had noticed when Rose had slipped down the back stairs and through the garden and hurried to the beach where the smaller fishermen's boats and island traders' sloops were drawn up on the sand. The first man she'd approached had agreed to take her across to St. Lucia that night; the distance was only twenty miles, the moon would be no more than a faint new crescent, and the gold guinea that Rose hesitantly offered was more money at one time than the man had seen in years.

The hard part came later, when she had to keep the guilty excitement from her face at the dinner table. She'd never been a particularly adept liar, and she'd blushed when she'd stood to excuse herself from the rest of the meal on account of a feigned headache. Nick's brow had instantly furrowed with concern, and it had taken all her willpower not to admit her falsehood. He had nearly carried her up the stairs to her room, and she had tried to smile as he'd tenderly kissed her good-night on the forehead, all the while knowing how angry and betrayed he would feel in the morning when he learned she was gone.

And how hurt. Lord, she knew she'd hurt him, but she was doing it all for his sake. She could only pray that by the time she returned, in a day at most, he'd be able to understand and forgive her. It was, truly, the only way.

But now that the Frenchman who'd brought her here to St. Lucia had vanished with her guinea, she wasn't as certain. How could she be? She was a woman alone, perilously alone, in the middle of the night in a makeshift town inhabited almost entirely by soldiers and sailors and prostitutes. Already she'd been accosted and propositioned by a group of sailors far too drunk to have acted on their offer, but she didn't want to wait to find others who could.

She took a deep breath and crossed the street to the tavern that the Frenchman had told her was the favorite of all the English officers. Unlike nearly every other place they'd passed on their way from the wharves, at least this tavern had no drunken men sprawled in the street before it, no raucous sounds of fistfights within or women shrieking from the open windows. The swinging signboard overhead was newly painted, bright with an elaborately gilded rampant lion that doubtless reflected the prices of the liquor served inside. If she'd find Lord Eliot anywhere on Pigeon Island, thought Rose, it would most likely be here.

Her heart pounding, she pushed open the door and stepped into a small, close hallway. The tavern's host, red-faced and sweating from the heat, sat on a tall stool near the stairs, his eyes narrowing as he studied Rose suspiciously by the light of the candle in the sconce behind him.

"Away with ye, ye hussy!" he said sharply. "We don't welcome your kind here. Begone now, and ply yer trade elsewhere."

"I am not a slattern," said Rose with a sharpness that matched his own. She drew herself as tall as she could and stepped more into the light of the candle. "I am Miss Rose Everard, the daughter of Sir Edmund Everard, and I have come to see Captain Lord Eliot Graham on most pressing business—private business—and I'll thank you to fetch him directly."

"Will ye, now." The man grunted, reconsidering her clothing and her accent. "We'll see what his lordship thinks, eh?"

He beckoned and she followed, down a narrow paneled hallway to a small back room. Though the windows were open, the air was so thick with tobacco smoke that Rose could barely make out the men clustered around the round card tables, with others leaning over to watch the game.

"Cap'n Lord Eliot," called the host. "Yer lordship, sir. This female says she's Miss Everard, an' wishes words wit' ye. Do ye know her, or should I toss her back into th' street that sired her?"

Every one of the men turned to stare, with boredom, irritation, curiosity or lust. They all seemed alike to Rose, these men with their powdered wigs and dark blue uniform coats with the gold braid. Not one of them looked familiar, not in the least, and she felt her panic rising by the second.

"Don't throw her back into the pond just yet, Weaver," drawled one of the men. "The dear little fish don't look big enough to swim on her own."

The other men jeered and laughed, pounding their open palms on the table, until one of them rose slowly to his feet, holding a tankard in his hand.

''Keep a civil tongue in your head now, Quinland,'' he said in a voice thick with liquor. ''My ravishin' bride's come at last.''

Chapter Fifteen

"A private room, Weaver," ordered Captain Lord Eliot Graham over the din of excited voices. "I wish to speak to my lady bride in private."

Rose stared as he came toward her, her mouth dry and her heart pounding. How had Lily ever loved a man like this? He was older than she'd thought, much older than any promising younger son had a right to be, with a full, florid face from too many late nights with too much rum and port. Although his uniform coat was expensively cut, all the tailoring in the world couldn't disguise the softness of his belly, bulging out against the white waistcoat. Tiny beads of sweat trickled from beneath the edges of his white-dusted wig, and he dabbed at his upper lip with the edge of a handkerchief bordered with lace.

"What I have to say to you will be brief, Lord Eliot," she said, striving to keep her voice from betraying her. "An hour of your time, that is all."

Unconsciously she was backing away from him, and he frowned, his chin turning slack above the tightly

·wound neckcloth. His pale eyes were small and close-set, his mouth wide with a smile that meant nothing. "An hour, my girl, when I've waited months?"

"I fear you've waited in vain, sir," she said quickly, "as my hour will explain."

The host, Weaver, bowed to Eliot. "Ye might have th' front room upstairs, if it please ye, my lord, seein' as ye do know the chit," he said with obvious reluctance. "But mind I run an honest house, my lord, with neither whores nor catamites, an' if she be not what she claims—"

"Oh, she's what she seems, all right, Weaver," said Eliot unpleasantly. "Cold and uncivil, a common little chit of a tradesman's daughter, complete with an overblown regard for her own maidenhead in direct proportion to her dowry. Hardly worth the six hundred pounds some fool clerk must have paid for her ransom for her to be here now. Six hundred pounds, I might add, that's ultimately come from my own pocket. Ain't that so, Miss Everard?"

Before Rose could defend herself, he had seized her by the arm and was yanking her from the room, away from the shouted encouragement and catcalls of the others.

"You are no gentleman," she cried, dragging her feet as she struggled to break free on the narrow staircase. "Not you, nor any of your fine brother officers! My father believed that by agreeing to this marriage he was improving our family, but I swear he would have done better to pluck a husband from a barnyard than—"

"That's enough," he said curtly, shaking her. "I don't air my dirty linen before publicans, and as my future wife, I advise you to do the same."

He threw open a battered door at the top of the stairs and Rose had a quick glimpse of a small room more meanly furnished than the public spaces below, with only a chair, a low bedstead, a washstand and a chamber pot.

"Here you are, Miss Everard." Then he shoved her inside first, so roughly that she stumbled across the uneven floorboards. Instinctively she reached out to catch herself on the chair, and as she did she struck her injured arm hard against the chair's slatted back. She gasped and sank to her knees, the pain so piercing that she feared she would faint.

"You are... *cruel*," she finally managed to whisper, dropping back onto her heels on the floor as she cradled her arm, the polished brass buckles of his shoes before her. "Unspeakably... vastly... *cruel*."

Miserably she thought of Nick, of how kind, how gentle he had been to her, how with him she had always felt cherished and protected.

"It won't be the worst you'll have, my girl," said Lord Eliot, unmoved, "unless you learn to hop right smart to my tune. What happened to your wing, eh? Stabbed with a dressmaker's sharp, or is that Sparhawk's doing, too?"

Carefully she pulled herself up into the chair. "It's a splinter wound, received when the vessel in which I was sailing was attacked," she said, hating him all the more for his callousness. "Not that it matters a fig to you."

"It does if you're damaged goods, unfit for breeding. Sparhawk should have taken better care of you than that to earn his six hundred pounds." He was sitting on the edge of the narrow bed, striving to strike a spark in the bowl of a stained clay pipe he'd drawn from his pocket. "When I agreed to this contemptible marriage, your father assured me there wasn't a smudge on you, and the old bastard better be telling the truth. Though what father thinks otherwise of his daughters, eh?"

He laughed at his own wit, a dry bark that gave Rose one more thing to despise. How, *how,* had Lily loved this dreadful man?

"Lord Eliot," she began, drawing the box with his ring from her pocket. "Lord Eliot. I shall not waste any more of your time than is necessary, and will come directly to my reason for being here."

"To marry me, you little fool," he said, amused, the pipestem clenched in his teeth. "I don't need you to tell me that."

"No, you don't, and no, I'm not going to marry you." She saw the startled look of alarm in his small eyes, and plunged ahead with her well-rehearsed speech. "Since my father made his arrangements with you, I have found my affections lie elsewhere, and that I cannot be the wife you deserve."

"Affections?" He laughed his scorn. "Do you truly believe I care if my wife loves me?"

She lifted her head sharply. "You did once. You loved my sister, and she loved you."

He turned his head to squint at her sideways through the haze of tobacco smoke. "Your beauteous tart of a sister would scarce let me touch her little finger," he said bitterly. "She agreed to wed me only because your father threatened her. I haven't a doubt she would have bolted and left me at the altar when the time came. Lily never loved me, not even my title, not for a moment."

"Then it was only for Papa's money that you asked for me," said Rose slowly, the truth making her head spin, "and not from love of Lily."

In one way she was glad that Lily hadn't loved him, but in another she felt her father's betrayal all the more keenly. Papa was too shrewd a man not to have recognized Lord Eliot for the kind of overbred fortune hunter that he was, but had Papa really been so eager for this union that he had lied to her about Lily even as he sealed her own fate in a loveless, scornful marriage? She bowed her head, her heart aching, and thought again of how endlessly fortunate she'd been to find Nick, her Nick, when she had.

"'Course it was for the money," said Lord Eliot flatly. "Whyever else would I do it? And it's a good thing you've come when you did, too. Even in this hellish place I've run desperate short."

"But Papa paid your debts," she said, bewildered. "He said it was hundreds and hundreds of guineas. How could you possibly need more?"

"A drop of water in the ocean, that was, considering how much the old miser must have with his bankers." His laugh was unpleasant. "But if you think I'll give my accounting to you, my girl, you're sadly wrong."

Oh, she was wrong, all right, thought Rose miserably, wrong from the moment she'd agreed to obey her father, wrong to have come here hoping to convince this man of anything. Two wrongs now she'd have to do her best to make right.

"Your father gives me the money," he was saying, "and I'll make you Lady Eliot before the parson. That's the sum of it, and always was."

"No, it's not," said Rose slowly, carefully, making sure he heard every word, "because I'm not going to marry you. Not now, not ever. And that, as you say, is the final sum of it. Good day, Lord Eliot, and I wish you joy of the next poor foolish woman you try to humbug."

She stood and hurled the box with his ring in his lap, and, with a final flick of her skirts, darted toward the door to escape. But for such a heavy man Eliot was surprisingly fast, lunging forward to block her path.

"It's Sparhawk himself, isn't it?" This close his words were stale with tobacco and bitter with hate, and his eyes glittered dangerously. "That bloody rebel pirate didn't just make you his prisoner, did he?"

"He didn't—"

"Don't deny it, you little slut, it's written broad all over your face. He may have had your maidenhead, the bastard, but I'll be damned if I'll let him steal your fortune from me, too!"

"Nick doesn't care about my father's money!" cried Rose. "He loves *me,* not my dowry!"

"So it's 'Nick,' is it?" he taunted. "If he values a shrewish little piece like you over your fortune then he's an even greater fool than I thought for letting you come here. Not that it matters, since he'll have neither you nor the money."

With aching clarity Rose remembered how Nick had told her not to come, and how yet she'd insisted. Why, why, hadn't she listened to him when she had the chance?

Swiftly her gaze swept the small room, searching for another way to escape, and stopped at the open window.

"I wouldn't advise it," said Eliot, guessing her intention but remaining close to the door. "How far would you get, I wonder, trying to climb down a sheer wall with one arm to support you?"

Rose's hands tightened into fists of frustration at her sides. "You can't make me marry you against my will," she said, panic making her voice shrill, "any more than you can make me your prisoner here!"

"You'll learn soon enough what I can make you do, my girl," he said, his smile chilling. "Before this next week is over, Miss Everard, you *will* be Lady Eliot. And as your wedding gift, the moment we are married I shall bring you the body of Black Nick Sparhawk."

* * *

The sun had nearly set on the following day when the hail came from the skipper of a small fishing boat, seeking permission in broken English to come alongside and aboard the *Angel Lily*. At once Nick himself was at the rail, ready verbally to tear the head off any fisherman who'd dare come hawking his wares today. But instead of some *Pierrotin du mer,* the man who climbed swiftly over the side was Michel Géricault, his handsome face unrecognizable beneath a carefully applied layer of grime and the rough fisherman's cap.

"We must talk, *mon ami,"* he said, glancing meaningfully at Gideon as he touched Nick's sleeve. "Your cabin, eh?"

But Nick shook his head, impatient with Michel's constant desire for secrecy. "There's nothing you can't say before Gideon. Damnation, Michel, don't keep me waiting! I've been sitting here idle the whole ruddy day! Where the devil is Rose?"

"Still on St. Lucia with Graham."

Nick swore and pounded his fist hard on the rail. "If that bastard's hurt her—"

"Miss Everard is unharmed," said Michel quickly, *"grâce à Dieu,* and as safe as the entire British fleet at Pigeon Island can keep her. But that is the problem. Though Graham has announced that they are still to wed, she is his prisoner, kept in a genteel lodging house and guarded by a party of women in his pay as well as by his men outside."

"Wedding, hell," said Nick furiously. "She went there to break the blessed match, not plan for it!"

"Vraiment," agreed Michel. "No one believes it to be a love match. The gossips are divided between those romantics who claim that Graham is so lovesick that he's loath to share his bride with the world before she is safely his wife, and the cynics who say that the bridegroom cannot afford to let her and her fortune stray from the reach of his creditors. But one thing is certain—the wedding is set for Tuesday evening."

"That's three days. We haven't a moment to lose." Nick's mind was already racing to make plans, relieved as he was at last to be actually able to *do* something on Rose's behalf. It would be the most difficult— and the most important—raid of his entire career, and he meant to leave as little to chance as he possibly could. "Will you lend me this fishing boat of yours, Michel?"

"Everything's squared away on board the *Lily,*" said Gideon eagerly. "There's not a man who isn't itching to take on the Britishers for Miss Everard's sake."

"Then let 'em scratch," said Nick grimly. "They signed on to fight for their country, not Miss Everard. Besides, do you think I'm daft enough to take the brig into their cove? They'd like nothing better than to blow us clear from the water."

Gideon shook his head. "You can't do this alone."

"I can, and I will," declared Nick. "I'll want you at hand off the coast, Gid, for when I have the lady with me, but I'm going into the town myself."

Michel frowned. "Very heroic, Nickerson, but also very dangerous, and not perhaps the wisest course, eh? Graham and his men will be expecting you to do this."

"They're expecting me with the *Angel Lily,* not by myself," said Nick confidently. "The English always make their own wars by the rules, and can't conceive of anyone else doing otherwise."

"Vrai," admitted Michel, "but you've already broken Graham's honorable rules by stealing his bride. There's nothing he'd prefer than to make good his threats to capture and to hang you. What good will you be to Mademoiselle Everard with your neck stretched as long as a gander's?"

"Then I'll make sure she won't have to find out."

"And she won't, not so long as I come with you." Michel's smile was charming, his manner the same as if he were politely insisting Nick take more brandy rather than what Nick suspected were his very considerable, very deadly skills as an undercover agent. "You will need someone to guide you into the harbor, to make the proper responses with the proper accent if challenged. You'll recall that St. Lucia is at heart still a French island, and only a captured bauble of the English for these past few months. If you wish, I shall swear to stay on the beach with the boat, but I cannot allow you to go otherwise."

Nick cocked one brow suspiciously. "Would my sister make life that wretched for you?"

Michel shrugged with resignation. "Let us say that I should not like to find out."

"Then come if you wish, Michel, but mind that I'm a lucky man, or I wouldn't have lasted as long as I have." He grinned wickedly. "Some swear the devil himself looks after me."

Only Nick heard the indignant squawk from Lily, somewhere above in the rigging, while the lines of concern on Michel's face deepened.

"I pray you're right, *mon frère,*" he said solemnly. "For however your help may come, you're going to need every last bit of it."

Stiff as a wooden doll, Rose stood balanced on the dressmaker's stool for the fitting, her arms slightly outstretched as she'd been bidden, while the woman and her two assistants fluttered in circles around her, plucking and smoothing the flounced hem of the cream silk lutestring gown for her wedding to absolute perfection.

"That is much, much better, Miss Everard," pronounced Mrs. Gawthrop from her chair with a finality that was unchallengeable. She was the rear admiral's wife, come to call at Lord Eliot's request, and Rose had quickly been made to understand that among the few other Englishwomen on the island, Mrs. Gawthrop expected to be treated with the same unquestioned deference that was accorded her husband. "Now you don't look so much like the ragpicker's daughter in borrowed clothes. You must have lost a stone at least on that voyage. You must do your best to put that flesh back, and soon. No gentleman wants to share his bed with a bag of bones, no matter how costly the bag.''

But Nick had liked her exactly as she was, thought Rose in silent rebellion, whether she was in coral silk or boy's breeches or even in only her mother's jewels, because he had loved *her,* just as she had loved every dear oversize inch of him, from his green eyes and black hair to his wicked grins and changeable moods to even the way he hated to lose at draughts. She loved it all and she missed it nearly as much. Yet her worst fear was that he would insist on coming after her himself, and unconsciously her shoulders drooped beneath the weight of her despair.

"No flopsy arms, missy," ordered the older woman sternly. "I won't venture to guess how you were raised, but if you're to be the wife of a lord *and* of the most promising captain in this station, you must learn to hold yourself as a lady of breeding."

Twice Mrs. Gawthrop nodded her powdered head, obviously satisfied with her own astuteness, and as she did the whalebone in her tightly laced stays creaked audibly. With all her "you must"'s the older woman was so much like Aunt Lucretia that any other time Rose would have laughed outright.

But not now. Now, Lord help her, she feared she'd never laugh again.

All day long she had waited and prayed and looked in vain for any chance to escape, a long, lonely, frightening day when the only people she'd seen were in Lord

Eliot's pay and beyond any cajoling or bribery. Even the gaunt-cheeked clergyman who was to marry them owed his living as chaplain on board the *Goliath* to Lord Eliot. He had ignored her pleas for help and instead merely counseled prayer for guidance to become a good wife. Her door was locked from without, her meals brought to her on a tray and in the garden below her window waited another guard to stop any escape.

An endless, exhausting day that had given her far too much time to remember the brief, idyllic hours she'd spent with Nick and to dread the future she could face with Lord Eliot. Though still she swore he could not force her to marry him, with each passing hour she saw the extent of his influence and power until she'd begun to doubt her own ability to deny him. Who would believe her if she did?

But she *would* get away. For Nick's sake and for the love they shared, she must.

"You shall learn to grace your role, Miss Everard," intoned Mrs. Gawthrop grandly. "You shall be like a prize jewel in your husband's crown of achievement, your every facet polished to make the whole shine all the more brightly."

Standing on the little stool, Rose could see through the open window, past the high palmetto trees that ringed the garden, to Gros Islet Bay and the fleet which was moored there. Beyond, a faint lump on the horizon, lay Diamond Rock and Martinique, not ten miles to the north. Martinique, and Nick, and the *Angel Lily,* all so close yet impossibly far. Yet again she cursed her own impetuous folly that had brought her here and away from him.

With an impatient sigh, she hopped down from the stool, ignoring the soft rush of objections from the dressmaker.

"You'll excuse me, Mrs. Gawthrop," she said tartly, her chin held high. "But I am weary, and wish to rest, so I shall wish you good-evening."

The older woman's eyes grew hooded with displeasure. "You can't dismiss *me,* you silly chit," she said sharply. Without looking away from Rose, she waved her hand at the dressmaker and her assistants. "Go now, all of you. I should like to speak to this *lady* alone."

The three women scurried from the room, barely pausing at the doorway to turn and curtsy before they fled.

"You may speak as you please, ma'am," said Rose, "but I'll not promise to listen."

"If you've any sense at all, you foolish jade, you will listen and listen well. When poor Eliot asked me to speak to you, I thought the gossip must have erred. How, I wondered, could so fine, so agreeable a gentleman be treated with such open disdain?"

"Because he is neither fine nor agreeable," shot back Rose. "He is a vile, cruel man who keeps me here against my will."

Mrs. Gawthrop sank back with her fingers arched over her breasts in a great show of shocked dismay. "So there it is, from your own lips," she said. "No wonder Eliot is so distraught! He has paid you the highest honor a gentleman can pay a lady, and you toss it back in his face!"

Stubbornly Rose folded her arms across her chest as best she could. "I do not care, because I do not love him, nor does he love me."

"Love!" The older woman practically spit the word with disdain. "How can you turn away from so favorable a match on account of *love?* The settlements have all been arranged and signed, the banns posted, the witnesses and guests are gathering from all over the Caribbean. Would you make a liar of your father as well as poor Lord Eliot and yourself all for some ridiculous poetical notion of *love?*"

With her unbandaged hand Rose began ripping away at the laces of the gown. "I'm not going to marry him, and nothing you say will convince me otherwise, for I do not love him and never shall."

"Flounce about all you wish, miss, but I vow you'll jig to a different tune tomorrow night, once you're Eliot's wife and he—"

"Tomorrow?" gasped Rose, horrified as she recalled the hideous wedding present he'd promised. "He said a week, not four days!"

"Tomorrow." Mrs. Gawthrop's thin-lipped mouth curled with triumph. "What greater compliment could your bridegroom offer? He cannot wait another day!"

And now, thought Rose fearfully, neither could she.

Chapter Sixteen

"I couldn't help coming, Nickerson," said Lily contritely as she glided along beside him over the dark, dusty paths that passed for streets on Pigeon Island. "'Tis my great weakness that I'm so tenderhearted. I know you have everything perfectly under control yourself, you and that lovely Monsieur Géricault, but when you left him with the boat and began to look so dreadfully forlorn by yourself I had no choice but to come comfort you."

"Forlorn, hell," said Nick crossly. "How the devil am I supposed to look?"

"I'd expected something more cheerful. You're going off to crack English skulls, a singular pleasure I thought you enjoyed beyond all others."

"I do," he said, shifting his shoulders uneasily beneath his coat. "It's just that—that, well, damnation, Lily, what if Rose doesn't want to be rescued? What if she came here meaning all along to stay, and marry her bloody lordling?"

"Oh, pish," scoffed Lily. "Now whyever would Rose do such a thing?"

"Nay, Lily, do I have to spell it out?" he demanded. "I love Rose, true enough, but how's that going to keep her happy the way a woman wants? I'm a wastrel and a wanderer on the losing side of a war with no end. My own parents will scarce receive me. I don't even have a home port to take her to, let alone a house with all the niceties she expects. What in blazes do I have to offer her, anyway?"

"Yourself, and your love," said Lily wistfully. "That's all Rose has ever wanted. You give her that much, and the rest will sort itself out."

He grumbled incoherently to himself, unconvinced. "Fat lot of good that does me now. Or her."

"But it will, as you know perfectly well in your heart already."

"Not that I've much choice." He sighed with resignation, halfway to a groan. "But that's what you've wanted from the beginning, wasn't it?"

"Of course, though I never meant to be so tediously obvious about it." Her smile was almost bittersweet. "But oh, Nick, you won't be needing me much longer, will you?"

He didn't answer until they'd passed a man and a woman drunkenly supporting one another down the street. Talking to himself wasn't the best way to make himself unobtrusive, even in the middle of the night.

"Don't desert me yet, Lily," he said at last. "Graham's not about to give Rose up without a fight."

"Ah, so now you wish my help," she said archly. "There was a time, my dear captain, when you swore you could save the entire world by yourself."

He snorted with disgust. "Would you like it better if I told you to go back to whatever black cloud you call home, and let me save your sister by myself?"

"Oh, be easy, please! I've no intention of abandoning you quite yet." She let her laughter fade, and her face grew more serious. "But before we begin, Nick, I would remind you again that I can do nothing on Rose's behalf. No matter what danger she tumbles into or mishap threatens her, I can only watch, helpless. *You* must be the one to save her."

"I'm doing my damned best, Lily," he said with weary patience. "That's all I can promise."

"Oh, my, my," she said softly. "Your best, dear captain, is more than I ever dared hope for."

Before the British had come, the town on the banks of Gros Islet Bay had been little more than a handful of buildings surrounding a sleepy, provincial harbor, and Nick had no trouble finding the lodging house with the green shutters that Michel had described.

The previous owner had been a French planter who'd fled farther inland when foreign warships had appeared in his bay, and the new occupant, a Mrs. Nason, had had the good taste to leave his elegant furnishings undisturbed. The widow of a captain recently dead from yellow fever, she also had the good sense to recognize the source of her personal largesse, and to cater to the whims and wishes of the officers with influence, both here and in London. Captain Lord Eliot Graham was one of these, and she'd been quick to find a solitary room for his future bride in the back of the house as he'd requested, away from the noise of the street and above the garden, where he'd thoughtfully placed an armed guard from his own ship so the lady—a pretty, quiet girl with sad eyes and a bandaged arm—could sleep in a strange bed without fear, her peace undisturbed.

This much, as well as a great deal of nervous giggling, Nick had heard from a young mulatto slave at the public pump in the street, where she'd been sent by her mistress for water. Now as he stood by the back gate of the garden, he could see that she'd been right about the guard, and hoped she had been as accurate about which room was Rose's. There were five windows overlooking the garden, all of them dark now that it was past midnight; Rose's, God willing, was the second from the end.

But first would come the guard. The man was a common sailor, clearly chosen for his fearsome size alone and not his abilities, for he sat on one of the garden's benches with his musket left forgotten on the nearby grass while he devoted all his energies to inspecting a hole in the sole of his shoe by the light of his lantern.

Nick glanced about for Lily, expecting her to be hovering about to watch the excitement, but to his surprise there was not the faintest wisp of her white gown. Well, he grumbled, so be it. He'd handled worse than this before on his own, and he would again. So why, then, did he almost miss the infernal, meddlesome creature?

Cursing himself for a fool, he drew from his coat a small bottle of rum he'd bought in a tavern and whistled sharply through the iron gate. Startled, the man leaped to his feet, grabbing the lantern in one hand and the musket in the other.

"Here now, who goes there?" he demanded, holding the lantern high as he peered into the shadows. "Come, show yourself, or be gone!"

Nick stepped before the gate and into the light, his hands raised to show he was unarmed except for the bottle in his hand. He grinned foolishly and swayed as if in the breeze, mimicking the drunkenness of nearly every man he'd seen since he'd landed. "John Stone, o' th' *Janus,* 44, Cap'n Henderson," he called, "an' I come as a friend, I swear by all that's good an' holy."

"Now why should I be believin' you, John Stone?" asked the man scornfully. But Nick noticed how he tipped the musket's barrel back against his shoulder, as sure a sign as any that he thought Nick was harmless. "What reason d'you have for swearin' anything at all to me?"

"Bein' one poor jack t' another, that's why." Nick thrust the bottle through the bars of the gate. "Th' whole ruddy fleet's makin' merry for your cap'n an' his lady, an' it don't seem fair for you to be left out of th' sport."

"Friggin' lot Cap'n Lord hisself cares," said the man as he took the offered bottle and lifted it to his nose to sniff. "Him an' them other gilded grandees, may they rot straight to hell. Do this be French brew, or Yankee?"

"French," said Nick, watching with satisfaction as the man tipped back the bottle and let the liquor pour down his throat. "Smuggled in this selfsame day from Martinico."

But the man didn't answer. The best he could do was slowly lower the bottle from his mouth, the last bit of the rum trickling untasted from his lips as he stared glassy-eyed at Nick, swaying, before he finally pitched forward to the grass. Michel had assured Nick that the mixture worked swiftly, and that anyone who drank it would be as if dead for at least six hours, but to be sure Nick waited a moment longer as the candle slipped from the lantern and its flame sizzled out on the dewheavy grass.

Then Nick was at the stone wall in an instant, effortlessly pulling himself up and over to land silently on the grass beside the unconscious guard. Swiftly he gagged the man with a rag, tied his wrists and ankles and dragged both him and the lantern deeper into the shadows, then he eased the musket into the ornamental pond in the center of the garden.

He lifted his hat long enough to drag his sleeve across his brow, and looked up at the house before him. To guard against thieves, the shutters of the first floor windows and doors were closed and locked for the night, but all five of the windows above, their sills part of the roof of the first floor piazza, were open to the breezes from the bay. With a final muttered prayer that he'd understood the slave girl's garbled, giggling French, Nick found a foothold in an espaliered rose tree, climbed to the roof of the piazza and, as quietly as he could, made his way along the roof to the window he hoped was Rose's. He slung one leg over the sill, drew his knife from the sheath behind his waist and slipped inside the darkened room.

"Rosie?" he called softly as his eyes grew accustomed to the shadows. "It's Nick, lass, and I've come for you."

Now he could make out the tall-posted bed, stripped of its heavy hangings for summer and left with only the ghostly gauze of the mosquito curtains. The coverlet was so neatly folded over the bedstead and pillows that clearly no one had slept here tonight, and this time, his disappointment keen, he cursed the slave girl's confusion.

He walked to the wardrobe and jerked open the tall doors, searching for clothes or any other sign that Rose had been in the room. Perhaps he had only missed her; perhaps she had been called to another room in the house, and would return soon. Perhaps—

The flying bundle of clipped velvet caught him hard in the chest as it hurtled into him, nearly knocking him off his feet as he staggered backward beneath the impact, his knife raised to defend himself.

"Oh, Nick, you came, you *came!*" gasped Rose in an ecstatic whisper as she tried to disentangle herself and miles of clipped velvet. "I didn't want you to—I even prayed you'd be sensible and stay in St. Pierre—but now that you're here I can't believe how happy I am to see you, and oh—oh, Nick, how I love you!"

She threw her good arm around his neck and kissed him, long enough and well enough that he briefly considered taking her directly to the bed on the other side of the room. The taste of her mouth, the sweet fragrance of her hair and skin, the soft, pliant feel of her in his arms—all things that were the more impossibly dear to him because he'd come so close to losing her.

"And I love you, too, Rosie." For a long, precious moment he buried his face in the dark silk of her hair before he forced himself to think of Graham and the danger they were in, and gently held her away.

"You're well, then, sweetheart?" he asked, searching her small face for any signs of ill treatment. "Graham hasn't hurt you?"

"He wouldn't dare," she said, her voice abruptly flat and joyless. "He wants my money too badly for that. And we must be quiet, too, for there's an odious old woman who sits in the hall outside my door to make sure I don't try to run away. But look, Nick."

Awkwardly she lifted up the lumpy velvet bundle she'd been holding when she'd thrown herself at him. "I've done the same thing as you did in Charles Town during the fire. I pulled down all the hangings from the bed and tied them together, and I was just going to wrap them around the window frame to climb out when you came.''

"You were going to climb from the window by yourself, swaddled in petticoats and with only one arm?" he asked as he imagined with horrifying clarity everything that could have gone wrong. "Didn't you know there was a guard with a musket below? And if you'd somehow gotten yourself over the wall to the street, what then? Where would you have turned in a town that's no more than a camp of drunken, randy sailors and marines?"

Her grin wavered uncertainly. "The guard, I know, often falls asleep on the bench at night, and I meant to wait until he did, but as for the rest, I—I—oh, Nick, they were going to make me marry that awful man tomorrow, and I couldn't stay and let them do it, truly!"

"Now you don't have to," he said gruffly, drawing her back into his arms. Lord, if he'd been fifteen minutes later, even ten... "Michel is waiting with a boat on the beach, and Gideon has the *Angel Lily* not far beyond the harbor. All you and I must do is reach them."

She looked up at him and smiled, melting every doubt from his heart. "We can do that. Together, of course. I don't doubt it for a minute."

"Good lass." Gently he pulled the bundled curtains from her hand and tossed them back on the bed. "This time we won't need these. Is there anyone else besides the woman at the door and the man in the garden?"

She shook her head, and he took her hand. "Then let's be off, Rosie."

Her heart pounding with excitement, she let him guide her across the flat roof of the piazza and then clung to him as he ordered while he climbed down the espaliered roses to the ground.

"I don't see the guard," she whispered. "He must be here somewhere."

"He is," said Nick as he led her across the wet grass, "but he's not going to trouble us. Now I'm going to have to boost you up to the top of this wall, and you wait until I can help you down on the other side."

"No, wait, Nick, there's a gate here to the side that's not locked," she said, breaking away to show him. "That's why there was a guard."

But as she scurried across the grass, holding her skirts above the dew, Nick heard the men's footsteps and voices on the other side of the wall, and instinctively he raced after Rose to grab her arm and pull her into the safety of the shadows. But before he could, the men were suddenly there by the second gate, two men in the uniforms of a lieutenant and a captain. As if caught in the spell of the moonlight, for an instant all four of them froze where they stood.

Then with a terrified little shriek Rose ran back to Nick, her eyes huge with fear. Swiftly Nick caught her arm and pushed her behind him, praying she'd have the sense to stay where she'd be safe, and then evenly met the gazes of the Englishmen before him. It was the captain who held his attention, a florid-faced man with mean, close-set eyes, a bully if ever he'd seen one.

He didn't need an introduction.

"Captain Lord Eliot Graham, if I'm not mistaken," Nick said softly, sweeping his cutlass from the scabbard. "I'm Nickerson Sparhawk. Your servant, sir."

"Damn your eyes, Sparhawk," spit out Graham, his hatred rising like a palpable thing between them. "You won't have the bitch!"

"There you're doubly wrong, Graham. Miss Everard is a *lady*," said Nick with easy, offhanded insolence, "and it seems she's already mine."

The lieutenant drew his own sword with a practiced flourish. "Let me take him, Captain," he said, his eyes narrowing with anticipation. "Don't sully yourself with the killing of a Yankee bastard like this."

But as the man charged toward Nick his heel slipped on the wet grass and he crashed backward, his head striking one of the large round stones edging the garden path. His wig tipped off his shaven head as his eyes stared emptily at the star-filled sky and the sword dropped innocently from his fingers.

"Useless," muttered Graham contemptuously as he kicked at the unconscious man's arm. "Damnably useless, the clumsy oaf."

Lily's laughter rang out across the garden, and Nick looked up to find her perched on the wall, her fan fluttering briskly with excitement. "Useless, indeed," she said cheerfully. "I've evened the balance for you, Nickerson. Now it's up to you to defend my poor sister's honor."

"My pleasure," he murmured, smiling as he briefly raised the hilt of his cutlass toward her in salute. "And thank you, sweet."

Furiously Graham ripped his own sword from its scabbard, his eyes bright with loathing. "The pleasure will be mine, you cocksure bastard!"

He lunged toward Nick, the blade glinting in the moonlight as it arced through the air. Deftly Nick caught and deflected the blow with a scrape of steel against steel, and shoved Graham back.

But instantly the Englishman returned, answering with a ruthless determination that forced Nick to focus his energies and begin fighting in earnest. Though he outranked Graham in size and strength, Nick realized at once that the man had experience and training on his side. He couldn't afford to grow careless, not when so much more than his life alone was at stake. He owed it to Rose to win, and, though Lily could save him, he wanted to do it without her help to prove to her—and himself—that he could.

Trembling with sick fear, Rose pressed her fingers to her mouth to keep back the scream that wanted to rip from her soul. She hated to watch, but how could she bear not to *know*?

One man would die. One would live. It was as simple, and as complicated, as that, for the one who lived would claim her as his. She thought back to the time when she'd grasped this same cutlass of Nick's in her own hands, playing with it as if it were no more than a child's toy. But it was no toy tonight, and this was no game. No wonder the wordless prayers for Nick came straight from her heart.

Again the two blades crashed together and scraped apart. Once again Lord Eliot surprised her with his agility, moving the heavy bulk of his body with a skilled quickness that let him deftly avoid the sure, steady slashes from Nick's sword. Abruptly he slipped to one side, catching Nick off-balance enough so that the hilts of their weapons crashed together, and Lord Eliot was able to use his advantage to shove Nick to the grass.

But before the Englishman could pull his sword back to use it, Nick grabbed him by the front of his coat and jerked him down with him. Over and over the two rolled across the dew-heavy grass, grunting as each struggled in a tangle of arms and legs and glinting blades to get the advantage of the other. With size on his side, Nick at last broke free long enough to drive his fist into the other man's cheek, and then roll back to his feet.

But Lord Eliot was far from done. Even as Nick rose Graham managed to whip his sword forward, dragging the tip of the blade across Nick's cheek as the Englishman, too, scrambled to his feet. Rose gasped as the blood stained dark on Nick's face, and impatiently he swiped his fingers across it, smearing it across his face like garish paint.

Around and around, back and forth across the garden the two men fought, grunting and gasping with exertion. Both men were tiring, both dripping with sweat as their blows grew wilder, and with sickening clarity Rose knew it would be luck, pure luck, that finally gave one of them the advantage over the other.

If only she could find some way to help Nick, she thought desperately, some way that would make her feel less helpless as he risked his life for her. In vain she looked about the walled garden for a branch or gardener's tool, anything she could use. Her gaze fell to the pond before her. There in the shallow water, surrounded by tiny darting fish, lay a musket. Without a thought for how the gun came to be there, she reached down and pulled it out with both hands by the barrel, cold, heavy and dripping. Then before the men could see what she'd done, she darted forward and swung the musket, droplets of water flying, as hard as she could at Graham's head.

She missed.

Lord Eliot didn't.

Catching her movement in the corner of his eye, Graham ducked and grabbed her around the waist. Deliberately he struck his fist against her bandaged arm and she shrieked with pain and dropped the musket. In a single swift motion he had locked her tight against his chest, the honed blade of his sword pressed to her throat.

"So, Sparhawk," he said, grinning with triumph even as he gasped for breath. "Who has—who has the bitch now? Move against me, and she dies."

Nick stopped, lowering his sword, and swore bitterly to himself. The terror in Rose's eyes as she mutely appealed to him was almost worse than the sight of the blade pressing into the smooth, pale skin of her throat.

"Let her go, Graham," he said as calmly as he could. "This is between us. Leave Rose out of it."

"Why should I, Sparhawk, when the chit's the cause of all my trouble?" He jerked Rose hard against him. "But maybe this is easier. Even if she dies now—the tragic victim of island thieves, say?—I'll have the papers fixed and witnesses sworn to say she couldn't wait until tomorrow and wed me tonight instead in secret."

"You would murder her yourself?" asked Nick hoarsely, appalled. "In cold blood, without mercy?"

"Why not?" said Graham carelessly. "This way I'll be rid of your little whore without having to give my name to your bastards, yet I'll still have her fortune."

"Oh, Nickerson," said Lily plaintively, hovering over Graham and her sister, "this wasn't supposed to end like this, not at all! I *told* you I couldn't help her, only you, and now look what has happened. You don't need my help. Oh, Rose, Rose, why couldn't you have stayed the frightened little rabbit just a little longer?"

But for once Nick scarcely heard her, his fear for Rose sweeping everything else away. Because she loved him, she had risked her own life to save his, and now he was powerless to help her in return. With his gaze never leaving her face, he thrust his sword back into the scabbard, unbuckled the belt and tossed it clattering at Graham's feet.

"There, Graham. You have my surrender. You can do whatever you want with me. Just let Miss Everard go free, my life for hers."

Graham snorted with disgust. "You disappoint me, Sparhawk. The way I see it, I already have you. Why should I bother freeing the chit as well? You'll hang as a pirate, with your body left to rot at the gibbet as a warning to others. Besides, I—"

But his words were drowned out by a strange rumbling noise from the tiled roof of the piazza. Frowning, Graham looked up, and as he did a large black cat, screeching with terror, leaped from the roof to sink its claws into Graham's shoulders. Swearing with surprise and pain, he staggered back, losing both his sword and Rose as he fought the animal clinging to his neck. The rumble grew louder, and the clay pot of red begonias knocked free by the cat rolled from the edge of the roof to crash directly onto Graham's head. With a groan he toppled to the ground, buried beneath a pile of broken crockery, red flowers and dirt as the cat bolted into the bushes.

"Oh, my, Nick," whispered Rose, her arms wrapped tightly around his waist as he held her close. "Oh, dear Lord in heaven. What *was* that?"

"Your sister, love." Nick sighed wearily and brushed his lips across the top of her head. She was safe, and that was all that mattered to him.

"My *sister?*" asked Rose uncertainly. "*Lily* did this?"

"It's too hard to explain just now," he said as he bent to retrieve his sword. Lily, of course, had vanished; not surprising, he thought, considering the extent of the damage she'd caused this time. He buckled his belt around his hips and took one final look at Graham, sprawled on the grass. "Another time, Rosie, when we're safe in the *Angel Lily,* and I'll try my best. But come, let's not keep Michel waiting."

Chapter Seventeen

"**Y**ou are indeed a lucky man, *mon frère,*" said Michel Géricault as he helped Nick push the little boat from the beach into the water. "At least half of me expected to never see you again in this life."

"I won't ask which half it was," said Nick, hopping over the side as the boat floated free. "And besides, we're not clear yet until we reach the *Angel Lily.*"

"A simple enough task," said Michel easily. "The tide's in our favor, and the winds, too. All we must do is look like any other nondescript little boat until we reach the deep water."

"Aye, simple enough if no one's chasing us," said Nick gloomily.

Michel chuckled as he drew a line taut. "You are a pessimist, *mon ami.* We'll be long gone before they find Graham's body. Without him to turn your capture into a vendetta, the interest in finding you will fade, especially since the entire fleet sails back to England within the next week or two. By the winter, when the hurricanes are done and they return, they'll have forgotten you ever existed. And maybe, if this extraordinary luck of yours still holds, the war itself will be through.''

Nick looked down at the tiller in his hand, lowering his voice so Rose wouldn't overhear. ''Graham's not dead, Michel,'' he said. ''At least he wasn't when we left the garden.''

''*Sacrebleu.*'' Michel's pale eyes turned coolly noncommittal, but the unspoken question hung between them just the same.

And outwardly, Nick didn't flinch. ''I know what you're thinking, Michel,'' he said evenly, ''but I don't do things the way you do. I've never yet willfully killed a man who was wounded or unconscious, and I wasn't about to begin tonight.''

Michel shrugged again. ''As you wish, *mon frère,*'' he said lightly. ''We each live our own lives, eh?''

But Nick knew precisely what Michel wasn't saying. Because he'd been so damned scrupulous about not dispatching Graham, the three of them were still in danger. Blast and hell, if only Lily hadn't interfered and he'd been able to kill the man fairly!

''Ah, *mademoiselle!*'' Michel smiled fondly at Rose as she cautiously made her way aft to join them. ''Allow me to congratulate you again on your delivery!''

''If I'd shown a lick of sense, I shouldn't have had to be delivered at all,'' she said sorrowfully, her shoulders bowing low with guilt. ''When I think of all the people who might have suffered on account of my foolishness—''

"Oh, love, hush," scolded Nick gently. "I won't hear it, mind? Now come sit with me, and no more of anyone's foolishness."

With a sigh she came to sit between Nick's legs while Michel moved forward in the boat to trim the sails. Shyly she curled closer against Nick's chest, relishing the feeling of being safe with him as he slipped his arm around her shoulders.

"You can babble on all you wish, Rosie, about who has suffered what for whom," he continued, guiding the little boat between two warships like the towering walls of a canyon. "But this night you risked your life to save mine, and no one, *no one*, has ever done that for me before."

She smiled happily. "How could I not do it, Nick? I love you so much I can't imagine my life without you in it. Of course I'd do all I could to keep you safe."

Suddenly her smile changed, and she drew her brows together, thinking. "What you said then, about Lily helping us. Did you truly mean that?"

He sighed, unsure of how best to answer. "So you do think I'm daft?"

"I didn't say that, Nick," she said slowly. "It's only that once you said you could sense her with us, and that sometimes you even saw her. Well, tonight when Lord Eliot was holding me, I felt Lily was somehow there. Maybe it was just because I was so frightened, but she truly seemed to be in the garden watching over us. And then when you said she'd made the cat jump and the flowerpot fall, it seemed so exactly like something that Lily would do that I almost wept.''

She tried to smile and ended up wrinkling her nose instead. ''Now I ask you, who's the daft one?''

''I'd say we've made a pair of it, Rosie,'' said Nick philosophically. ''No one else would have us.''

''I suppose not.'' Lightly she ran her fingers along his arm. ''Not that I shall complain. I rather like it this way. Being so thoroughly besotted with you as I am only makes the arrangement that much better.''

''Aye, it does at that.'' He cleared his throat, remembering all the vows and promises he'd made to her in his mind during the time they'd been apart. It should be easy enough to speak them now, but damnation, he didn't know where to begin, and he cleared his throat again.

She sat upright to look at him. ''Have you caught a chill?'' she asked, faintly accusing. ''You're quite rumbly to lie against. When we're back in the *Angel Lily,* I'll make you hot tea with sugarcane.''

''You'll have to make coffee instead. Good Yankees don't drink tea any longer on account of the tariffs your people inflicted on mine.''

''Very well, then,'' she said promptly. ''I shall make hot coffee with sugarcane, as hot as blazes, if you can bear it, and I shall make you drink every last, blessed drop.''

The image of her trying to make him drink hot coffee in his cabin made him smile, especially since he was picturing her once again in her mother's necklaces and little else, sitting poised on his knee with a silver tea-spoon held daintily in her fingers as she coaxed him to open his mouth just a little wider, please, only a little more....

He was so blissfully enthralled with his dreaming that he didn't hear the first cannon from the encampment on the hill they'd left behind, or the second one that answered it. What he did hear was Michel swearing, in both French and in English as he struggled to bring the little boat around on a fresh tack, and belatedly Nick leaned against the tiller.

"*Mordieu*, Nickerson, it's past time for that," shouted Michel. "Haven't you eyes in your head?"

And at last Nick saw the harbor washed in the cool, lemony light of first dawn, the shallow hill of Pigeon Island bright on one side and still in darkness on the other, the gulls wheeling and mewing overhead as they fought over the trash cast overboard by the fleet. And at last, too, he saw the final frigate they had to pass before they would leave the harbor for clear water, a small frigate with only thirty guns, yet impressive enough with all fifteen here on the port side run out, and marine sharpshooters ranged along the rail and in the tops, and dear God in Heaven, every one of those guns and muskets was aimed at *them*.

"*Mordieu*, we were almost clear," said Michel, his face wooden as he stared at the long line of guns. Blindly he fumbled inside his shirt for a locket on a chain and opened it to a miniature of Jerusa, rubbing his thumb around and around the polished gold frame.

"If they'd meant to take us as prisoners, they would have lowered a boat by now. *Sacristi et Jésus.*"

"Then they're going to kill us instead," whispered Rose. "Because of Lord Eliot, because of *me,* those men are going to kill us."

Nick stared at the frigate, unwilling and unable to believe what his eyes told him was true. They were nearly even with the larger ship, and at this range the gunners would not miss. Before they could sail clear on this tack, to Gideon and the *Angel Lily,* they'd be dead. It was as horrifyingly certain as that. There was no chance of going over the side to swim for safety, not in waters this transparently blue, not at dawn, and not with Rose with her heavy skirts and bandaged arm. They were going to be slaughtered where they sat, their little sailboat smashed to pieces and them with it.

So this, then, was how it would end for Rose and him, he thought furiously, end before it had really begun. He stared at the rows of guns, cursing the fate that had brought his life to this end, while his soul turned heavy as lead at the heartbreaking unfairness of it.

Unsteadily Rose climbed to her feet. "If I must die, I won't go weeping and wailing," she said, though her voice quavered with tears. "Here, Nick, stand with me, so I'll be sure to die at your side. Bravely and gallantly, Nick, oh, please, the way I've learned to be with you!"

Standing there in the light of the rising sun, she was the most beautiful woman he'd ever seen, her dark hair streaming around her shoulders in the wind and her silver eyes defiant as she tried to face her destiny.

He loved her, loved her with all his being, and he didn't want her life to end like this. He couldn't let her believe that this was all there was, and gently he pulled her back down and into his arms.

"You've learned to be brave, Rosie, aye," he said, his voice rough with emotion. "But I'd rather you'd have learned more from me than that alone. We've not much time, I know, but I'd ask you instead to think of when this war will be over and done and our two countries are at peace. Think of yourself as my wife, and us living in a pretty little house in Newport, near the water so we can see the ships come and go from our parlor."

She shuddered with a sigh that was halfway to a sob, a sound that tore at his heart. "I would like a yellow house, Nick," she said softly. "A yellow house with white shutters always looks very fine and trim."

"Then yellow it shall be." They were coming closer under the guns, and he turned her face to his chest so she could not see, smoothing her hair gently. "You can have a garden with all the flowers you like, too, since flowers prosper most amazingly well in Newport. Children do, too. I'm only one of six, you know, and look at me."

"I would have liked that very much," she said sadly, her voice muffled by his coat. "We would have made vastly fine, fat babies between us, I believe."

"Aye, we would indeed." Damnation, why the devil didn't the bastards fire? Why didn't they go ahead and end this *now?* "I love you, my own White Rose, sweet little Rosie."

"And I love you, Black Nick Sparhawk," she whispered. "Dear Lord, how I love you!"

Desperate to treasure this last moment with her, his mind was slow to realize what was happening, but after a lifetime at sea his body sensed the change at once. The wind was shifting, gathering and blowing up from nowhere on this cloudless morning to whip the waves higher, high as a midwinter gale as their little boat raced along before it toward the mouth of the bay. Nick let Rose go to grab at the tiller with both hands, struggling to hold the boat steady while Michel wrestled to control the sails.

"Oh, Nick, look, look at the other ships!" cried Rose as she clung to the side. "Oh, my God, *look!*"

The same wind that was making them fly across the waves had caught the frigate with too much sail aloft, and she lurched crazily toward the waves, marines and sailors and guns jerked free from their moorings all tumbling and rolling across the slanting decks as the canvas overhead shredded to tattered rags.

But in as much disarray as the frigate was, the rest of the fleet was suffering, too. As far as Nick could see were shattered masts and ships wrenched free of their moorings, and torn sails whipping in the wind like laundry on the line. With their anchor chains broken, seventy-four-gun ships of the line crashed into their sisters, the bowsprits jabbing into one another's rigging as lines and cables snared together into hopeless tangles. No battle could cause so much destruction in so short a time, and no one storm had ever been so costly to so many ships in one place.

Not one storm or battle, thought Nick grimly, but what were they compared to Lily?

"Oh, pish, I know perfectly well what you're thinking," she said mildly as she appeared beside him in the sternsheets on the other side of the tiller from Rose. "It's not nearly as bad as it looks with everything jumbled together like this, and I took care that not a single innocent fellow was injured. That took some doing, I can assure you, but I did it just the same. *You've* been so wondrously saintly, how could I dare be otherwise?"

Mutinously he scowled at her, unwilling to speak before Rose.

"Oh, go ahead and say it, if you wish," said Lily as she patted at her hair. "Since this will most likely be our last time to converse, neither Rose nor Michel can hear a word from either of us."

"Well, then, why the devil did you go through all *this?*" He waved his hand back toward the harbor. "Why didn't you end it with Graham in the garden?"

"Because I wanted to see if *you* would," she said, prodding him gently with her folded fan as if to share a humorous jest. "Thank goodness you didn't, or I don't know what I would have done. You were quite surpassing noble over that, and if you had killed Lord

Eliot I wasn't quite sure what I would have done. But this way, he's been supremely discredited and shamed for ordering ships to sea in such dreadful weather, especially on a personal matter. He'll be court-martialed for sure, and sent back to Britain in such disgrace I'm certain he'll never find another heiress. I only pray he's not given to *me* to reform next."

Nick looked at her curiously. "So you really are clearing off, then?"

"That's what you've wished from the first time I rescued you, isn't it?" She tipped back her head and laughed. "Oh, my, I never expected calf's eyes and a long face from you!"

He smiled wryly. "It's not as bad as all that, Lily. It's going to be a powerful relief to know my water pitcher will stay where I put it. But you brought me Rosie, and I'll never be able to thank you enough for that."

"No, most likely you won't," she agreed amiably. "But then, you'll recall I did promise you happiness."

"That you did, and I will thank you for not giving up on me before I found it." He smiled, surprised by how much he truly would miss her. Without thinking he reached out to take her hand, only to have his fingers pass through to the side of the boat.

"None of that now, Captain." She glared at him with feigned indignation and slapped his fingers with her fan, a fan as ethereal as the rest of her that nonetheless left his fingers smarting. Then she smiled, her blue eyes growing misty. "Oh, but I shall miss you, too, my dearest, darling Nickerson! I vow I could almost be jealous of my little sister. Just mind you marry her before you start bringing that litter of jolly babies into the world.''

"*Grâce à Dieu!*" cried Michel excitedly as he pointed to the familiar ship that lay directly before them. "It's the *Angel Lily!*"

"Why, so it is," agreed Lily, slipping the loop of her fan over her wrist. "I suppose that means it's past time I said my farewells."

"Damnation, Lily, wait!" Unable to resist the sight of his own ship, Nick looked briefly to her familiar outline on the water and then back to Lily. But the seat beside him was empty, and Michel was seizing his hand to congratulate him.

"*Vraiment,* Nickerson, you are the single most fortunate man I have ever known," he said with amazement and something close to outright awe. "I would not have believed it had I not seen it for myself. How all those other vessels were damaged, while we escaped unharmed." He shook his head with fresh wonder. "*Grâce à Dieu,* it comes perilously close to a miracle, eh, *mon frère?*"

Shyly Rose slipped her hand into Nick's, her little fingers twining familiarly with his.

"If you begin to believe in miracles, *monsieur,*" she said as her gaze never left Nick's, her eyes bright with the unspoken secret they shared, "then next you may find yourself believing in angels and goodness knows what else."

Nick bent and kissed her then, unable to resist, and tasted the promise of the love and the future they'd share together.

Michel cleared his throat, and reluctantly Nick lifted his lips from Rose's. "I didn't know you'd fallen in with another ship, Nickerson," he said, pointing to a privateering schooner with an American flag, sailing just beyond the *Angel Lily*. "But then you Rhode Islanders never cease to surprise me."

The schooner surprised Nick, too, until he realized it was the *Charity* from Bristol, the one vessel he knew in the entire thirteen states that could boast a clergyman for a captain, an Anglican minister who'd rebelled against his church as well as his king and gone to sea instead. But rebel or not, the man was known still to keep his hand in his former trade, baptizing the stray sailor or preaching a sermon if he felt the need.

Or performing marriages without bothering with banns or licenses. Doubtless that was what Lily had heard, anyway, to arrange it like this, and Nick laughed out loud from sheer joy. Why, he and Rose could be husband and wife before supper, leaving plenty of time for taking hot coffee with sugarcane and other such important duties for a captain and his wife.

He slipped his hand around her waist and drew her close. "I have another secret to share, Rosie love," he began, "one about the captain of that schooner."

But Rose wasn't listening, instead staring openmouthed past him to the figurehead of the *Angel Lily*, rising high on the bow before them.

"I don't know how it can be, Nick," she said softly. "Or is this another one of your miracles?"

Slowly he lifted his gaze to follow hers. The gilt and paint were as bright as ever, the gown fluttering gracefully and the fan spread above the perfectly arched wrist. But by the clear light of the morning sun, there was no doubt at all that the figurehead of Lily Everard was winking.

Aye, thought Nick as he winked back at it, he believed in miracles. He believed in true love and happiness and jolly babies in a yellow house in Newport, too, when it came right down to making declarations.

And angels, both ones with wings like Lily and those of the more earthbound variety like his own dearest Rose. Oh, aye, he'd always believe in angels.

Always.

* * * * *

BRIDE'S BAY RESORT

UNLOCK THE DOOR TO GREAT ROMANCE AT BRIDE'S BAY RESORT

Join Harlequin's new across-the-lines series, set in an exclusive hotel on an island off the coast of South Carolina.

Seven of your favorite authors will bring you exciting stories about fascinating heroes and heroines discovering love at Bride's Bay Resort.

Look for these fabulous stories coming to a store near you beginning in January 1996.

Harlequin American Romance #613 in January
Matchmaking Baby by Cathy Gillen Thacker

Harlequin Presents #1794 in February
Indiscretions by Robyn Donald

Harlequin Intrigue #362 in March
Love and Lies by Dawn Stewardson

Harlequin Romance #3404 in April
Make Believe Engagement by Day Leclaire

Harlequin Temptation #588 in May
Stranger in the Night by Roseanne Williams

Harlequin Superromance #695 in June
Married to a Stranger by Connie Bennett

Harlequin Historicals #324 in July
Dulcie's Gift by Ruth Langan

Visit Bride's Bay Resort each month wherever Harlequin books are sold.

HARLEQUIN ®

BBAYG

HARLEQUIN®

Don't miss these Harlequin favorites by some of our most
distinguished authors!
And now, you can receive a discount by ordering two or more titles!

HT #25645	THREE GROOMS AND A WIFE by JoAnn Ross	$3.25 U.S./$3.75 CAN. ☐
HT #25648	JESSIE'S LAWMAN by Kristine Rolofson	$3.25 U.S.//$3.75 CAN. ☐
HP #11725	THE WRONG KIND OF WIFE by Roberta Leigh	$3.25 U.S./$3.75 CAN. ☐
HP #11755	TIGER EYES by Robyn Donald	$3.25 U.S./$3.75 CAN. ☐
HR #03362	THE BABY BUSINESS by Rebecca Winters	$2.99 U.S./$3.50 CAN. ☐
HR #03375	THE BABY CAPER by Emma Goldrick	$2.99 U.S./$3.50 CAN. ☐
HS #70638	THE SECRET YEARS by Margot Dalton	$3.75 U.S./$4.25 CAN. ☐
HS #70655	PEACEKEEPER by Marisa Carroll	$3.75 U.S./$4.25 CAN. ☐
HI #22280	MIDNIGHT RIDER by Laura Pender	$2.99 U.S./$3.50 CAN. ☐
HI #22235	BEAUTY VS THE BEAST by M.J. Rogers	$3.50 U.S./$3.99 CAN. ☐
HAR #16531	TEDDY BEAR HEIR by Elda Minger	$3.50 U.S./$3.99 CAN. ☐
HAR #16596	COUNTERFEIT HUSBAND by Linda Randall Wisdom	$3.50 U.S./$3.99 CAN. ☐
HH #28795	PIECES OF SKY by Marianne Willman	$3.99 U.S./$4.50 CAN. ☐
HH #28855	SWEET SURRENDER by Julie Tetel	$4.50 U.S./$4.99 CAN. ☐

(limited quantities available on certain titles)

	AMOUNT	$
DEDUCT:	**10% DISCOUNT FOR 2+ BOOKS**	$
ADD:	**POSTAGE & HANDLING**	$
	($1.00 for one book, 50¢ for each additional)	
	APPLICABLE TAXES**	$_____
	<u>**TOTAL PAYABLE**</u>	$_____
	(check or money order—please do not send cash)	

To order, complete this form and send it, along with a check or money order for the
total above, payable to Harlequin Books, to: **In the U.S.:** 3010 Walden Avenue,
P.O. Box 9047, Buffalo, NY 14269-9047; **In Canada:** P.O. Box 613, Fort Erie, Ontario,
L2A 5X3.

Name: _____

Address: _____ City: _____

State/Prov.: _____ Zip/Postal Code: _____

**New York residents remit applicable sales taxes.
Canadian residents remit applicable GST and provincial taxes.

HBACK-AJ3

Bestselling authors

ELAINE
COFFMAN
RUTH LANGAN

and

MARY McBRIDE

Together in one fabulous collection!

OUTLAW
Brides

Available in June wherever Harlequin
books are sold.

Harlequin® Historical

If you're a serious fan of historical romance,
then you're in luck!

Harlequin Historicals brings you
stories by bestselling authors, rising new stars
and talented first-timers.

Ruth Langan & Theresa Michaels
Mary McBride & Cheryl St. John
Margaret Moore & Merline Lovelace
Julie Tetel & Nina Beaumont
Susan Amarillas & Ana Seymour
Deborah Simmons & Linda Castle
Cassandra Austin & Emily French
Miranda Jarrett & Suzanne Barclay
DeLoras Scott & Laurie Grant…

You'll never run out of favorites.

Harlequin Historicals…they're too good to miss!

HH-GEN

What do women really want to know?

Trust the world's largest publisher of
women's fiction to tell you.

HARLEQUIN ULTIMATE GUIDES™

I CAN FIX THAT

A Guide For Women
Who Want To Do It Themselves

This is the only guide a self-reliant
woman will ever need to deal
with those pesky items that
break, wear out or just don't work
anymore. Chock-full of friendly
advice and straightforward,
step-by-step solutions to the
trials of everyday life in our
gadget-oriented world! So, don't
just.sit there wondering how to
fix the VCR—run to your
nearest bookstore for your copy now!

Available this May, at your favorite retail outlet.

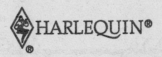

HARLEQUIN®